Dancing

with the

Devil

Marie James

Copyright

Acknowledgments

Book #24!
Without all of the amazing people supporting me, encouraging me, and listening to me when I ask myself why I keep doing this, I would've called it quits a long time ago! I'd be able to read more books and take more naps, that's for sure!

My amazing, loving, and sometimes extremely annoying husband, thank you for supporting me through another release! Love you to the moon!

My girls, Laura, Brittney, MaRanda, and Steph thank you for always being there! Sanity isn't possible without you!

BETAs girls! Mary, Brenda, Shannon, Laura, MaRanda, Michelle, and Jamie, you guys totally rocked this book! Thank you for all of your hard work and attention to detail!

Shout out to RRR Promotions. Thank you for your help on this release! It was last minute, but you rocked it like you always do!

Stalkers! You gals are THE BEST EVER! Thank you from the bottom of my mostly dark soul for supporting me, entertaining me, and helping me when I need it. You are the reason the Indie community is so amazing!

ARC readers, thank you so much for getting on top of this and being excited about this release!

Bloggers, thank you so much for sharing, reading, reviewing, and just being all around awesome!

Until next time!

~Marie James

Ravens Ruin Series

Prequel Book 1: Desperate Beginnings:

Book 2: Sins of the Father

Book 3: Luck of the Devil

Book 4: Dancing with the Devil

Synopsis

I thought leaving her in that room covered in her attacker's blood would teach her a lesson.
I thought she'd be more careful about her safety.
Little did I know that she's seeking pain and humiliation.
Well, it's her lucky day because pain is sort of my thing.
I can hurt her much more than she's able to hurt herself.
The twist is we'll both enjoy every second of it.

Epitaph

"Destroy the part of you that searches for angels in places you know
only monsters exist"
~ Erin Van Vuren

Prologue

TJ

She's stunning, the most gorgeous creature I've ever seen, but it isn't her long blonde hair scattered on the pillow or the plumpness in her lips as she lies in repose that heats my blood and kicks my heart up a notch. Her nakedness, the bare curves of her body, and the dusky-rose nipples, drawn tight by the coolness in the air, are merely adjectives, accessories to the real allure.

"Look how fucking sexy that is," I mutter, shocked at the sound of my voice because I hadn't meant to praise her perfection out loud.

"Sick fuck," Briar mutters beside me.

He doesn't see what I see. He can't appreciate the transcendent sight of the girl on the bed. His concerns lie elsewhere, which is fine. It gives me more time to admire her.

The sight of her covered in blood has to be the most beautiful thing I've ever seen in my entire life. The only displeasure I allow to seep in is the fact that it's not her blood.

Or mine.

My cock thickens behind my zipper at just the thought of covering her milky smooth skin with my own blood.

"Are we going to leave her there?"

What the hell does Briar expect us to do with her?

"Let her wake up in this mess," I say without pulling my eyes from her. "Maybe she'll learn her fucking lesson."

Honestly, she's just too superb to disrupt.

The problem, also Briar's main concerns, are the three dead guys at our feet and the currently living one whimpering in the corner. I ignore all of it as I step over the gore and get closer to her.

"You should be safe at home reading a book or something, beautiful." I push her hair from her cheek so I can see her face better. "Now, you're here covered in blood."

She whimpers, her hazy green eyes fluttering open for only the briefest of seconds before her long lashes rest once again on her rosy cheeks.

"You want to be identified?" Briar hisses from the other side of the room.

Ignoring him, I swipe my finger through a splash of blood on her arm before lifting it to her face. "It was my pleasure saving you."

Chapter 1

Kaci

"Ms. Stewart?"

I don't know how long I've been here. My head is foggy, like thick vapor. Nothing seems real. The world around me is a fabrication of reality, and if I'm being honest, I'd love to live in this dream state forever. Nothing hurts here. Nothing is hurting me, and I'm not thinking of hurting myself. The change of pace is comforting.

"Ms. Stewart?" I look up at the female glaring down at me. "Take this and wipe your face."

I saw myself in the mirror before the police arrived at the house party earlier. The ghostly, ashen face that stared back at me was unrecognizable, much like the bodies scattered around the floor.

The heart drawn in blood on my face is both terrifying and soothing, placed there by an angel who had no idea I didn't want to be saved. Even though I'm reluctant to remove it, I press the damp cloth to my cheek as instructed.

"Why did you kill those men?"

A humorless chuckle erupts from my throat. "Kill them? I didn't kill them."

"You were the only other person left alive in the room." The male police officer that has been standing on the other side of the room closes the distance, placing his hands on the table directly in front of me. He crowds my space as if this intimidation tactic is going to work on me. "Three men have been brutally murdered, and you want us to believe that they left you alive for no reason?"

I don't bother answering. The female police officer looks at me with pleading eyes, as if she's saying she's on my side. I've watched enough damn TV to know the whole good cop, bad cop routine.

"I don't know anything."

"Did your boyfriend do this? Did he catch you upstairs ready to spread your thighs for three men and lose his shit?"

"I don't have a boyfriend." Plain, simple truth.

"So some random person comes up there, hacks three people to bits, draws a sick fucking heart on your face, and I'm supposed to believe you had nothing to do with it?"

The female officer's eyes cut to the man in my face, irritation clear in her eyes, but she doesn't say anything to reel him in.

"The last thing I remember is dancing downstairs. I don't even know how I got in that room." I swallow thickly before continuing. "I-I think they drugged me."

"Did they rape you?" The female officer pushes away from the wall to get a better view of me.

"I-I don't know." I grip the scratchy blanket I was provided at the house tighter around me. "Can you take me to the hospital?"

"Fuck my life," the male officer huffs before standing and backing away.

"Give it a rest, McGee. Look at her. She can barely hold her head up. I told you she should've been taken by medical before she was brought here."

If looks could kill, the female officer would be dead on the floor. Seems her counterpart doesn't like to be corrected.

"Do you know, or have you had any prior encounters with Dean Smith, Edgar Romeo, or Chance Brown."

My head shakes, but Officer McGee doesn't seem impressed. There isn't anything I could say right now to make him change his train of thought. I imagine the video evidence could be presented of someone else murdering those guys, and he'd still come after me.

My head shakes again, but the effort is no longer enough to keep the flashes from invading my vision.

"Hey, gorgeous. I'm Max." I look up at the frat boy I'd noticed earlier in the night. "You look thirsty."

My hand trembles as I reach for the red, plastic cup. I know what happens after this, not from experience, but from stories I've heard and read about recently. I know it wasn't vitamins I watched this guy pour into a cup very similar to this only moments ago.

"Thanks," I say with a sweet smile before tilting the cup to my lips.

"I don't know any of them," I explain when all McGee does is stare down at me. "I met a guy named Max downstairs."

"Max wasn't one of the victims." McGee spits the words through clenched teeth. Clearly, he's easily flustered, but I can't tell them more because I don't know any details. I'd never be able to explain that I suspected I'd end up in that room with those guys.

The possibilities send a jolt of unease up my spine. Drugged and taken advantage of by Max was a self-destructive bitter pill to swallow, but knowing there were at least three guys up there is a horror I don't want to consider.

McGee looks over his shoulder at his partner, and I see the slight shake of her head.

"Can you go check on that lead?"

The female cop shakes her head again. "Let's get Ms. Stewart to the hospital for an examination, and then I'll be free to follow-up."

I mouth a thank you to her while McGee is still staring at her. She's refusing to leave me alone in the room with him, and I'm beyond grateful for that.

"Send her in a cab," McGee huffs when the officer holds a hand out, indicating for me to stand and follow her.

"I'm taking her. We need to know the results of the rape kit."

"Rape?" McGee huffs with incredulity.

His eyes sweep up and down my body. I shiver at the perusal, even though the blanket on my shoulders is wrapped tight and touching my knees. I'm naked underneath, but it feels as if he has x-ray vision and can see straight down to my soul.

"Those boys are dead, murdered in cold blood," McGee says to his partner, his rotund body blocking my path to the door. "And no matter what the exam results are, this department isn't going to taint their memories."

"Give it a rest, McGee."

I slide past both of them and wait in the hall for the female officer. It takes several long minutes before their whispered, yet heated argument comes to an end.

"I'm Detective Abigail Martin."

She doesn't bother holding her hand out to shake because she's well aware that my hands are tangled in the blanket.

"I wish we had some clothes here at the station."

I watch her back as she begins to walk down the corridor, unsure of where she's leading me. She's acting nice right now, but I'm sure it's a ploy, just another part of the good cop, bad cop skit she and her partner have perfected over the years.

"Follow me, please," she says over her shoulder when she realizes I'm not following her.

The walk to her car is short and filled with a heavy silence.

"McGee is a dick," she mutters as we close ourselves into the car.

"That's not going to work with me," I advise as I struggle to clip my seatbelt over the blanket without having to expose any part of my skin.

She sighs, nodding at the same time, and I can't tell if she finally understands that she isn't going to get anything out of me, or if she understands that I'd never trust her. Either way suits me.

"Can you just take me home?"

"You need to be seen at the hospital." The sound of her blinker echoes in the silence. "Don't let what McGee said back there keep you from finding out what happened in that room tonight."

"It doesn't matter." My eyes are trained on the darkness outside the window.

At a red light, I can hear more than see her shift her weight in her seat.

"It matters." I don't bother looking at her. "If those guys drugged you and brought you upstairs with the intent to rape you, they got exactly what they deserved."

Even without my eyes on her, I sense some truth in her opinion, but she still can't be trusted. Cops will say anything, *do* anything, to get you to confess.

She sighs again when I don't engage, but before long we're pulling up to a small hospital.

"Have you been to the hospital here before?"

"Where are we?"

"Haverhill. I can walk you in, or you can go alone, but either way, the emergency room has to be used since it's the middle of the night."

"I'll be fine."

Climbing out of the car, I expect her to follow me inside, not to help in any way, but to get whatever evidence she could to take back to McGee to use against me. I'm still stunned that I'm entering the hospital rather than being tossed in a jail cell. They may not have enough evidence to hold me now, but I'm certain they'll somehow find something to charge me with.

With one last look over my shoulder, I see Detective Martin pulling away. The sight of her taillights as she creeps through the mostly empty parking lot strengthens my resolve.

Why should she stick around? She doesn't care about me. No one does.

Chapter 2

TJ

Not thinking things through, or more specifically, not caring what happens is sort of my thing. I've been this way for as long as I can remember. If an idea pops in my head, I go with it. Why worry about the *what ifs*? Fate, karma, whatever people want to call it, always has a way of sneaking in when you're not looking and destroying your life anyway.

I was six years old when a toy gun caused my mother's death. I barely remember her face, and I can no longer hear her voice when I squeeze my eyes closed. I think her blood covering me as a little boy is what kicked off my obsession, but I'm no psychologist. I know I'm fucked up. Everyone knows I'm fucked up, but pinpointing the cause isn't really a concern of mine.

My motto? Have fun while there's fun to have because life will eventually turn to shit in the blink of an eye. I may need to tweak that a little bit before Hallmark prints it, but at the end of the day, I know it'll be a bestseller.

Not planning, not thinking, not caring is why I'm not questioning dropping Briar off at the clubhouse, only to turn right back around and head to Andover. After only fifteen minutes back home to scrub all the blood from my skin, I was on the road again.

We'd spent two days following the douchebags that drugged and attempted to rape my little sister Molly, but once we knew they were all at the same place, hosting another party where no doubt they were going to try something with another girl, we knew we had to intervene.

As I drive to the hospital closest to the frat house, I don't let myself focus on what those pieces of shit may have been up to in the weeks since my sister returned home. The simple truth is, they won't hurt anyone else.

My SUV idles in the darkness of the almost empty parking lot. The emergency room is the only entrance open this late, but there isn't a cop car to be seen. After twenty minutes of no activity, I pull away, heading toward the police station. It's been a couple hours since leaving that pretty girl in the frat house, but I can't I understand why they haven't taken her to the hospital.

Arriving at the police station just in time to see her walk to an unmarked car, she tugs the blanket closer to her skin before climbing inside. Only now does the cop car take the route to the hospital in Haverhill.

She has been drugged, has woken to a horrific sight, and yet it takes hours for them to get her medical care. My fingers twitch to open the door and slit the cop's throat after she drops the girl off. The officer couldn't even be bothered to go in with her. My hand is on the gear shift, ready to follow her to her demise, but the officer drives her car around the lot, putting it in park in the closest space to the entrance. Parking lights glint off the early morning dew beginning to accumulate on the other cars.

So we both wait. What feels like a lifetime later, the blonde walks back through the door. She's now wearing a set of scrubs that swallow her tiny frame. Her hair is pulled back in a low ponytail, but even from this distance, I can see the honey-blonde streaks still coated with blood. My cock stirs in my jeans.

Wavering between what I want to do and what I should do, I watch her face fall. Alone in front of the hospital, her shoulders sag with resignation. She's realizing she's going to have to walk home.

Before I can climb out of the truck and do the creepy thing by asking her if she needs a ride, the cop I'd forgotten was still in the lot pulls in front of her. A grin spreads across my face when I notice her face fall even more. Clearly, she's not fond of the cops either.

With no other options, she climbs inside, and they pull away. This is exactly what I needed, the only thing that will feed what is quickly becoming a new obsession. Keeping distance from the cop car, I follow them out of Haverhill and back toward Andover.

Unease settles low in my gut as I watch the cop car pull up outside of an unkempt house. The larger than normal driveway is an indication that this house has been transformed, more than likely, into several studio apartments.

She doesn't look back at the car after closing the door, but the officer doesn't pull away until she retrieves a key from under the mat, unlocks her door before placing the key under the mat once again, and closes herself inside. Stubborn, naive girl. Doesn't she know how corrupt and dangerous the world is? Did she not learn her lesson mere hours ago?

The urge to go to her, to teach her a lesson about self-preservation lights my skin on fire. The need to show her just how bad things can be if she isn't careful with her safety begins as a twitch in my knee. I stare at her door, leg bouncing with jittery agitation because at this very second, there's nothing I can do to correct her behavior.

The world is starting to wake up. Traffic is increasing on the roads as the sun lifts on the horizon, which means I have to wait. I've waited all night to see her again, to be close enough to reach out and touch her. When there is only one crappy car parked in the oversized driveway, I climb out of the SUV and bury my face and hands deeper into my coat, more to shield my identity from others than a need to get warm. Heat is the last thing I'm thinking about because my blood is already on fire for this girl. Her carelessness makes me want to shake her until she understands the dangers, or at least until she's frightened enough to take precautions.

She weighs almost nothing. I could tell from the way the full-sized bed at the frat house nearly swallowed her, so subduing her if she came at me would be child's play. As if I own the place, I scoop the key out from under the mat and let myself into her space. Just as I suspected, the one-room apartment allows me to observe her from the door.

She doesn't stir when the door closes behind me. Surely, her exhaustion from last night has taken over, and she's down for the count, but upon further inspection, I notice the prescription bottle of Ambien on her bedside table.

In the time I waited for the house to clear out, she's taken a shower. Blood no longer decorates her skin. It no longer enhances the delicate glow of her blonde hair. I miss it immediately. Fighting the urge to replace it with my own, I walk to her kitchen. A purse she wasn't carrying earlier sits on the cramped countertop. Knowing that she's out like a light with the help of a sedative, I upturn the bag and pour the contents out.

Two things draw my attention, her small wallet and her cell phone, neither of which I imagine she had on her tonight. Imagining what those guys were planning to do with her after they'd had their fun only serves to reignite the turmoil I felt when I left her there to take Briar home. From my vantage point, I see no pictures, no snapshots of friends or family members. A quick search of her phone, not password protected by the way, provides the same dismal results. Either this girl has purposely isolated herself, or she has no one to rely on. The result, however, is the same. There's a good chance that no one would look for her if she disappeared. If those guys finished her off after their playtime ended, no one would be the wiser, a missing girl no one would look for. She wouldn't even be a blip on the police radar.

The realization is both jarring and filled with so many possibilities.

After taking a picture of her driver's license, I upload a tracking app on her phone, hiding it in a folder labeled "Shit I'll Never Use."

When she entered this place, I'd sat and dreamed about all the things I'd find inside. I imagined the information, the secrets her belongings would reveal to me. Standing in her dismal home, I'm disappointed but struck at the same time with a revelation. This girl may not have anyone to look out for her, but whether she likes it or not, she's now stuck with me.

I don't question the attraction or the allure she has that no other woman has even come close to.

I see her.

I want her.

I'll have her.

Simple.

It takes everything in me not to mark her with my own blood. The sight of her cheek, the heart I'd drawn missing, is almost enough to break a rule I may not be able to recover from. I don't know her enough to trust leaving another heart behind. I don't have enough power or control over this situation to leave my DNA on her silky cheek.

"Until next time, Sweetheart."

I press my lips to her warm forehead. Unlike when I touched her at the frat house, her eyes remain closed. My time spent outside the hospital, police station, and her apartment isn't rewarded with one last flutter of her gorgeous green eyes.

I walk away craving with needs unmet, leaving the key to her apartment on the cluttered countertop rather than returning it under the tattered welcome mat outside.

It's hard to walk away when all I want to do is curl around her in the bed and promise to protect her. Make sure she knows she's mine. Make her swear that I'll be the only one to hurt her.

She'll know this all in good time.

Chapter 3

Kaci

Waking up with a hangover when you didn't have the luxury of enjoying a couple of drinks has always been the negative side effect of taking a prescription sleep aid.

The growl of my stomach chimes in with the familiar chorus of my neighbors arguing. I don't have to look toward the single window in my tiny apartment to know that night has fallen. The drunken bickering always starts late in the evening, and by the time the sun kisses the ground, they are at each other's throat.

"The joys of having neighbors," I mutter to myself as I climb out of bed and head straight for the shower.

Although I scrubbed every inch of my skin before I crashed into my bed, I still feel dirty. I always feel unclean, which makes me grateful utilities are included in my rent. Nothing has changed from when I woke up yesterday, I realize as I climb out of the shower.

Swiping my hand across the frameless mirror hanging above the bathroom sink, I stare into my empty eyes. Waking up surrounded by bodies, getting interrogated by the police, it hardly even registers. It's not a common occurrence, but the brutality of what happened in that frat house yesterday wasn't my initiation to the darkness. Hell, it wasn't even the worst thing I've seen in my life.

That's what I mutter to myself as my eyes slam shut. Bile rises in my throat, burning a path from my stomach until, unable to hold it back any longer, I'm bending over the toilet and dry-heaving.

This is also part of my daily pattern, only today the sequence of actions doesn't take much effort. I don't have to concentrate or dig deep into my past. I don't have to hyper-focus on past touches, violations, or abuses. Purging myself of the filth, both from the inside and the invisible layer that perpetually stains my skin come effortlessly today.

I smile at the mirror, ignoring the dark circles under my eyes, as I rinse my mouth. Makeup easily covers the purple proof of my restless sleep, but I don't bother with it this evening. I have no one to impress, no trouble to find myself in tonight. There's always some mischief to entangle myself in, but after last night, although I feel like it's admitting defeat on some level, I need a break.

And tacos.

With wet hair and my mother's tinny voice bouncing around in my head warning of illness, I grab my wallet and leave my apartment. A five-minute walk from my house is a little restaurant that makes the most amazing street tacos. Formerly a food truck turned success story, Tito's Tacos has quickly become a staple in my life, and the walk in the dark over uneven sidewalks just happens to feed my hunger for danger.

"My cock gets hard every time you walk past here."

I roll my eyes at the old bum as I pass the liquor store. He's as familiar as the smell of pot from the alley, and the stench of burning plastic from the crack users a couple streets over. The vagrant smacks his dry lips at me, but like every other day, I just keep on going.

You'd think the liquor store would be a dangerous place for a woman to stroll past alone, but around the corner is Pappy's. The coin laundromat is the real test of courage. Kept warm with the use of the dryers inside, the laundromat attracts all the people not allowed to stay inside the liquor store and consume their purchases.

Any other day, I'd walk right by the cracked picture window, head held high and daring anyone to mess with me, but tonight I'm still raw from my choices twenty-four hours ago. Instead of turning the corner and crossing the road a few blocks down, I cross right after the liquor store and keep to the shadows along the closed storefronts opposite of the laundromat. None the wiser, the degenerate population inside drink from cans stuffed in paper bags and don't even raise their heads from their card game as the sinister darkness turns into a more respectable area of the neighborhood.

The paper-thin divide separating the contradictory areas of town on Parker Street are always battling for dominance, but lucky for me, tonight isn't one where either side is wrestling with the other. Tonight, the streetlamps and the lone light in Tito's small parking lot are lit, and there are no teenagers looking for trouble across the street to hassle people needing to walk by.

The false sense of security crackles around me. It's not a good thing no one is out causing trouble. It's curious more than anything. The air is different, crackling at the wrong time, surrounding me in a bubble that's sure to pop at any minute.

Blaming the cold, I shiver when I step inside of Tito's, but the malevolent sensation doesn't subside even when the tinted door closes behind me. A collection of spices invades my sinuses, and I know, if only for a few moments, things will be fine. It's amazing what the promise of tacos can do to a person. Getting two tacos, fries, and a drink for just five bucks isn't a deal many people would turn down.

"Can I get the special, beef with extra pico?"

The cashier behind the counter jots my order down on a generic menu pad. "To go?"

She may not know my name, but every other time I've stepped in here, I've asked to have my food packaged to carry back home. The idea of being caged in this windowless building has always teetered on the edge of too confined for me. Tonight is different, however. Tonight, going back outside is what activates that low hum of fear deep in my gut. It's the promise of what could happen that forms the response on my lips.

"To go, yes."

The same fear that drove me to cross the street earlier than normal mere moments ago is the same one that urges me back outside immediately after collecting my bag of food and Pepsi from the counter. My life is spent in a never-ending game of chance. Last night I almost lost. Most often, I somehow manage to slide through unscathed. Those nights are the ones I find most disappointing.

Still focused on their card game, the guys in the laundromat don't so much as give me a passing glance when I cross in front of the window. The homeless man that has become a permanent fixture on the front stoop of the liquor store isn't around either.

Silence in a busy town is eerier, more alarming than gunshots and arguing as far as I'm concerned. You expect the violence, the raw and uncensored humanity of people unhappy in life and no real means to change. The people around here don't hide who they are. They don't bite their tongues until a later time when voicing an opinion contrary to their current company is appropriate. If an emotion bubbles up their throat, they spew on the sidewalk as if it's their God-given right to let the world know they are unhappy, or sad, or pissed they caught their best friend on her knees in the alleyway sucking a cock that didn't belong to them just for that bump they needed to make it through the night.

What *is* unusual right now is the false tranquility that seems to engulf the entire neighborhood. There's a sinister energy surrounding everything. Like dogs who can sense the tornado and impending storm just by sniffing the air, the folks up and down Parker Street seem to be taking cover.

Chilled both from the early spring air on my bare arms and the vibe that's crackling around me, a soul-deep shiver runs down my spine as I cross the street from the liquor store. The headlights of a car blind me as it closes the distance. I stare straight into the blinding light. momentarily wondering if the vehicle will pop over the curb and strike me down. A grin forms on my lips at the thought.

Disappointment clouded only by a tinge of relief washes over me as the car zooms past. Like all horror movies, the night comes alive again in a flash. A cat screeches in the distance, someone bangs the lid of a trashcan, and an argument over whose turn it is to watch the kids surrounds me.

All of it normal.

All of it more calming, more comforting than the quiet that surrounded me as a child.

It isn't until I'm certain I hear my name whispered over the buzz of the neighborhood that my skin tingles with the urgency to get back home, but I'm stubborn. So instead of increasing my pace and focusing on the lone light on the front porch of the house I live in, I slow to a crawl, hoping and praying, just like in that ridiculous Jeepers Creepers movie that something swoops down from the sky and carries me off.

Chapter 4

TJ

Like a magnet to jeopardy, Kaci walks in the dark, wearing a thin tank top and yoga pants. Less concerned about the cold air, I'm focused on the sharp jut of her nipples as she leaves her apartment and walks, in the dark no less, down the sidewalk.

This gorgeous girl, less than twenty-four hours ago, was on the verge of being gang-raped. Now, as if she doesn't have a care in the world, she's prancing down the street freshly showered and tempting every man she walks past.

I'm a sinner on my best day, not caring who I hurt or plow down on my way to have a good time, but I've always drawn the line at hurting women unless they legitimately deserve it of course. Those infractions usually come with a healthy dose of club betrayal. That being said, and I'm not one to blame the victim or start an argument on rape culture or suffer through opinions about why women should be able to wear whatever the fuck they want without fear of being assaulted, but the sight of Kaci walking down the road, her hair wet and dampening her back just enough to make it clear she isn't wearing a bra is almost enough to persuade me to take her against the wall of the alley she's fixing to walk past.

"My cock gets hard every time you walk past here."

I can't see her face, but there's no change in her posture that even hints at hearing the man even though I'm yards behind her, and he didn't bother to whisper his confession.

Clearly homeless, the man is dirty, emitting an odor that only shows up after too many missed showers. It's chilly outside, but he seems to be wearing numerous layers of clothing, probably everything he owns. He doesn't throw sexual innuendo at me as I pass him. I must not possess the same appeal as the green-eyed blonde a few yards ahead of me.

"Hey man, can I grab a smoke?"

My feet pause in front of him, but my eyes stay on Kaci's back as she walks across the street, turning left down the block.

"She's sexy as fuck, right?" My blood heats with his comment. I'm angered that he'd even chance looking at something that belonged to me, much less open his filthy mouth and speak the words aloud. "One of these days, I won't let her get away. How about that smoke, man?"

He nudges my shoulder like we're best buds.

I grin over at him when my prey disappears from sight. A sparkle lights his eyes as if he believes he's just found someone either with a cigarette or the same lack of morals when it comes to persuading members of the opposite sex.

Ignoring the urgency to get Kaci back in my line of sight, I pull loose change from my pocket and show the man my hand. "Sorry man, I don't smoke."

Like I knew he would, his eyes narrow on the tiny packet in my palm.

"Looks like you have something better." He literally licks his lips like the lion in a cartoon as he visualizes the zebra turning into a slab of meat.

"Not here." Two simple words. Not one of them an invitation, but the man sticks close to me when I walk around the corner of the liquor store and let the alley swallow me in darkness. By the time I turn back in his direction, he's so close to me the mildewed stench of his clothes burns my nose.

"What-a-what do you want for it?"

His eyes dart lower before raising up to mine. I can't tell if it's an offer or a refusal, but I'm not remotely interested in his lips on my cock.

"Tell me more about that girl." I urge as I shove the change back into my pocket and hold the tiny baggie between us.

"You want a taste, too, huh?" His eyes follow the sway of the bag between my fingers as if I'm a doctor giving him a neurological exam with a pin light.

"Do you know her name?" His head shakes, eyes still entranced with the plastic baggie.

"Nope." His jaw works again. "But it won't stop me from tasting her one of these days."

"You think she'd go for that?" He grunts. "She didn't seem too interested a few minutes ago."

"They all want it," he confesses with an enthusiastic squeal when I lower the product into his dirty gloved hands. "They may fight a little at first, but that's what makes it so much fun."

Another predator mere blocks from Kaci's front door. Protecting her will be impossible.

"You got a light?"

"Sure, buddy." The light of the moon glints off the blade I pull from my waist rather than the flame he's hoping for. He mustn't register the difference because he doesn't so much as make a peep when my hand surges upward, the metal piercing the bottom of his chin before reappearing out of the top of his head.

Unblinking eyes glaze over as his brain finally tells everything else that the game is over and it's time to shut the factory down. Getting him off my knife and into the dumpster we're standing beside is easier than I'd expected. The numerous layers of clothing contribute to my wrong assumption about his size. I have no clue when the trash runs around here, but it's cold enough still that he won't start stinking for at least a few days.

I don't believe in God. Hell, I don't believe in right and wrong most days. I believe in my club. Plain and simple.

But, there's something mystical or paranormal that, if you're paying close enough attention, you'll notice surrounding someone who dies. The air either charges or loses all energy. It's really hard to tell, but tonight is no different. Other than the rusty squeal of the dumpster lid when I entomb the dead guy, not another sound can be heard. The mice that scampered away when I lured him down this alley are silent, as are the natural noises of the neighborhood. Even the constant drone of the dryers at the laundromat a block over halt. It's as if the universe is having an unscheduled moment of silence for the piece of shit predator I just cleaned from the streets.

Drawn back toward the street, I lurk in the shadows, making it to the mouth of the alley just in time to see Kaci walking back by, her face lit by the bright light of a passing car. She's a gorgeous, pixie-like creature. She's going to be the death of me, a siren singing her song of seduction without having to open her mouth with the effort.

"Kaci," I pant, my lips moving without my brain engaging.

I trail her, the rest of her trip taking much longer than it actually should. She seems nervous or scared, her back tense with the emotions, but they only serve to slow her down rather than make her walk faster to the false sense of security behind her wafer-thin front door.

I smile, reveling in her new self-preservation when she doesn't bend at the middle to retrieve her door key. The smile immediately slides away when, without pulling a key from somewhere, she turns the knob and steps inside of her apartment.

She hasn't learned a fucking thing. I've killed four people in the last day to protect her, and she relentlessly continues to channel trouble, repeatedly exposes herself to threats as if she's seeking them out. She'd be better off putting a gun to her head and pulling the trigger. At least the death would be quick and almost painless, something better than this long drawn out hobby of testing fate.

A dog barks in the distance, but my eyes never leave her apartment. My weight doesn't shift even when my feet begin to hurt about an hour into my observations. Adding to her growing list of infractions, I notice she has only a sheer curtain hanging over her single window. Each and every time she gets off her bed to cross the room, her hazy form is easily recognizable. I both love and hate the easy view into her privacy.

Hate will be the winning emotion tonight, because it merely means that I'm not the only one who would be rewarded by simply walking down the street. Hate because she shouldn't be giving away for free what I'm willing to work so hard for.

I don't reach into my pocket to grab my phone until after the sixth or seventh text rings out.

Briar: We have trouble.

I huff a humorless laugh because trouble follows the Ravens Ruin MC like the fucking black plague. There isn't a week that goes by without incident. We never get a break. Someone always fucks up. Someone is constantly needing a reminder of who is in charge. We run fucking drugs in the majority of the northeastern United States, and yet we spend most of our damn time babysitting people.

"I should've gone to college," I mutter as I decide that the chances of Kaci leaving the house again tonight are slim.

Before my impulsivity gets the best of me, I pull my eyes from her window and walk back to my SUV. Shaking her and making her see the light doesn't seem like it will be well received, so I have to figure out a way for this damn woman to take her life and her safety more seriously. I have a feeling it's going to be an uphill battle, but it's a sacrifice I'm willing to make.

Chapter 5

Kaci

The best thing about fear is the rush of adrenaline, that ten-foot tall and bulletproof feeling you get right before fate decides if your fear is warranted or not. It's what makes people jump out of planes, hike mountains with little ability to breathe, and drive at break-neck speeds around a track. It's the threat of death and injury that makes your heart pump wildly in your chest. It's the knowledge that just one miscalculation could end it all.

It's why it's also an addiction, better than any drug on the face of the earth, as far as I'm concerned. My body has experimented with almost everything you can imagine and nothing, absolutely nothing, compares to the rush I get when I'm afraid.

Due to the addictive nature, it's also why it has to be fed. It's why, instead of staying home and numbing out to the latest Netflix series, I'm coating my eyelids with color as dark as soot and painting my lips crimson. I'm not a makeup expert. I don't have the newest Naked palette by Urban Decay. The three-dollar charcoal shadow I grabbed at the drug store works just fine.

In my experience, the guys at the parties I hit to get my rush don't honestly give a shit what I look like. It's the level of inebriation and pliability that concerns them more than anything else. Believe it or not, a huge percentage of college-aged men are just one bad decision away from Brock Turner status where no means maybe, and the inability to protest equals consent.

It's a fucked-up mindset, bordering on entrapment putting these guys in situations like I do, but I figure if they were stand-up guys in the first place, I wouldn't even be a temptation for them. The guys I go after are the ones that would hurt any other female, and it's that level of ego and entitlement I'm looking for tonight.

My hand trembles as I dab a tissue to my lips to remove excess lipstick. Anticipation thrums through my body, forcing me to attempt picking up my cell phone twice before I have it safely in my hand. Impatience fills my blood as I wait for the Uber driver to arrive. I have a car, but I have no idea how the night will end, so I walk right past it and climb into the back seat of the hired car.

After giving him the address listed on the chat thread in a popular group online, I sit back, eyes closed, and imagine all the things that could happen tonight. Filtering out all the positive outcomes, I pick and choose the most horrific scenarios and let them play on repeat until the driver informs me we've arrived.

I don't stand on the curb and analyze my choices or give myself a second to rethink. With clear focus, something that needs to be remedied immediately, I stride up to the house and push myself through the open door. Even the cool air from outside doesn't alleviate the damp heat stifling the room from those dancing and standing in tight groups to talk.

The beat of my heart echoes in my ears as my claustrophobia kicks into full gear. I aim toward the kitchen for my first drink of the night. I usually pre-game, but my liquor supply back home is low. Being one hundred percent sober heightens my anxiety, and the buzz alone is enough to encourage me to stand in the middle of the room, close my eyes, and let it take me to my happy place, but I know myself better. The longer I wait, the more I increase my chance of running out of here.

"You look good enough to eat."

I turn, smiling at the first guy to approach me tonight.

"That so?" I lick my bottom lip to entice him further, but his focus is on my tits. Men are so fucking easy.

He nods before lifting his beer bottle to his lips, almost as if his mouth needs something in it.

"How hungry are you?"

"Go upstairs with me and find out," he challenges, his eyes looking past my chest for the first time. Shock fills his eyes as if he's surprised I even have a head.

"Are you asking me or telling me?" His face is angled down again.

"Asking?"

"No thanks." I spin around and refocus on the kitchen.

"It's a madhouse in there. Take mine." A red cup appears right in front of my face.

He's cute, maybe twenty-one tops, but the cockiness of just expecting me to take his drink is exactly what I'm looking for. The other thrill I'm seeking is evident on his face.

"I'm hoping for something a little stronger."

His grin widens as he lifts his other arm showcasing a half-empty bottle of tequila.

"Even stronger than that." I brush my fingers under my nose, and it's all it takes for him to understand.

"I got just what you need, baby." Isn't he adorable with the pet names? "Follow me."

Anticipating going to a quieter part of the house, I'm shocked when he tells a few guys to move before plopping down on the sofa in the middle of the living room. The cup of beer and bottle of tequila drop down on the table, and he's pulling out a vile of coke before I can plant my ass down beside him.

My mouth is watering by the time he dumps the contents out on a magazine and scrapes it into three lines. He produces a rolled-up dollar bill from thin air, much the same way he did with the cup of beer earlier.

"Ladies first." Taking it from his hand, I give him a coquettish smile.

"Such a gentleman." His wicked 'just you wait' smile betrays his chivalrous actions.

"Let me help you," he says as I lean down and swipe the bill across two lines. His hand sweeps my hair from my face.

His anger in me taking liberties with more than one line is evident in the punishing grip of his fingers tangled in my hair. He doesn't relent as I lift my head and bring the back of my fingers to my nose.

"You're a greedy little girl, aren't you?" I want to huff at his little girl comment, but the glorious burn from the coke is subsiding and numbing my throat.

His tongue licks at his lips, and I'm cognizant enough to notice he's a handsome guy. One I'm certain many girls around here would willingly let him do anything he pleases to them, but that kind of thrill isn't his game. He's made a mistake if he thinks I'm going to say no or tell him to stop. I never do. Playing victim isn't part of my adventures. I don't imagine he'd pump the brakes anyway. As far he's concerned, he just paid for my time and bought himself a little extra considering I snorted a line he'd intended for himself.

"You want the last one?"

His tongue licks up the side of my neck, and an uncontrollable shiver runs down my spine. This is the best part, knowing, even though he's good-looking, I'm not attracted to him in any way.

"A drink first," I whisper loud enough for him to hear and hope I can use the tequila to choke down the bile quickly rising in my throat. The thrill of the fear, of the unknown, of the possibility that this asshole could finally be the one to cause lasting damage is putting my fight or flight through its paces.

"There's my girl," he praises, raising the bottle to my lips and pouring the warm liquid down my throat. Releasing my hair for the first time, he nudges my shoulder when my eyes drift closed and angles his head toward the table. "Last line."

He smiles with the reminder, not even bothering this time to hide the sinister glint in his eyes.

"Who do we have here?" a new voice asks.

The sofa shifts next to me as I lift and tilt my face to the ceiling to enjoy those first few seconds of the blow hitting the back of my throat. The bass pounding through the amateur sound system rattles and pops, leaving the beat and words of the song undecipherable, but I'm high enough to imagine my own music in my ears. My swaying is interrupted when a hand falls on each of my knees. I'd laugh at them for starting so far away, but I'm more concerned that I misjudged the red solo cup guy.

"So frisky," I giggle and bat the first guy's hand away to test him. Guy number two is circling my inner thigh with the tip of one single finger, but at least he's made it under the hem of my skirt.

"No stopping me now," red solo cup mutters as he clasps my wrist and forces my hand down between us. His hand lands on my knee again but moves quickly up my thigh.

The fear of him being too nice is replaced by the uneasiness his aggression has caused. I close my eyes and revel in the pounding of blood in my ears. Combined with the coke, my heart is on overload.

"Drink."

A bottle is once again lifted to my lips, and I take a long swig without even opening my eyes. There could be a third guy involved by now for all I know. I don't sputter when my mouth fills faster than I can swallow. I just let the liquid run down my cheeks and neck.

"Fuck yeah," someone grunts.

Rough fingers tug on my thighs, and I fight him a little. Not because I'm saying no but angering red solo cup a little will ensure marks are left on my skin. Waking up with injuries increases the thrill the next time I want to go out. I live for it.

"Keep 'em open," red solo cup warns in my ear with another harsh tug to my leg. "You're about to get fucked in front of all these people."

His menacing chuckle pales in comparison to others I've encountered. The threat of assault in front of an audience isn't new to me, and his puppy threat is nothing compared to the rabid bulldogs I've been introduced to.

"Take another drink." A cup is tilted to my lips, and the beer does little to hide that metallic taste I'm all too familiar with. I drain the drink before I can second guess myself, and my heart somehow manages to beat even faster. My eyes open and meet red solo cups'. "Hey, baby. Ready to have some fun?"

"Shouldn't she be awake for that?" I hear from across the room before the laced beer forces my eyelids to drop.

Chapter 6

TJ

"Where the fuck are you?" Briar's agitated voice fills my ear as I stand across the street from yet another fucking house party.

Kaci is inside according to the tracker I put on her phone. Grateful she's actually carrying it with her tonight, I breathe a sigh of relief, forcing me to realize I'm still on the phone when my breath ricochets in my ear.

"TJ?"

"I'm around," I mutter. "You aren't my fucking father. Quit checking up on me."

I hit the end button and shove my phone back into my pocket before he can utter another word.

"It's more fun inside," a twinkly voice says beside me. "Join me?"

Cold hands tug on my bare forearm until I pull my hand free from my jeans pocket. A pretty girl with blonde hair similar to Kaci's but having the wrong color eyes smiles up at me. In a past life, or a mere couple of weeks ago if math is your thing, I wouldn't have joined this girl inside with the other partiers. A couple of weeks ago, I would've bypassed the front door altogether and urged her into the shadows with me. Fucking her against the side of the house, no matter who was around, would've been my first goal, but I'm not here for this chick.

"Why are you out here alone?" The question is second nature, especially considering why I'm here in the first place. These damn college chicks are supposed to be educated, but they don't seem to have any concern for their safety.

"I'm not." Her brow furrows as she looks around and realizes she is in fact alone. "My friends must've gone inside already. Come on it's cold, and I need some alcohol to warm me up."

The only reason I let her tug me across the street and up the steps to the house is that Kaci is inside, and I can't protect her ass from outside.

That voice in my head that's been telling me to leave her the fuck alone since I dumped that bum's body in the dumpster silences immediately the second I turn my attention to the living room. Sandwiched between two assholes, Kaci's head lolls on her shoulders. With the crowd surrounding them, you'd think these guys would take her someplace a little quieter considering consent is the last thing she can manage right now.

The only thing making her seem animated at all is the jerks one guy is causing from using her hand to stroke his exposed cock. It's clear he's doing all the work, yet, not one person in the room is stopping them or voicing an opinion about what's going on. Society is so fucking broke these days.

I'm making my way across the room when the guy on her other side pulls his hand from under her skirt, spitting on his fingers before attempting to slide them back between her legs.

Red-hot anger fills my vision as I shove the last few people standing between me and her out of the way.

My first fist is aimed at the guy with his hand up her skirt. His head snaps back, but I lose it even more when he refocuses and has the fucking balls to be surprised I hit him.

"Dude? What the fuck?"

My fist meets his pretty-boy face twice more, and then again when he tries to speak. Getting the message, his jaw snaps shut.

The guy on the other side, so drunk or high, hasn't even noticed me pummeling his friend. He's overly concerned with Kaci's hand and its inability to stroke his half-limp cock to climax.

Normally, I'd give it a minute, say something smart-assed to get his attention, but seeing her like this is killing me. I opt for a quick knee to the face. This guy actually has the courtesy to pass out with the first hit. Clearly, he's smarter than his sexual assault companion.

"Thank God," someone in the crowd mutters. My eyes snap up to try to determine who it was. "Glad someone stopped it. That chick has been passed out for the last ten minutes."

My eyes narrow on the guy across the room. Shock and dread wash over his face as I make my way in his direction. Hitting this fucker in the face is just as satisfying as the first two. I grip him by the hair as he falls to his knees.

"If you see something wrong going on," I kick the stupid fucker in the gut, "then you fucking put a stop to it."

I lift my eyes to my captive audience. "Quit being fucking sheep!"

People grumble and turn to look away. I fucking hate people.

"Give me your keys," I tell the guy, shaking him by the hair still in my fist.

His hand pats his pocket, and less than a breath later he's pushing a keyring into my palm.

"Now get the fuck up and show me where you parked."

I release him, but the guy must be an all A student because he doesn't try to get away. He even waits to the side while I lean over and scoop Kaci up. She's dead weight in my arms, and I hate that she's put herself in this situation, but even more so because showing her how I feel about her behavior wouldn't even be remembered by morning time.

"Will you return it?"

"Fuck no," I grunt. He opens the passenger side door, so I can lower Kaci inside without jostling her too much, and for some reason, I'm less angry because of the kind gesture. "I'll park it back on the street in a couple hours."

"Thank you."

Ignoring him, I walk down the block to grab my cut and jacket off my bike.

"That's badass," the guy praises when I slide the double layers of leather over my back. "I've always wanted to be in a motorcycle club."

"You don't have the fucking nuts for it."

With that parting declaration, I hop in his truck and take off.

I strapped Kaci into her seatbelt, but with each sharp turn and equally crappy road I take, her head just rolls back and forth. I should've strapped her into the middle seat so I could put my arm around her to keep her steady, but the console between us is loaded down with shit.

I slam on the brakes, noticing the stop light mere seconds before blowing through it. Paying attention to Kaci instead of the road nearly just caused a wreck.

"Ughhh." My eyes snap to her again.

She's moving her hands a little but making no effort to open her eyes. Either she's been out of it for a while, or they didn't give her much. My teeth clench.

"I'm getting you home safely."

She makes a sound like a snort, but she doesn't say another thing. She doesn't jolt when I place the truck in park, or when I open her door. Goosebumps sprout all over her exposed flesh, but I'm too pissed right now to even enjoy the sight of her pushed up tits and the way the skin pebbles there.

As fucking usual, the key is under the goddamn mat. I don't know why she fucking bothers to hide it. She might as well just hang it on a damn string from the doorknob. Not locking the door at all would require the least amount of effort.

"You're gonna end up dead," I hiss when I unlock the door of her studio apartment and push it open with the toe of my boot.

"Sounds like a good time," she mumbles.

Without conscious thought, my head shakes, and my mouth tilts up in a frustrated smile.

"Why would you put yourself in harm's way like that? Those guys could've hurt you tonight."

She doesn't bother to open her eyes, but her lips tilt as if what happened tonight happened exactly as she'd planned.

"I think you were drugged again."

She sniffs, more clearing her nose like a coke user than as if she's getting sick and in need of a tissue. I have a long history with my dad being a user. The signs are all over this girl. "Happens a lot."

"You drive me insane," I grumble, shifting her weight in my arms so I can pull back the covers of her bed. I'm surprised the thing is made with how chaotic her life is.

"You'd still fuck me if I spread my legs for you." Her words are low, without a hint of seduction. "You'd probably fuck me even if I didn't. Just like those guys would've tonight."

Her words are heavy like she's using all of her strength to get them out, but her eyes never open again.

Leaving her on the bed, I enter the small but tidy bathroom, grabbing and wetting a washrag before returning to her bedside.

"Do you believe in angels?"

When I first place the warm cloth against her cheek, she tries to pull back. I cup her other cheek with my palm and soothe her the way I imagine you would a startled child.

"I think a better question," I begin as I press the cloth to her closed eyelid, "is why do *you* believe in angels?"

Her small smile grows.

"Angels keep saving me from myself." My hand stills, the washcloth covering one cheek. "I wish they'd leave me the fuck alone."

Chapter 7

Kaci

Tears warm my cheeks before my eyes even open. My head is pounding just like every morning after going out, but the pain radiating behind my eyes isn't the cause. Waking up, plain and simple, is what upsets me. Within minutes I'm sobbing because I know I'm in my own bed. I'm not waking up in an alleyway, or some abandoned house. It's clear by the familiar scent of my own sheets that I'm home and safe.

It would be a relief for most people but knowing what day it is makes being alive even more unbearable. I wanted last night to be the night all the pain and guilt finally ended. As much as I want to die, ending my own life isn't an option. I'm not religious or not considering suicide because of some tainted vision of what the afterlife holds. I'm just incapable of doing it. All my attempts in the past have been failures, and somehow, I know living and waking up each time I put myself in danger is part of my punishment. It's penance for what happened nine years ago.

Remorse and my need for continuous suffering are why I climb out of bed and make preparations to go to my parents' house. I strip out of my clothes from last night and cry harder when I look in the mirror and see no reminders of last night. There are no bruises or scratches anywhere on my body. I have nothing to beat myself up for, and I know it only means that I'll be forced back out of the house sooner than usual.

Ice-blue eyes fill my head when I climb in the shower, and they don't dissipate when I towel off and get dressed. I'm haunted by them but tormented even more by not knowing who they belong to or what purpose they serve in my life.

The people from the party last night wouldn't recognize me. Hell, taking one last look at myself in the mirror, I no longer see the girl who's wearing a prim dress with knotted hair at the nape of her neck. Even though that's exactly who's looking back at me, my reflection is as fake as the actress that will go home and pretend life is the opposite of what it actually is, however, with any luck, I won't have to pretend to be someone else today.

The car I drive to my parents' house is the same one I was gifted in high school. The hand-me-down BMW has seen better days, but I'll continue to drive it as long as it continues to crank. It fits in my life just like everything else that could be upgraded but hasn't. Smaller rundown houses transform into nicer homes before transitioning once again to large estates as I leave Andover and draw closer to Newbury.

My childhood home brings bittersweet feelings when it comes into view. I hate coming here, but at the same time, I need the shame that settles on my shoulders the second the gate swings open, giving me access to the last place I'm welcome. This isn't home. This is where my parents live in their own grief and blame.

True to form, my father merely grunts when he opens the door and sees me standing here. He doesn't let his eyes linger for even a second before turning back around and refilling his whiskey glass. Almost as if I'm allergic to this house, my throat constricts the second I step inside and close the door behind me.

"Why are you here?"

"You know why I'm here."

I don't see Mother in the living room with him, and I didn't really expect to, but knowing she's isolated somewhere in the house makes my gut clench.

"You shouldn't have come," he grunts before turning his tumbler up and draining the glass.

Inwardly, I wonder how much he's drank today, or if he even stopped from the glasses he poured last night.

I don't respond to him. Once a year my shadow darkens his door, but for him, that's one time too many.

"Where's Mom?"

He doesn't answer me.

"I put money in your account every month, so I don't have to see your face."

It burns even more that there isn't a trace of emotion in his voice. His demeanor isn't angry or aggravated. He's had decades of perfecting his responses to coincide with political requirements. Even at home, he has the ability to school his face. It's been years since he's had any viable political aspirations, but most of the time he remains in character.

"Of all days, today is the worst time for you to show up here."

"It's Seth's birthday." My words are almost a whisper, but I know he heard them because he flinches, his eyes closing tightly before he can shove the emotion away. My words hit their target, and I tense waiting for what I know is coming.

"So you think the reminder that you killed my only son is something that I need?"

Swallowing repeatedly doesn't remove the lump in my throat. I shouldn't be upset. Coming here and being treated like this is exactly the reason I show up year after year. The reminder of what I did nine years ago feeds my pain for a while.

"Kaci." My mother's dry, weak voice forces another wave of chills over my skin. "You look nice, dear."

I don't bother running my hands down my dress to make sure it's sitting just as it's supposed to. My mother gives me empty compliments every time she sees me, but they don't mean anything. Years ago, she wasn't like this. Before Seth died, she was brutal in her reminders on how a lady is required to act, and I never once met her standards.

"How are you, Mother?"

"Good."

I know better. Her hair is a mess, blonde, natural curls springing from her head in all directions, and the sagging clothes on her body don't even coordinate. This is the woman she became years ago with the help of Vicodin and vodka, and she shows no signs of slowing. Like myself, my mother also has her own ways to fast track herself into oblivion. The drugs and liquor are her own slow spiral into death. We all have our methods.

"It's Seth's birthday," I whisper the reminder just like I did with my father, only her reaction is stunted. Her eyes were already glassy when she walked in, and there isn't a change even now.

"Is it?" I'm not surprised she wasn't already aware. Most of the time she doesn't even know what month it is, much less the actual date.

"Are we doing lunch?"

"I don't want you here, and I'm definitely not sitting down at the table with you."

Mom nods her agreement with my father, more out of habit than understanding of his words.

"I'm your only child." I know reminding them of this is only twisting the knife deeper into his gut.

"You murdered my son!"

Only now do his eyes turn to me, and his emotions begin to show.

Last year when things took this turn, I reminded him that Seth died from choking on part of a toy he bought for his three-year-old son. I made sure he remembered that mother had told him that the toy airplane had an eight to ten age range, but he put her in her place, making sure she knew he'd buy Seth whatever he wanted.

"Seth is smart enough to play with the damn plane," he'd said to her before they left the house with me in charge of watching him. Just like always, she agreed because, in her eyes, he was always right. My father's word was the law in his house, and no one was to contradict him.

Three hours later, I was making him a grilled cheese sandwich while my parents were at a town council meeting, my little brother died with one of the plane's tires lodged in his throat.

In my father's eyes, I'm one hundred percent to blame. Something he reminds me of each and every time I see him.

The yelling brings me back to being fifteen again, alone in the house while I tried desperately to get him to breathe while waiting for the ambulance. My efforts were hopeless, and the blame was immediate. I didn't fault my father for pinning me with the blame. His anger was warranted. If I hadn't answered the phone that day, things could've turned out very differently, but after hearing rumors around school that he liked me, I'd been anticipating Desmond's call for days.

Shaking my head to clear it of the past, I just watch my father. The tips of his ears redden, and his grip on the whiskey glass in his hand is so tight his knuckles begin to lose color. Apparently, he's easier to anger than he was a year ago, so I don't bother to remind him that the toy plane was his idea.

"I'm going to go lie down." I don't bother to acknowledge my mother as she leaves the room, and neither does my father.

"I want you gone. You never should've come back six years ago." His words have a drunken edge to them, but the fire in his eyes makes it very clear that he's speaking his true feelings.

That reminder is a slap to the face. He's always blamed me for Seth, and I've always shouldered that. My guilt weighs me down every day over what happened to my little brother, but my father bringing up six years ago is a low blow, even for him.

Having fulfilled my yearly need of disgrace from my family, I don't utter another word as I walk out of the house. I don't even bother closing the door behind me, knowing it will anger my father to no end for disrespecting his house.

If I'm lucky, this will be the year he cuts me out completely. Having nowhere to live would be the icing on my shit cake, but I know that won't happen. My father will continue to pay my bills if only to prevent me from coming back home.

Chapter 8

TJ

"You seem agitated tonight."

I'm beyond annoyed, but it's not Legs's business that I've been grounded to the damn clubhouse like a child. Lynch's order earlier in church is still ringing in my ears, but I know why he commanded everyone to stay close tonight.

Tomorrow we head down to Richmond to meet with Luis Jiménez's crew. Not long ago Jiménez practically forced a contract for cocaine down my brother's throat, and in two days we're handing over a ton of cash for over thirty-five kilos of coke. I'm not upset about the run. Thanks to the ever-raging war on drugs, riding down the highway with enough snow to land me in jail for the rest of my natural life is a thrill I look forward to. It's the distance and my inability to get to Kaci if she pulls some more stupid shit that frustrates me.

"We can always go back to your room." The coo in Legs's voice and the brush of her hand down my arm is driving me insane, and not in the *strip your clothes off and let me fuck you* kind of way either.

I haven't been an angel in the last couple of weeks. I've dabbled with some of the girls at the club. I mean a man has to come, or he'll go mental after all, but these women here no longer bring the same thrill I used to get from them. Thinking of teaching the girl in Andover a lesson or two is all my cock gets excited for these days. I know once I have her things will go back to normal, but it's all I can focus on in the meantime.

"Hitting it kinda early aren't you?" I ask Briar as he plops down on the sofa across from me, spilling whiskey out of his glass because he's too wasted to know he's got the damn bottle in his other hand.

As if realizing he has both, Briar tilts the glass up to his lips before dropping it on the wooden table between us.

I know why he's acting like a surly bastard. The man is head over heels for my little sister. I've known it for a while. Lynch, my older brother and club president, asked me about them the other day, and even though I confirmed we both had the same suspicions, he wasn't ready to do anything about it. If it weren't for the VP's oath of celibacy and his loyalty to the club the last ten years, he'd be in the fucking ground already. In the meantime, it's an absolute fucking blast to mess with him.

"I saw Molly at the vet's office today." I know I hit him in the right spot when he narrows his eyes and lifts the bottle to his lips.

Molly recently got a job at a vet's office in town, and the animal doctor has garnered some of her interest. It's eating him alive, because there isn't shit he can do about it without going against a direct order from his president.

"She seems to like him, I mean likes working there." He doesn't acknowledge me, and before I can say something else, a leggy brunette blocks my line of sight to him. I stare at her back as if I do it long enough, I'll be able to see straight through her.

Legs huffs next to me, and I can't be bothered to feel guilty that I forgot she was even sitting beside me. I also don't realize she has her hand on the front of my jeans. My dick doesn't even respond to her. Picky motherfucker.

I grunt before moving her hand from me and placing it back on her lap. "Don't ever touch me without my permission."

Her head snaps back, and I know why she's baffled. I've had this woman in every way imaginable. Her blood has flowed over the blade of my knife more times than I can count, and each and every time she begged me for more. A couple weeks ago, I was seriously considering making her my old lady, or choosing her to entertain me exclusively. Things changed when I saw Kaci lying in that bed covered in blood. I can't explain why, but an immediate connection was formed, and I'm just as confused by it.

"You're wasting your time," I tell the girl vying for Briar's attention. "Briar doesn't—"

"Hey, doll," he slurs as he pats his lap.

"Well then." Surprise and anger fill my voice as I watch the brunette take the proffered seat, and when Briar grins at me, it takes everything I have not to stab him in the neck. Acting this way now is getting him closer and fucking closer to a visit to the basement.

"I thought he didn't—" Holding up my hand to silence her, I continue to glare at my brother's best friend. VP or not, he's going to be in a world of hurt if he doesn't get that girl off him.

"Can I suck your dick?" I hear the brunette ask.

All of my focus is on him and this new girl. I'm waiting for him to tell her yes, but the words don't come. His only saving grace is the sour look on his face as she wiggles her hips. He must be trying to prove a point, either to himself or to me. The fact that he might be letting this shit happen, so I don't get suspicious about him and Molly calms my racing heart a little.

Being the asshole that I am, I pull my phone from my pocket and snap a picture of the girl on his lap. If he's doing this to prove a point, either to my little sister, or to me, having proof of his indiscretion isn't a bad idea.

"What are you doing?" The strain and fear in Briar's voice make a wide smile spread across my lips, and I full out laugh when I see him push her a little to get her off his lap. She doesn't budge, but I commend his effort.

"I'm documenting your return to manhood." My words are sugary sweet, but I know he can read the look on my face, and it clearly says *take this any further, and you won't have to worry about the celibacy vow because you won't have a dick to fuck with.*

"I'm next," Legs says.

"Better find someone else to fuck tonight, doll." I sneer down at Legs. "You won't be getting a piece of me or a piece of him."

Legs huffs but is smart enough not to throw an insult or argument as she stands and walks away.

The girl on Briar's lap says some stupid bullshit, playing the innocent card, and I snort a humorless laugh. The girl can't play virginal when the first thing she said to the man was offering her mouth to be fucked. At the same rate he pulls in air to his lungs, he tilts that whiskey bottle to his lips. At the rate he's going he won't have to worry about making a decision. The alcohol will render his cock useless.

Just as I expected to happen, ten minutes later he's passed out, head laid back on the sofa and soft snores coming from his parted lips.

"Oh shit," Ronan spits when the front door slams shut.

My eyes snap from my sister, to the girl licking Briar's neck, and back to my sister again.

"Hey, Princess."

After noticing the girl on Briar's lap, my sister glares at me as if she's expecting me to do something.

"You aren't the only one who knows how to handle a knife, big brother, but I won't be as disciplined or discerning as you." Another smile spreads across my face. People underestimate Molly because she's so tiny, but they fail to realize she was raised in the brutality of this club just like Lynch and me. She can handle herself, and I have no doubt she means business when she takes a half step toward the girl still attached to Briar's neck.

"You can't ruin the man's good time," I tease as her cheeks redden.

"Oh fuck." Ronan must see the angry tremble in her fists because he shoves the chick getting ready to suck his dick away and stands to cross the room. "Hey, honey?"

The newest patched member to the club circles his arms around the brunette's waist, and I flinch when Briar doesn't move. He's so fucking drunk he doesn't even realize the chick was there. My gut clenches because I beat the shit out of three guys the other night for doing this exact same shit to Kaci. The double standard hits me in the face a little too late. Jesus, I'm just like that asshole who didn't say anything when those two fucks were assaulting my girl.

"Eighty-sixed. You got it, Princess," Ronan says before carrying the girl out the front door.

Briar jolts awake when Molly kicks his boot, but he's slow to respond.

"Baby?" The pain and love I hear in his voice is all the confirmation I need for the way he feels about her.

"Where did she go?" Briar asks the same time my sister reaches for him and says, "A little help, TJ?"

I can't help the chuckle that slips out because this situation is just as messy as the one I placed myself in with Kaci.

"Why were you letting that girl lick all over him?" Molly asks as I help hoist Briar's heavy body up to standing.

Irritation flares. I can't be fucking responsible for every damn person in the world. I'm not Briar's keeper.

"He's a grown man," I remind my sister. "I'm not his mother or his warden."

"He was passed out, shithead," she snaps.

"Such a pretty mouth saying such nasty things," Briar slurs.

"He wasn't passed out when they got started." Pain multiplies like pressure in a dropped can of soda in my gut when I see her face fall. Apparently, she'd let herself believe that chick was acting on her own accord without an invitation.

Hurting Molly is the very last thing I want, but sometimes the asshole in me escapes before I can close my mouth.

"I was going to kill her instead of you," Briar whispers. He's talking to Molly, but his head is right beside my ear, so I hear the words meant only for her.

Briar is a brutal motherfucker, but he'd never lay a finger on a woman unless she deserved it, and although he didn't really want that chick tonight, she didn't do anything to deserve being hurt. I take his words as a joke, even though the thought of what it means in my head makes me want to cringe.

"You drank a little too much to be murdering anyone's pussy, bro." I cringe at my words as I help Molly get Briar onto his bed. My sister is grown by legal standards, but she's a few years past ripe for club standards. Lynch and I got an extra early start when it came to sex. I pray Molly is untouched, but it's not something I want to think about.

"You coming?" I ask her as I back away from the once again passed out VP.

She shakes her head as she continues to stare down at Briar.

"Be careful, Princess," I warn as I kiss her forehead before leaving the room.

Against my better judgment, I whistle at Legs from the entryway to the living room. She pops off Hornet's dick as if it's spring-loaded and follows me down the hallway. I can't even revel in his curses as we walk away. I have no ties, no strings to anyone, but guilt still washes over me when I close us into my bedroom.

Chapter 9

Kaci

I fed off the pain my father's words stabbed me with for the better part of a week. Today, I'm restless once again. I don't often drink alone, and recreational drugs are meant to be used in social settings. I'm not so far down the rabbit hole that I snort coke when I'm home alone, but today I'm considering it.

I eat my tacos from Tito's at the restaurant all while pretending I'm interested in the soccer game playing on the widescreen TV above the bar. The guy that is always standing on the front stoop of the liquor store was nowhere to be seen when I walked by earlier, and even the laundromat was missing its usual criminal vibe.

I'm waiting in Tito's until the sun fully sets. Maybe the deviants don't come out until the light leaves the sky. Normally, I'm not roaming around this early, but my fridge is empty, and I can't be bothered to go grocery shopping.

Walking home delivers the same less than stellar thrill that walking to the restaurant did. It's quiet, and unfamiliar, but the sinister feeling of someone lurking in the shadows doesn't hit me tonight. It's as if the slums of Andover have grown a conscience since my last trip down the street.

The creepy vibe I couldn't find on the way to get food renews full force when I reach my door. A card is closed in the door, and from the looks of it, the only way that could've happened is if someone opened my door to put it there. I pull the card out and push my door open, but I'm only greeted by darkness. Whoever it was didn't bother to lock the door, but they don't seem to be waiting inside either.

The rush of my blood echoes in my ears as I step inside and close the door without bothering to turn on a light. Standing in the middle of the room seems ridiculous after several long minutes of hearing nothing but my own breaths, so I click on my bedside lamp and stare down at the card. When I finally get around to turning it over to read, I realize just how crazy it is to be invited to party on a hand-written note. I don't have friends. There isn't anyone I speak to with any regularity. Hell, I only see my parents once a damn year.

What I don't think is crazy is my rush to get ready because the card says free alcohol and free transportation. Worcester is over an hour away, so whoever is throwing this little get together wants me there badly if they're sending someone to pick me up.

I have to admit, I'm a little disappointed when an Uber driver pulls up outside, rather than some mysterious town car, but I force myself to consider since a car service like Uber is seemingly friendlier, it could be intentional, a way for the person who invited me to set my mind at ease so I'll actually get in the car.

"Who hired you?" I ask the driver as soon as I climb in the back.

"Lady, I just go where they tell me."

He doesn't say another word to me the entire drive to Worcester. I still tip him generously even though he assured me he'd been compensated. Although the music in the dive bar is loud enough to be heard from the parking lot, the lack of cars, even for a Tuesday night, is concerning. Assuming this was going to be some big to-do was clearly a mistake, but I let my high-heeled shoes carry me inside anyway. I'm not going to miss free drinks for anything.

These people inside must've traveled together because dozens of smiling and half-drunk faces look my way when I enter the bar. Women dressed in tiny strips of clothing filter through big men wearing leather cuts. I have no firsthand knowledge of bikers, but everything I've read and heard about the guys in this area say they're nothing but trouble.

My smile grows as I walk deeper into the room. These guys are clearly used to women throwing themselves at their feet because even though I'm dressed to the nines with tons of skin showing, some don't even bat an eye when I saunter past them on my way to the bar.

"Tough crowd," I murmur as I wave down a waitress and order a tray of shots.

Men hate to see a woman drinking alone, and I know just how to lure in the most dangerous ones.

Just as promised, the bartender doesn't ask for money, but I shove a twenty in her tip jar anyway. Wasting daddy's money is the least I can do for the way he treated me on Seth's birthday. I toss back a shot, and when the guilt doesn't wash away with it, I tilt another one up. The waitress only smiles and replaces the two empties with two new ones.

"Be careful in here," she warns. "These guys are bad fucking news."

She tilts her head as if indicating I should look behind me, but I give her a bright smile. "My favorite kind of men."

I walk away, carrying the tray loaded with shots to an empty pub table near the dance floor. Several women are dancing seductively, putting on a show for a couple of guys paying them attention. I swear if there was a pole in the middle of the room, they'd all be fighting over it. That thought only makes me smile harder because men watching easy women are the ones I'm after.

"Party favor?" I grin when a tiny bag of coke is shoved in my face, but only because of the drugs. I've been hungry for a line for days, but it's a female offering me the coke, not a man with ulterior motives. I don't turn her down because there's still the chance she was sent by one of the guys in here to get me loosened up. Wouldn't be the first time it's happened. A shiver runs down my spine, but I push the memories away.

"What do I owe you?" I reach into the small pocket of my jeans, but her hand covers mine before I can pull cash out of it.

"Girls don't pay here."

I look at her, shocked, and a little turned on by her sultry voice, which is curious because I've never been attracted to a woman before. Granted, I'm rarely attracted to anyone, and the pull I get at parties has more to do with the possibility of getting hurt than the looks of the person doing the damage. I'm met with vibrant blue eyes and a grinning smile.

"I'm Xena." She offers me her hand, and I take it. When she pulls hers away, the tiny little baggie of coke is left in my palm.

"Thanks, but I don't have—"

"Here," she offers pulling a small mirror and rolled up bill from her purse.

"Are you here to butter me up so one of the guys can swoop in and fuck me?"

She seems like the kind of girl that appreciates honesty, and I just can't seem to keep my mouth shut tonight, which is unusual for me. Normally, I want to be left alone to get high while others circle me like prey. My need to socialize tonight is why the Uber driver refusing to chat irritated me so much.

"They won't."

"What?" I pull my head back before I can get the coke up my nose.

"They usually don't try to get my girls."

I grin at her but lower my head to snort before I comment on that.

"*Your* girls?" My voice squeaks because of the burn in my nose, but my new friend doesn't seem to mind.

"Xena's mouth is legendary." Another girl slides up to the table I've commandeered. She tosses two shots from my tray back before speaking again. "I'm Vixen."

I shake her hand also, but this girl isn't looking at my tits like Xena did when she first walked up.

"Kaci," I offer to both of them since I just realized I didn't tell Xena my name when she introduced herself. My head is already spinning, but I look to Xena to ask for more. "Can I get another?"

"Give it a minute," she answers. "Our shit is really strong."

"I know my limits." Why I'm arguing with the girl who just got me high for free isn't something I can concentrate on right now.

"Give it a minute," she repeats but hands me a shot glass in substitution.

Both girls are smiling at me when I set the shot back down on the tray.

"Wanna dance?" The question is moot since they each have one of my hands in theirs, and they're already dragging me to the dance floor.

The sound system is a million times better than any frat house I've partied at, and for once, I'm having a good time rather than looking for trouble to get into. The night is young, however, and in my experience, I know trouble will still be waiting for me when I decide to seek it out.

We're three or thirty songs in, I'm too fucking high off one line of coke to keep count when the entire bar explodes in a roar. From what I can tell, a couple of popular guys walk in, but I can't see them through the others dancing around me.

"Who's here?" I ask the girl closest to me. I don't know if I introduced myself to her yet or not. Honestly, between the coke and the shots, I don't know if I could introduce myself. The only thing I can focus on is the sway of my hips and liquid feeling of my body as it moves along with the music. Did I mention the ecstasy tab? These people have the best fucking drugs.

"TJ, Ronan, and Boston," the chick slurs beside me.

"Stay away from TJ unless you like getting hurt." She leans on me so much, I nearly topple over.

"I'm not an emotional kind of girl," I inform her, but her head shakes back and forth almost violently.

"He may fuck with your emotions also, but his knife is what does the most damage."

"You've had enough," Xena says as she loops her arm under the girl and carries her off the dance floor.

My mission has changed. Ten minutes ago, all I wanted to do was dance and have a good time. I was numb enough to just exist in this moment with people I don't know, but the mention of pain, something like knife play that can do serious damage, and my focus is adjusted to meet my desires.

Chapter 10

TJ

The fanfare when Ronan, Boston, and I walk into the bar is a little over the top, but it's expected. A brief shower is all we managed when we got to the clubhouse before driving to Worcester to meet up with everyone else.

The drops in New York went off without a hitch, and now it's time to relax and have a little fun. My aim is on the bar. Not for the liquor, but because Molly and Zoe are standing there talking. Checking with my family is usually my number one focus, but I'd be a liar if I said my senses weren't heightened with the thought that Kaci will be here. The invitation was a little over the top, but the prospect I trusted to set it up assured me he did exactly as instructed. Her key was under the mat just like usual, so leaving it with tempting and menacing flare was easily accomplished.

I know Kaci's game already. The woman is hell-bent on getting herself hurt, and I'm hoping she wouldn't resist the invite.

"Sister. Sister-in-law," I greet, kissing each of them on the temple.

I ignore Zoe's half step away from me. Seems she hasn't gotten over the little incident in the basement. She'll come around in her own time, I guess.

"Where's Lynch," Molly asks innocently like I can't read her like a book. She isn't asking about our older brother. She's more interested in his road partner this trip.

"He and Briar are still in Detroit. Won't be home for a couple more days." I hold my hand up to signal the bartender, and just as I'd hoped, she heads my direction.

"I hope you don't plan on sticking around up here. Service is shit for us when you bring out that smile." Zoe doesn't look in my direction as she focuses on the other side of the bar.

"You said this was invite-only." As a group, we all turn around to look at Legs. Like an angry little monkey, and just as clingy, she has her arms crossed over her chest. The agitated tap of her foot is a little over the top, even for her.

"It is," I answer, but that doesn't stop Legs from turning to point in the direction of the dance floor.

"Who is that?"

"How should I know?" I pray they don't hear the huskiness in my voice as my eyes land on the blonde that all my recent fantasies are made of. I map the delicate curve of her neck and slender shoulders, imagining my knife trailing down her milky skin. My cock jumps in my jeans.

"I'll tell her to leave."

Images of me driving that knife through the bum's head flashes in my mind, only the filthy creature who so vocally spoke of raping Kaci is transformed into Legs.

"You'll leave her alone," I grunt, grabbing her by the upper arm with enough force to make her flinch.

"Okay," she breathes. She loves the roughness, but my focus is still on the girl across the room. I don't bother acknowledging her hand as it skates down my shirt to rest right above my belt buckle.

The only reason I know she's still with me after grabbing my beer and crossing the room is because she tries to sit in my lap when I take a seat beside Ronan.

My focus is solely on Kaci as her head pops up, no longer lost in the music. She frowns, looking around as if she's just now realizing she's on the dance floor alone. Her lips turn down even more when she walks to a table overflowing with empty shot glasses, but the disappointment doesn't last long. She saunters, the sway of her hips hypnotizing me with every step she takes, up to where my sister and her friends are still chatting.

"Do you know her?" Legs is still clinging to the front of my shirt, so I bat her hand away. She can sit here all she likes but wrapping herself around me in an attempt to put some sort of claim on me isn't going to happen. She rests her hands on her lap, not pressing her luck with me. I was exceptionally brutal with her before leaving for Richmond, and I feel bad about it. She loved every minute, but that still didn't keep me from hurting her to ease the uneasiness I felt about leaving for several days.

"Are you going to answer me?"

Fuck, is this what being married feels like? If nagging and someone being up my ass 24/7 are what it entails, I'll be fucking single forever.

"No." I tilt my beer back to my lips, smiling as Kaci gives the group a little wave before shimmying her hips.

"You're staring at her like you want to fuck her."

"Don't have to know her to fuck her," I counter.

Ronan snorts, and we clink the necks of our beers together.

Kaci stays at the bar talking to everyone for a few minutes before she follows Zoe to the booth to continue their conversation. My sister hits the dance floor, and it doesn't take long for her to be swarmed by people. The club whores want to be her, and every idiot hangaround wants to fuck her.

I snap a quick video because a picture just wouldn't do it enough justice and send it to Briar. He's hours away, and there isn't a damn thing he can do about it. Knowing he'll be pissed makes me smile a little wider. I shoot him a picture when he asks what Zoe is doing. Thankfully she's being a good little girl sitting in the booth and talking with Kaci. I know he's hoping she's misbehaving as well so he can get Lynch riled up enough to head back this way.

Several songs later, and I've switched from beer to soda because I know I'm going to have to get Kaci home tonight. They've left the booth and are on the dance floor laughing and having a good time. I want to shoot the fucking DJ because each and every song he plays is more seductive than the last. Legs has disappeared, and I'm grateful for my ability to stand and go to the blonde luring me in without hearing her bitch about it.

She doesn't look back when I lock my hands on her hips and roll my body with hers. She smells delicious with hints of clean sweat from exertion, whiskey, and the body wash she keeps in her shower. I spent more time than I'm comfortable admitting to standing in her bathroom sniffing her lavender vanilla soap.

She turns in my arms, and her small smile grows. At first, I think she recognizes me from when I brought her home a week ago, but she doesn't say anything. Her hips move, legs widening until her skirt is hiked so high, it probably isn't covering her ass from behind so she can grind on my thigh.

"I'm Kaci," she pants so close to my lips I can smell the liquor on hers. "Nice to meet you."

She grinds even harder on my leg, and my cock grows jealous.

"Hi," I tell her with a smile.

As if she has come to her senses, she presses both of her hands against my chest. It only makes me hold her tighter. When she shoves at me again, I lower my arms and grip her ass. A wicked smile crosses her lips and realization slams me in the gut.

This is exactly what she does at the frat parties. She tees a guy up and revels in the abuse she suffers when she rejects him.

And I thought I was fucked up.

Her smile fades when I take a step back.

"Aren't you angry with me?"

I don't bother answering.

"What drugs have you done tonight?"

Everything she ingested here had to have been taken of her own free will. The guys in this fucking bar know what will happen if we catch one of them trying to drug a woman. We didn't have to tell them what almost happened to Molly months ago, they know it's wrong. The old Ravens Ruin crew wouldn't bat an eye, but these guys know better.

"A little of this, a little of that." Her hips keep moving, and when she realizes I'm not going to force myself on her, she closes the distance and wraps her arms around me again.

I should push her away and refuse to play her sick fucking games, but I'm anything but hypocritical since I'm a fan of some pretty twisted shit too.

"I'm TJ," I finally say, and smile when her brow scrunches up.

"The knife guy?"

My eyebrows hit my hairline in surprise. "What do you know about me?"

"I heard you like to hurt people with your knife." Her teeth dig into her bottom lip, and once again I'm infatuated with a girl who's nothing but trouble.

"I can make you come with just the tip of my blade."

She somehow manages to get closer. "You seem arrogant enough that I'm sure you believe you're that good, but I doubt you can make that happen."

"Are you challenging me?" My head tilts down further, and we're a fucking breath away. All she has to do is raise her head a couple of inches, and our mouths would connect.

"I just know my body." Her breaths grow shallow, and in my grip, I can feel her muscles tensing. The small tremble in her arms doesn't go unnoticed either as she clings hard to my back. "You can cut me, but I won't come. They never let me come."

Hatred for every man who has ever hurt her fills my blood to the point I have to take a step back.

"Let me take you home."

Her lip tilts up on the right.

"Let me freshen up first."

She turns and makes her way to the bathroom, and like a fucking dog I stand near the entrance and wait so long, I'm heading in the direction of the bathroom by the time she reemerges. Her steps aren't as sure as when she left fifteen minutes ago, and when I see Xena walking out right behind her, I know she's probably snorted more coke.

I let her lean on me as we make our way to the SUV. I strap her in beside me this time because I just know she's going to pass out before we get back to her place.

"Hi," she giggles as I click her seatbelt. "I'm Kaci."

She offers her hand to me, and I know for a fact that just like all the other times she's seen me, she won't remember tonight either.

Chapter 11

Kaci

My fingers tap against the note I found wadded up with my cash from my skirt last night. Google tells me that the address is exactly what I suspected. The Ravens Ruin clubhouse is out in the middle of nowhere near Purgatory Chasm. Rumor has it they don't even call the police if bad shit goes down on the property, which means it's my kind of place.

Yet, I've been sitting here contemplating about going for the last half hour. As many times as I've hoped each trip out would be my last, this place holds the most potential for actuality, and I can't bring myself to get off my bed.

There's a phone number written on the slip of paper along with Xena's name, but she wouldn't be my reason for going. Those ice-blue eyes I've been infatuated with and comments about knives are all that I've thought about since waking up this morning.

TJ brought me home last night, and although I reintroduced myself in his vehicle like I couldn't remember him, he didn't take the bait. He carried me inside, situated me on my bed, and covered me with blankets. He didn't let his eyes linger. He didn't take my clothes off with the excuse of making me more comfortable. He didn't molest me or touch me without permission.

To build my courage, I grab my flask from my bedside table and take a long pull. As the tequila burns down my throat, I refocus on the millions of questions I have for him.

Why do I feel like I know him even though I only met him last night?

Why didn't he hurt me?

Why didn't he use his knife on me like he promised?

A shiver of anticipation rolls down my arms at his dark promise.

I can make you come with just the tip of my blade.

I want exactly that, and that scares me more than walking into a frat house with the hopes of being hurt. Wanting someone is new to me, and the sole reason I haven't gotten off my bed to head to Ravens Ruin territory.

A few more slugs of tequila and my perspective changes. Within thirty minutes of making my decision, I'm in the back of a cab and arrowing toward the brutal biker's property. I don't give myself a second to think or wonder about how I'm going to get home. When the cabbie pulls up to the gate, I slide my card and jump out. He can't seem to get away fast enough, leaving me standing on the road with the gravel dust swarming around me.

"Hey there, gorgeous."

I smile at the guy standing just outside the door of a small guard shack.

"I heard there was a party here tonight." I give him my sweetest smile. I don't have to flirt very hard. My clothes, or lack thereof, do all the talking for me.

"Ever been here before?"

My head shakes, and his smile grows wider.

"You're in for a treat then. Tonight, is one of the few nights the guys let people in without formal invites." Reaching inside the shack he does something to activate the gate, and it's sliding open to reveal the Ravens Ruin clubhouse.

I must stand there staring at the building and the rows of motorcycles to the left of the parking lot because the gatekeeper sidles up beside me and whispers in my ear, "I'd tell you that the guys in there don't bite, but I don't want to disappoint you."

He chuckles when I can't hide a full body shiver.

"Clubhouse rules," he begins, "no fighting with the other girls. No touching the VP. No touching the Prez unless Zoe says you can."

"And everyone else?"

"They're all fair game, darlin'." He gives me a little push to get me started, and honestly, I need it. I don't think I'd begin walking toward the door otherwise.

The gate begins to close, startling me. When I look back over my shoulder, I realize he's closing me inside. My blood pumps harder, and the familiar sound of my raging heart pounds in my ears. I make my way between a couple of SUVs in the lot and pull my flask from my small clutch, frowning when I bring it to my lips, only to remember I drained it during the cab ride over here.

"Get some rest, my beautiful broken girl."

Those were the words TJ left me with last night when he pressed his soft lips to my temple, and the thrill of him being here tonight is enough to motivate my legs to move. Why I want to seek out the one man who somehow threatened me with a knife, but turned me on at the same time is beyond me, but being in his arms on the dance floor last night was the most alive I've felt in almost a decade. I'd be a damn fool to not find him.

My heels come to an abrupt stop as I realize exactly where my head is. I don't want to like him. I don't deserve the thrills TJ gave me last night.

"Hey, sexy."

My head turns, finding some guy standing in the shadows of another vehicle. His eyes rake me up and down as if he's appraising the value of something he's already purchased. The tremble in my hands is immediate. The sweat pooling along my spine despite the cool air is a warning telling me to get away from him. So I do what I've always done in these situations. I smile and ask him his name.

"Spencer." He holds his hand out, pulling me roughly by my wrist.

I tumble against his chest, and his hands immediately find my ass, fingers skimming along the narrow fabric between my thighs. Bile rises in my throat, and my eyes burn with the effort to swallow it back down.

"Wanna have some fun?" I don't answer him, but I also don't put up too much of a fight when he leads me through the darkness to a building similar to a garage for auto repairs.

I'm terrified, as I should be. When he closes us inside the building and blackness fills my line of sight, and all I can hear are his panting breaths, I realize I'm too sober to let this happen. As much as I love the thrill of being hurt, of being ignored when I push someone away, I always have the drugs to cushion my bad decisions. The tequila alone isn't enough for me tonight.

"Don't." I push against his chest, and true to form of every guy I've been in this position with the last couple of years, he only holds me tighter.

"Don't get cold feet, baby. Play nice, and I'll make you come."

Leaning back, an attempt to keep his harsh puffs of breath from invading my nose, I realize he's situated us against a wall. I have nowhere to go. The second my arms and legs begin to shake as if I'm convulsing, I know I'm in deep trouble.

"Stop." I push against him again, but unlike the frat boys who just grip me harder and whisper bullshit about enjoying it, Spencer pulls his arm back before hitting me with the crushing blow of his fist.

Someone cries out, but it doesn't sound like my voice. My knees give out, and by instinct when my body begins to crumple my arms come up to protect my face. I haven't experienced this kind of violence in six years. How could I have forgotten how much it actually hurts to be hit?

His foot reaches back, and the tip of his boot hits me in the ribs before I can protect them. That same person screams again, and this time Spencer only laughs.

Bruises, scratch marks, and bite marks are a common occurrence. Punches to the face and kicks to the stomach have their place as well, I realize. Before he reaches his arm back to hit me again, I lower my arms and smile up at him. His first blow must've split my lip because the taste of iron fills my mouth. I lick at my wet lips, my teeth digging into them when he hits me again.

"You crazy bitch." The hits keep coming until a door is opened and Spencer is haloed by an aura of light.

Is this it? Is this where it finally ends? Had I known it would take more physical pain to bring my demise, I would've sought it out long before now.

"What the fuck?" A gruff voice echoes around the room before Spencer is pulled back.

I reach out for him, disappointed that the abuse has transitioned to him. He doesn't deserve to be kicked and beaten. Those are my kicks and blows.

"Me," I choke out, the pain of speaking forcing my arms to wrap around my waist.

"Jesus Christ," someone mutters before I feel my body being lifted.

"Death," I whisper as my body is jostled when the guy stands with me in his arms.

"You'll be okay. Let's get you cleaned up."

Only then do the tears start to fall. I don't need to be saved. I don't want it. Sharp intakes of breath make my head spin, and before I can tell the guy to just throw me away, darkness clouds my vision.

This is perfect, I think as my body succumbs to my injuries.

Chapter 12

TJ

My cock is hard before I can even climb into the SUV. Leaving Kaci last night was harder than it ever should've been. Not touching her after the way she moved against me on the dance floor was a test I normally would fail.

I wave to Sonic, the new prospect manning the gate as I drive through and press the buttons on my phone to bring up Kaci's tracker. The ass end of the SUV fishtails when I stomp on the gas. She isn't at her studio in Andover or getting into trouble at one of those fucking frat houses she frequents to get her rocks off. She's a quarter mile back at my fucking clubhouse. Patience isn't my friend when I slam on the brakes to get to the only section of the road wide enough to turn around.

"Forget something?" Sonic asks when I pull back up to the gate.

"You could say that," I grumble. My fingers tap with agitation on the steering wheel as I'm forced to wait for the gate mechanism to engage and drag it open enough to fit the width of the vehicle.

"Cut it close," Sonic yells when I drive through with only an inch or so to spare.

I ignore him and the gate closing back up when I climb out of the SUV and head for the front door of the club. She's either here because one of the girls invited her, or she's looking for me. I huff a humorless laugh at the thought. The girl will not even remember who I am so that only leaves one reason for her being here. My blood is boiling before I reach the front steps to the clubhouse. I normally don't hurt women unless they beg for it, but if I find Xena with her mouth or hands on Kaci, I know I'll lose my shit.

Angry voices pull my attention to the left, and I plan to only give them a passing glance, but I spot Hornet walking toward the side door of the clubhouse with a woman in his arms. It's not unusual for women to get so drunk they have to be carried to a bed to sober up, but I spot the woman's shoes. They're the same pair of black heels Kaci was wearing last night, and consequently the only thing I stripped from her body before pulling the covers up to hide all of her tempting flesh.

I'm off the porch and barreling toward him when he's spotlighted by the flood light focused on the parking lot. Bruises are forming on her face and a ring of blood coats her mouth even brighter than the red she's known to paint her lips with.

"What the fuck happened to her?" I ask as I reach them and yank her out of his arms. She doesn't even groan when I cradle her to my chest.

"Some piece of shit hangaround was in the garage just whaling on her, man," I growl at him when he reaches over to straighten her shirt. I should kill him for seeing her exposed breast where her shirt is ripped, but my focus is on getting her to safety. Hornet takes a step back, knowing I mean business.

"I got her," I hiss. I know I should take her inside and get her cleaned up but explaining to the other members why I'm concerned with her isn't a conversation I have the energy for tonight.

I spread her out on the middle seat of the SUV and strap her in with the two seat belts near the doors before pulling my phone from my pocket. After sending off a quick text, I assess her injuries. Bruises on her ribs are beginning to turn purple, but they don't look deep enough for internal injuries. I pray that I'm right because I'm not taking her to a fucking hospital. All that would bring are questions I can't answer and suspicion I don't deserve.

"Fuck, man." I don't lift my eyes from Kaci as Ronan steps in close. "You taking her to the hospital?"

"Did you get what I need?"

He holds out the bag of supplies but doesn't release it immediately. "I think this is out of your wheelhouse, man."

"Go back inside," I grunt. "I'm all she needs."

Being the smart man that he is, Ronan turns and walks away.

"I'm taking you home, my beautiful broken girl."

It's not the first time I've called her that but fuck if she doesn't meet the requirements in the flesh tonight.

***

"Don't," I tell Kaci when she grumbles and tries to knock my hand away. "I'm not here to hurt you."

I hit the vein in the back of her hand on the first try, but I'm not surprised by my success. Knowing which places to cut without hitting something major is a skill I perfected years ago. Sometimes I need to end things quickly, but more often I need to know where not to cut.

"It's just a banana bag," I tell her even though she's fallen still once again. I don't bother explaining that it's the same shit you can get in those fucking hipster clinics when you're feeling a little low on vitamins. She doesn't seem the type that would care about shit like that since her normal thrill-seeking adventures include getting herself hurt.

Speaking to her calms me, though, and I'm doing my best to forget about that motherfucker back at the clubhouse that hurt her. Taking care of her is my primary focus, but that still doesn't keep me from wanting to drive back home and dismember that piece of shit limb by limb.

"We use them back at the clubhouse when we need to ride and are too drunk to get on our bikes."

She doesn't stir. I hang the bag of fluids on the inside of her lampshade and click it off, so the bulb doesn't melt the bag. I'm twisted, wondering if I should push painkillers, but at the same time, I want her to feel the pain, so she doesn't pull shit like this again. I'm a sick fuck, just like that mom on the TV show Molly made me watch years ago. The girl was in labor, and her mother was trying to talk the doctor out of giving her an epidural because feeling the pain was something the mother thought would keep her from getting knocked up again. Back then, I thought the mother was a piece of shit for wanting her daughter to suffer. Tonight, I'm understanding her in a different light.

She doesn't make a sound, but tears stream down her face when I press sterile gauze dipped in saline solution against her split lip, and it's all the motivation I need. I pull the vile of morphine out of the kit Ronan brought to me and push two milliliters of morphine into her IV port. Within seconds the tension in her muscles settles.

Going back to the cut on her lip, I realize it looks worse than it actually is and use Steri-strips to close the wound rather than the suture kit I was gearing up to use. There's nothing I can do about the blood in her hair, but I use a comb I found in her bathroom to get the grass and other debris from her blonde locks.

"Why did you let this happen to you?" I'm not blaming her, but after the way she responded to me last night, I know she had some hand in pushing this guy to violence. Just the thought of doing something to end up like this makes my gut clench. "What happened to you?"

My own fucked up childhood contributes to my fucked-up perversions, so I'm certain she's had something just as tragic happen to her, and I'm hell bent to find out what it is.

I clean up the packaging and supplies on her bed before curling up beside her. I don't touch her other than to brush her hair away from her face. I lie and watch her breathe until the vitamin bag is empty. Only then do I climb out of her bed and remove the IV from her hand, making sure to clean the puncture wound before covering it with gauze and tape.

I want to stay with her, to be here when she wakes up, but I know I can't. The sun is already shining through her only window, a reminder that I have to get back to the clubhouse. After what happened last night, I know church will be called the second Lynch crawls his ass out of bed. I'll be expected to be there, and since I have no plans of telling them more than I have to about Kaci, my ass better be in my chair the second the meeting is called to order.

I leave her key on the small counter, just like I've done the other times I've carried her home, and lock her inside. I didn't bother parking down the road like I normally do, and it's apparent I've pissed someone off by blocking them in. I take the threatening note from under the windshield wiper and toss it to the ground before climbing inside and hauling ass back to the clubhouse.

Chapter 13

Kaci

The pounding on my door matches the pounding in my head, as well as the pain radiating from my ribs and face. That guy last night did a real number on me, and I can't wait to get a look in the mirror. My eyes slit open but swelling keeps them from opening all the way.

"Kaci, open the door!"

I don't recognize the female's voice outside, so I don't bother getting out of bed. Also, I don't know if I can walk, and whoever it is isn't important enough to find out.

The doorknob rattles before the banging commences. I'm surprised the damn thing is even locked. I normally don't bother to do it when I'm home.

When it doesn't seem like she's going to stop, I climb out of bed, groaning because of the pain all over my body and slowly make my way across the small room before ripping open the door.

"What the fu—?"

My words die on my lips when I see the female cop from the other week standing in my doorway. There's never a good reason for a cop to bang on the door, and even less of a reason for Detective Abigail Martin to be standing in front of me right now.

"Jesus." She takes in my face before sweeping her eyes down my body. "Who hurt you?"

Her hands tighten into fists as if she's struggling to keep from reaching out for me. I don't spend a second analyzing the flash of need to be soothed, and in a fraction of a second, I shove it down and stare back at the cop.

"What do you want?" I'd slam the door in her damn face, but if she's here to arrest me, I don't think she'd take that very well. Adding a new charge wouldn't help me any.

"I tried calling." I stare at her. "Did you block my number?"

I don't bother telling her I blocked a number last week. I had no idea it was hers, but the caller never left a message. I figured it was some damn telemarketer that wouldn't get the message that I wasn't going to speak with them.

"Why are you calling me?" I'm afraid she's going to tell me she found the guy who cut those frat boys up. After the dreams I had last night, I'm fairly certain TJ was involved somehow, and the last thing I want is him paying for the trouble I got myself into.

"I wanted to check on you."

"I haven't remembered anything else." Her foot blocks the door when I try to close it.

"I'm not here about the case, Kaci."

My lips turn down in a frown. The tactic she's using by saying my name isn't lost on me either. It makes the conversation more personal, a way to draw in the person you're speaking with, provides a familiarity that isn't actually there. It's politics and interview techniques 101, and I'm not falling for her shit.

"I don't need you checking up on me."

"Who hurt you?" I don't respond, just like the first fucking time she asked. "Does this have something to do with what happened back at that house?"

"Listen, *Abigail*," I spit her name out turning the table back on her, "I don't need you coming here to check on me. I'm fine."

"You look it." My swollen eyes turn to slits when she glances over my body. Her head angles toward my right arm. "Did you go to the hospital for these injuries? Report the attack?"

My eyes follow hers, and for the first time, I notice the gauze taped to the back of my hand.

"Am I under arrest?"

"No. Why would you think that?" Once again, I don't respond. "Do I have a reason to arrest you?"

Her foot blocks the door once again, and it takes everything in me to hold back a growl.

"Unblock my number, Kaci."

"No thanks."

"Then I guess I'll need to keep swinging by to check up on you then."

Her threat is a challenge, and I get the feeling she'll do exactly what she says she will if I don't comply.

"Fine," I huff, but this time when I close the door, she pulls her foot back and lets it shut in her face.

"Be safe," I hear her say on the other side before she walks away.

One glance in the bathroom mirror is all it takes for me to turn out the light before stripping all the way down. It's been years since I looked this battered, and as much as I normally revel in my injuries, I can't stomach the sight of myself today. The memories that guy brought back are enough to suffer through without the visual reminders.

My hypersensitive skin burns with the rush of the water, and for the first time in as long as I can remember, I want the pain to go away. It's too much this time. I took it too far. Either that, or he didn't take it far enough. Once again, I'm teetering on the edge with no end in sight.

I know TJ brought me home last night, or at least I think he did. His soft voice is like a mist in my head when I close my eyes, but that's how it usually is. I have no real, clear and cognizant memories of him. All I have to focus on are the ghostlike whispers and the soft brush of his skin on mine. He can't be real. A real man wouldn't take care of me. Real men damage everything they touch. Real men torture with words and threats, knowing that the promise of injuries is just as damaging as the blows with their fists. It's all real men have ever done in my life, so the angel that doctors me and gets me home safe must be a figment of my imagination. It's the only explanation.

It's this realization that makes the tears form in my eyes and mix with the hot spray of water as it cascades down my battered face. Only in my dreams and fantasies would someone like him exist. I hate that I've conjured him in my mind because I don't deserve the reprieve from the pain he brings when he shows up to nurse me back to health.

With my demons fed, I opt to order delivery rather than using the energy it would require to walk down to Tito's. When the food arrives, I find out quickly just how damaged my lip is because it's too painful to chew.

I give up on the food and try to numb out to the TV, but I can't think of anything other than TJ. Against my better judgment I reach for my phone, and the slip of paper Xena gave me with her number on it. I spend the next hour typing out messages, each one more ridiculous than the next before giving up on the idea altogether.

The TJ from the bar and the man that protects me can't be the same guy. I've somehow managed to transform them into one singular person, but that can't be right. One I was warned to stay away from, and the other protects me like it's his job.

Sighing with frustration, I toss my phone to the floor and try to sleep. I'm used to being alone, used to making sure I'm on my own ninety percent of the time, but it's the last thing I want right now. I want my protector here with his arms around me, or even better I want to feel the tip of TJ's blade slicing my skin after he makes me come with the tip as he had promised.

A sharp thrill runs through my body, and I recognize it as arousal even though I haven't been seriously turned on for ages. I felt a hint of it the other night dancing with TJ, but the coke overpowered the ecstasy and just kept me mostly numb. Just the thought of being high and the fun I had dancing at that shitty bar in Worcester makes me crave another night like that, but leaving the house in my condition isn't going to happen.

Even the shithead guys who want to hurt me don't want to be seen dancing with or hitting on a girl with cuts and bruises on her face, and the idea of climbing out of bed to find some trouble to get into just exhausts me more. It took all the energy I could manage just to answer the damn door when the delivery guy showed up with my pizza.

Sleep is about the only thing I can handle right now, but the prospect that I may dream of TJ brings a smile to my battered face as I close my eyes.

Chapter 14

TJ

"That was brutal," Virus mutters as we exit church and head back into the living room.

"I need your help." I tilt my head in the direction of his and Boston's office.

He follows me inside, but I'm already changing my mind about asking him for background information on Kaci. I hate people being in my business or giving them anything that can be held against me at a later date. The memory of her face after the beating she took last night forces my mouth to open.

"I want you to find out everything you can on Kaci Stewart."

"Okay." He doesn't move, merely stands beside me as if he's waiting for more information or has something better to do and plans to work on this later.

"Like now."

"Okay." He drops down in his desk chair and stares at me over the top of his laptop. "Got anything to get me started?"

I relay the information I've memorized from her driver's license, along with her phone number.

My eyes narrow when Virus snorts at whatever he's looking at on his computer screen.

"What?" I spit. I normally fuck with people, and some tease me as well, but there isn't a damn thing comical about what I'm asking from him right now.

"She just doesn't seem your type, is all." He doesn't lift his eyes from his computer screen as his fingers continue to fly over the keys.

"What the fuck do you know about my type?"

Why wouldn't a broken girl with a death wish be my type? As far as I can see, we're as close to The Joker and Harley Quinn as two people can get.

"A little prim and proper is all."

"What?" Not giving a damn about his personal space, I round the desk and look at his computer. "Take that fucking privacy screen off."

If it were humanly possible, my jaw would unhinge and hit the floor. The dark screen transforms, and in front of me are dozens of pictures of a girl I hardly recognize. Gone are the low-cut tops and skirts that barely cover her ass. The girl smiling back at me from the screen is jubilant and wearing pastels and fucking cardigans for Christ's sake.

Oddly, seeing her this way still makes my dick twitch in my jeans as fantasies of her in knee-high socks, plaid skirts, and pigtails infiltrate my brain. She's a knock-out in her private school getup.

I cough, clearing my mind of Britney Spears and all things resembling *Oops, I did it again.* I'll save that shit for later, right after kicking my own ass for not googling her earlier. I don't focus on my regret of refusing to be concerned about her past right now.

"Who the fuck is that?" Pointing at the screen, I wait for Virus to click on the image.

"Her parents. Former mayor of Newbury, Royce Stewart and wife Victoria."

"I can find all of this shit myself," I mutter. "Dig deeper."

Walking across the room, I fall into Boston's office chair and let Virus get to work.

Of course she's from a political family. Why would she make this any easier for me? Disappointment settles in my gut at the realization that she's just another girl with daddy issues. Granted, she's destroying her life to get her family's attention, but a spoiled brat seeking validation from her most likely neglectful parents does nothing for me.

"Holy shit," Virus hisses.

He has my attention, but my discontent keeps me rooted in the chair. "What?"

"Her baby brother died when she was a teenager."

"That sucks." And it does, but we all suffer loss along the way. It still doesn't explain her self-destructive behavior.

"She was the one watching him when it happened." I continue to watch his lowered head, but he doesn't look up from his computer. "Reports claim she valiantly tried to resuscitate him and failed."

"What happened?" I ask because it feels like the thing to say.

Maybe we have more in common than I thought; both losing someone we loved right in front of our faces. I don't wish her heartache, but my need to have some connection to this woman increases if she suffered the way I did watching my own mother die because of me.

"Choked on some toy." His fingers continue to click for a long moment before he speaks again. "Her father was already running for office, but he switched campaign strategies from industrial revitalization to child safety and education. It propelled him into the spotlight, and he was elected mayor by a huge margin."

"Did *she* give him the toy?"

His eyes snap up to mine. "Why does that even matter?"

I glare at him until his eyes narrow and refocus on his computer.

"It says a friend of the family gave the toy, but it doesn't go into further detail."

Could she have killed him because he was pulling her from the limelight and she demanded that attention, or is it just the guilt of being responsible for him when he died that is driving her self-destruction?

"Jesus Christ."

"Did she kill him?"

"What?" Confused, Virus looks back up at me, but he only holds my eyes for a split second before he looks down again. "You're not going to believe this shit. Who is this damn girl to you?"

His words are enough to get me out of the chair and back around behind his desk.

"What the fuck?"

Virus clicks on the screen, enlarging the article, but I can't stop looking at the dirty, bruised, and emaciated image of Kaci-fucking-Stewart on the screen. The only semi-clean parts on her body are the lines washed away on her face from her tears. *This* is the broken girl I've become familiar with over the last several weeks.

"Tell me what happened," I demand past suddenly dry lips.

Virus does some clicking on the laptop before turning slightly. A desktop screen to his right flashes to life, and he's smart enough to realize I can't stop looking at her, so he turns and focuses on the other screen for details.

"Abducted at eighteen during a family vacation in Honduras. This article doesn't go into much detail about what happened to her, but it hints at sexual slavery. She was gone for nearly ten months before she was rescued by—" My eyes snap to him when he pauses. "Fucking Cerberus."

That information is almost enough to make me pull my eyes from her haunting image, but not quite.

"During a rescue mission," he begins to read from the article, "for Colby Davis, the twenty-year-old daughter of actress Gwen Davis who was abducted from a beach in Costa Rica two weeks prior, six other girls were also recovered from a compound in Venezuela. She was one of them."

"Ten months?" I swallow back the bile rising in my throat. That's too much for any one person and a complete contradiction to what she's been putting herself through lately. My palm stings with the urge to spank her ass.

"One girl they rescued had been there for over two years," he mumbles quietly as he reads more of the article. My eyes stay fixed on the image of the broken girl. "She killed herself."

"What!" My throat is on fire, heart slamming against my chest as my hands reach for my phone. When I'd left her this morning, she was fine. If it was internal injur—

"Colby Davis." Virus points to his desktop screen at an image of a beautiful, smiling brunette. "A week after she was rescued, they found her dead in her apartment. She overdosed on pain pills."

"Fuck." I'm both sickened that they got to her like that and for the relief washing over me that he wasn't talking about Kaci.

"I can't even imagine what those girls went through," Virus says as if he's inside my head and speaking for me. "I knew a girl in high school once that got hooked on drugs and ended up a hooker."

"It's not the same fucking thing," I spit as I step out from behind his desk and reach for the office doorknob. "Keep looking. I want to know everything there is to know."

"This about sums it up." He's pointing at the screen when I spin around to glare at him. "I'll keep looking."

My first instinct when I walk out of the office is to jump on my bike and head straight back to Kaci's place, but I know that seeing her right now while I'm feeling murderous would only have negative results.

I don't understand her behavior at all. She doesn't act the way you'd expect a victim of sex trafficking to act, but that's the problem, isn't it? Trauma takes on all sorts of disguises. I should know. Pointing that play pistol at the police when I was a kid made me realize guns would never be my thing, but it didn't prevent me from transforming into the man I am today. Guns are impersonal. Knives require a certain kind of finesse, and when confronted by a man with a knife, his intentions are very fucking clear.

I can't even begin to understand her psyche or dictate how she should act based on her experiences, but knowing that she was hurt years ago makes me sick to my stomach. Realizing she was mere yards away from my home last night when she was hurt again is what forces me to my knees in my bathroom.

Chapter 15

Kaci

"Fuck, fuck, fuck," I grunt as I slowly turn over in bed.

The pain all over my body has only doubled in the last twenty-four hours. It reminds me of that bunk scene in *Full Metal Jacket* as I wonder if someone snuck in last night and beat the shit out of me with a bar of soap in a sock.

I stiffen, blood running cold when I hear the rattle of a plastic bag and realize it was that very same sound which woke me up. I'm nearing heart attack territory when the door snaps shut with force, but my back is facing the intruder, and I'm too scared to turn around.

I locked the door last night. I know for a fact I did because I felt creeped out lying in bed, too sore to move, but too awake to go to sleep while staring at the unlocked deadbolt. On my last trip to the bathroom, I made a point to flip the lock into place.

"If you stay in bed all fucking day, you'll never get better."

Tears burn the back of my eyes as I wait for him to attack. More plastic rattles, but when I realize the sounds are coming from the other side of the room and not getting closer, I chance a glance over my shoulder just in time to see a tall guy with sandy blonde hair shrug out of a leather vest before swinging it over the back of the single chair in my make-shift dining room.

It's not just any damn leather vest, I realize as the demented eyes of a raven stare back at me.

He isn't facing me, but I know immediately who has invaded my space just by instinct. If I close my eyes and concentrate long enough, I'm certain I could conjure his heady scent from my murky memories.

"Sit up," he grunts. "I brought you soup."

Piercing blue eyes catch me staring in his direction, and if that isn't enough to keep me frozen in place, he turns and flashes me a devious grin.

"A-are you here to h-hurt me?" I stammer.

"Soup first."

I'm certain I hear sarcasm in his voice, but at the end of the day, this guy just broke into my house, and I seriously doubt soup is all he has in mind.

"Sit up," he urges as he walks across the room with a bowl in his hands.

My stomach grumbles with the aroma of what I'm sure is chicken noodle, but I'm reminded of my injuries when my tongue slips out to wet my lips to dab at the scabbing.

"I'm not hungry." My stomach growls in protest, and I'd beg it to do it on repeat when his face softens, his smile transforming from sinister to something resembling compassion.

"I can feed you if you're too sore."

He closes the distance, sitting on the edge of my bed. I attempt to tug the blankets closer to my chin, but his weight keeps me from hitching them up higher. I regret climbing into bed last night with only a tank top and panties.

"Feed me?" I cough. "H-how did you get in here?"

"Door wasn't locked." He shrugs as if I'm crazy before dipping his head and blowing on the soup.

My eyes, fixated on his mouth, water unexplainably. I don't cry in front of people. Normally his threatening presence would thrill me, but I came too close to the end the other night, and as much as I hate to admit it, dying here in this shitty studio apartment is the last thing I want.

"The door was locked," I finally manage.

"You keep the key under the mat." He shrugs, shoulders lifting a fraction of an inch, obviously unconcerned. "Sit up so you can eat."

"Why are you here?"

"I brought chicken noodle," he says, ignoring me as he pulls the spoon out of the soup showcasing an egg noodle and a chunk of carrot. "The jambalaya looked great too, but I didn't think you'd be up for something spicy."

Are we in the twilight zone? Am I dreaming? It's like we're having two separate conversations.

"I also brought a chai tea latte, but the fucking lid came off outside, and I dropped the fucker on the ground."

"I don't drink chai tea lattes," I mumble absently.

Only now does his focus turn to me. "You used to."

Cold chills sweep over my arms at his words. "How do you know that?"

"Sit up."

Ignored again.

Short, panting breaths escape my lips when I don't move, and in turn, he places the bowl of soup on my bedside table before turning back in my direction. As if time stands still, I contemplate fight or flight, knowing deep down neither would end with me victorious over this man. Even if I were fully healed and functioning at a hundred percent, I have no doubt this man could overtake me without breaking a sweat.

His kind smile, nor his eyes so blue they're reminiscent of husky puppies, are enough to fool me. His strength is evident in the long, lean muscles that move and bunch under his Henley shirt and in the length of his sure fingers as they reach out and grip the edge of my comforter.

"What are you doing?" I whisper when he folds the blanket away from me before reaching out to me. Instinct takes over, and I release the blanket. Yielding, even in the face of harm, is the only thing that kept me somewhat safe when—

I squeeze my eyes closed, shutting down those memories. They won't help me here.

"Do you need help sitting up? I imagine you're pretty fucking sore."

"W-who are you?"

"You know exactly who I am."

I expect frustration not the humor in his voice.

"TJ." He winks a bright blue eye at my confirmation. "I thought you were an angel."

"You'd do better thinking about real estate a little further south." He grins. "I mean Hell, gorgeous. There's nothing angelic about me."

"I knew what you meant," I mutter. He's a damn liar though. His voice, the scent rolling off him, even his calculating grin are tiny bites of heaven.

"Let's get you sitting up."

His hypnotic voice is familiar and strange at the same time.

"Why are you here?"

I cringe when his cold fingers gently sweep under my arms, lifting until I'm sitting against my headboard. I should be worried about his impending attack as he touches me, but instead, I'm wondering when I shaved my damn underarms last. He doesn't move away immediately, and although I can't feel the warmth of his body, his face is close enough I can hear soft pants on his lips.

"I was in the neighborhood." The gravel in his voice nearly lights my skin on fire.

"Liar." I freeze immediately, worried he's going to hurt me even more for being rude, but when he sits back his face is fixed with that sweet grin of his.

"Yeah," he agrees. "You don't have any food allergies, do you?"

Food allergies? What the hell? Next, he'll be asking my favorite color and if I'm a cat or a dog person.

He picks the bowl back up from the bedside table, and a second later the spoon is being lifted to my lips. I'm unable to hide my wince when I open my mouth too far and feel the tender tissue in the corners split again.

"I can't." I hold my hand up in front of my mouth. "I'm sorry."

And I'm apologizing to my future attacker. I'll take the most fucked things in the world for two hundred, Alex.

He nods once, places the bowl back on the bedside table, and walks across the room. From the inside pocket of his leather cut, he pulls out a paper sack with a familiar pharmacy logo on it. My mouth begins to water immediately.

"What do you have there?" I'm not to the point where I'd climb off the bed and tackle him for a Percocet, but I also can't deny my increased heart rate.

"Aleve." My face falls as fast as it did the year I didn't get a puppy for Christmas.

"Aleve?"

"For the pain."

My frown doesn't dissipate as he reaches into my fridge, and it only deepens when he walks back in my direction with a bottle of water and two blue pills.

"What's that look for?" He offers the pills and the bottle of water, but I don't take either. "You saw me get them out of the brand-new package. I'm not trying to drug you."

I almost want to snort at his choice of words.

"Some of those party favors like I had at the bar the other night might be a little better in this situation," I counter.

"Why?" He asks as he presses the pills to my lips until I open my mouth. He hands me the bottle of water. "So you can tempt me to hurt you while you're high?"

Ice cold water dribbles down my chin, and my quick movements to correct my error only make me hurt more.

"You pushed me away the other night, and me being me didn't appreciate it, but your eyes flared when I refused to let you go." He pulls the bottle from my hands after I swallow the pills and screws the lid back on the bottle of water. "You were getting off on the fear."

Getting off on it? I almost correct him, but somehow manage to keep my response to myself. Getting off is so far from the truth. I hadn't even felt a hint of arousal until I was pressed against him on that dance floor, and that memory is groggy at best.

"You purposely put yourself in harm's way."

His eyes stay on me even when his hand moves to place the bottle of water beside the now cold bowl of soup.

"I had a bad night," I mutter.

"You've had a lot of bad nights recently." He leans in, but there's something different in his eyes. It's nothing like looking into the eyes of those frat assholes I'm so familiar with. It's threatening all the same, but there's also a thrill in his irises, an unexplainable promise of so many unspoken things.

"You were there that night." The words leave my lips the second my brain knows it's true.

"Which night?"

I don't shy away from him when his fingertip traces a design on my cheek.

"You killed those men." My voice is nothing but a rasp.

"Are you afraid of me?"

"Terrified," I confess.

He pulls back the very next second, giving me his back as he walks across the room, and I realize I've never felt fear before in my life until he turns back around with a gleaming knife in his hand.

"You're a very smart woman then."

Chapter 16

TJ

I have to look over at Kaci twice to make sure she's still breathing. I haven't hurt her or anything. Other than sweeping my fingers over her cheek ten minutes ago and helping her sit up in the bed, I haven't touched her. Resisting the urge has become a full-body workout.

I know it's the knife. Most smart people are terrified of it, as they should be. Her fear doesn't keep me from twisting the tip into my palm, but I know she hasn't taken her eyes off it for a single second.

"I'm not going to hurt you." I almost follow up the statement with the truth but specifying *today* right now doesn't seem like it would be very productive.

"You threatened me at the bar." There's more than fear in her voice right now, and I know immediately what she's referencing.

I almost say the words out loud, almost taunt her with my delicious threat, but before I can get the words, *I can make you come with just the tip of my blade* out of my mouth, I'm reminded of her response that night.

You can cut me, but I won't come. They never let me come.

I thought she was referring to the men she sought out at the frat houses and parties she went to, but after what Virus discovered, I can't help but think it's those ten months in captivity that she was speaking about.

My eyes refocus on the TV. Some stupid sitcom is playing, but neither one of us has made a move to turn up the volume. I haven't because I'm enjoying the sound of her frantic breaths. She's probably too afraid to move, but at the same time, I think she lives for the adrenaline she must be feeling.

"I woke up this morning planning to kill my sister's lover."

Lover.

What a simple word for something so fucking complicated.

Fuck, even after watching Briar so willing to die for Molly this morning, the thought of my kid sister having sex still kind of makes my skin crawl. I don't even understand the sentiment, but I appreciate his dedication to her.

Kaci's frantic breaths stop, but I don't say another word until she's near passing out and forced to gasp for oxygen.

"Lynch, that's my older brother and the club president," I explain, "had the rope around his neck, and I was just biding my time, waiting until I could sink my blade into his skin for not being man enough to confess his feelings to us. I had to wait. There's a hierarchy in the club. Lynch is number one, but man was it a sight to see his number two, his best friend and VP, teetering on his toes with that rope around his neck."

Closing my eyes, I let my mind drift back to this morning.

"What happened?"

My teeth scrape over my bottom lip to keep from smiling at her question. She's a curious little kitty.

"The fucker was willing to kill himself so my sister wouldn't feel the pain of knowing her brothers were responsible for his death."

She huffs a humorless laugh, and I bite the inside of my cheek to keep from smiling. At this rate, I'll have sores all over my mouth.

"What?" Turning my head, I look her in the eyes, hating the swollen lids and purple coloring on her cheeks. "You don't believe in love?"

"Love doesn't exist," she replies without a second thought. "It's all an illusion."

"That's not true."

Her eyes widen as much as her injuries allow.

"What?"

"You just don't seem to be the type to *love*."

"I'm capable of love." Her eyebrow rises. "I love my sister."

The right corner of her lip tips up. It's not a full smile, but I'll take what I can get in the situation.

"What's going to happen to your sister's guy?" she asks after a long silence.

"Other than pissing blood for a couple of days and nursing some fractured ribs?"

An urge to bite her throat hits me when she swallows roughly.

"Nothing." My shoulder hitches in a half-assed shrug. "Unless he hurts her."

"Do you think he will?"

"I don't normally put much faith in people," I confess. "But Briar is the most loyal man I've ever met."

"But you were willing to kill him?"

"My sister is off-limits. He knew that going in." Unfamiliar calmness washes over me, and I know it has everything to do with just sitting here talking to her. No expectations. No disappointment in unmet needs. I close my knife and toss it onto her bedside table. "The cost of betrayal is death. That's how it works in the club."

"Yet, he's still alive." I don't respond. It's her exact conclusion that may also compromise our club. "Are you regretting it?"

"Regretting what?" My eyes find hers again.

"Letting him live."

"Not yet." Her body sags, the tension she's had since I arrived finally leaving her body. "But it hasn't been twenty-four hours, and the day is young."

"The sun is setting," she counters. "How long are you going to stay?"

Her voice is heavy and sleep-filled, and when she yawns my jaw tightens with the effort not to mirror her.

"It's a mistake to think I'll ever leave."

Unbidden, my jaw unhinges and a small yawn escapes. She smiles, eyes focused on my mouth long enough that my cock begins to thicken, but too soon she looks away. Her eyes flutter, lids heavy.

"Lock the door when you go."

Her mumbled words fade away at the end. I don't know if she has grown comfortable enough with me here to fall asleep, or if her injuries have exhausted her to the point that she couldn't stay awake even if she tried.

If she's smart, it would be the latter, but it doesn't stop me from hoping it's the former.

Her breathing is calm at first, but quickly grows more ragged, so I shove the blankets away and help her lie down. With her head flat and chin no longer tucked into her chest, she breathes easier. Comfortable or not, falling asleep while I'm still here is dangerous, and I realize just how true that is when it takes a long moment of staring at her naked legs before I'm able to pull the blanket back over her body.

She snuggles deeper when the warmth of her covers surrounds her, and I watch as her hand slides across the mattress. If I were some romantic asshole with hearts and fucking flowers dancing around in my head, I'd let myself wonder if she's reaching for me.

I'm not. All it makes me want to do is prick the tip of her finger with my knife to see if she draws back into her body or if she'll press it harder against the blade.

Although I know I should walk out and let her sleep, I busy myself with putting the soup back in its original container and popping it in the fridge so she can have it later. The sun has set, and that means things will be livening up back at the clubhouse. The liquor will be flowing, and club whores will be walking around with their tits and asses out; every hole they have ready to be fucked.

The girls back at the clubhouse have been a staple in my life since I was thirteen, an avenue to visit when I need a release and nothing more, yet the prospect of doing that tonight doesn't even make my dick twitch. The promise of warm lips wrapped around my cock, or Legs's blood dripping from my knife doesn't stir a damn thing. I've never even envisioned what it would be like going home and not carrying a bottle of whiskey and woman to fuck back to my bed, but that's been exactly what I've done much too often recently.

It has to be her fault. Consequently, it makes me want to wake Kaci up and shake her for ruining whores for me. I'm only ever reminded I even have a cock these days when she's near, or I'm alone imagining the silky canvas of her unmarred, virgin skin and the tip of my knife running across it.

Now I'm hard.

"Fuck," I hiss and run heavy, unforgiving hands over my face and the top of my head.

Leaving now isn't an option. Convincing myself she's going to wake up in an hour or so in pain and will need more Aleve, I settle beside her, closer than I was before and stare at the muted TV.

I'm lying to myself again when she reaches for me, and her hand settles on my thigh. Something funny happens on the TV, I reason with myself. That's the only reason my lips turn up in a grin.

***

I don't realize I'm asleep until a pained groan makes my eyes jolt open.

"Kaci?"

The TV turned off automatically at some point, and the only light filtering inside her apartment is from the curtain less window.

"Are you hurting?"

"Yeah." Her fingers flex against my stomach, but she doesn't pull her hand away.

I grip her wrist with my right hand, preventing her from moving it as I reach to the bedside table for medication and the bottle of water. I can't hold her forever, and it becomes clear when I shift to hand her the items, and she has to sit halfway up to swallow.

"You're not scared of me anymore?" I ask when she hands over the bottle of water and settles her cheek on my chest.

She doesn't answer, and I assume she's asleep again when my eyes start to close. It's the middle of the damn night and way too late to get on my bike for the hour drive back to the clubhouse.

"I'm more afraid of you being nice to me than the pain I know you're capable of." She swallows loud enough for me to hear. "But I'm tired, so maybe wait until the morning to hurt me."

Her slender leg slides between mine, and my fingers tease the soft skin of her outer thigh. This girl drives me absolutely insane, and I can't imagine being anywhere else right now.

"It's only because I'm so tired," I mumble as I let myself drift to sleep with perfection in my arms.

Chapter 17

Kaci

"You're making this a habit," I grumble, not bothering to look up from my phone when TJ lets himself into my apartment.

His only response is a quick grin as he shrugs off his jacket and leather vest.

He's empty-handed, which makes me frown. He's been bringing food because I haven't left my place in over a week. The last time I walked out of my front door I had to be carried back in after my run-in with the asshole at TJ's clubhouse.

"You have nothing better to do than drive an hour just to sit in my apartment?"

"I enjoy the scenery." His eyes roam from my socked feet to the top of my messy head, and I know he isn't talking about the curving roads and fields on his way over. "And I haven't been here every day. I didn't come yesterday."

I don't admit to him that I waited with my eyes on the door almost the entire day hoping he'd show up as I flip my cover over to hide my legs. He'd sent a pizza to my door instead. It wasn't much of a consolation prize after the all the consecutive days of spending time with him. I'll also never confess that I tossed and turned last night because his warmth wasn't heating my side as I fell asleep. The luxury of that comfort shouldn't be wasted on me.

He's always gone by morning, but I've grown accustomed to resting my head on his chest and dozing off to the rhythm of his heartbeat and the cadence of his breathing against my cheek.

"Did you miss me?"

My brow creases when I look up at him. "What?"

"Did you miss me when I didn't show up."

"No," I answer too quickly, and it's reflected in the blue of his eyes. "It was nice to watch what I want on TV for a change."

"I missed *you*."

His simple words do more to me than I want to admit, so I opt to change the topic instead.

"How did it go?"

Before he'd fallen asleep in my bed Wednesday, he'd talked about the way his sister was treating him differently since his meeting, as he calls it, with her lover Briar.

"Lynch set the club straight, but I can tell it's going to take a lot more than our blessing to make her trust us again."

"Trust is hard to build once it's broken," I whisper, and immediately clamp my mouth closed. Talking out of turn and saying more than I should, has become a problem recently. He's invaded my life like he has a right to be here, and I've just let it happen. I've clung to his affection and presence like a lifeline, and I think I'm losing my sanity because of it.

"Kaci?" I pull my eyes from my phone and look up at him. "Are you going to answer me?"

He frowns and crosses the room in my direction when I don't answer. How can I? I'm so stuck in my own damn head, I didn't hear him talking.

"I said I'm hungry."

I swallow thickly when his lids fall and only the tiniest slit of his irises can be seen. He has to be talking about food, right? He hasn't made any other move on me in the last week. Sure his hand grazed my thigh more than once when we were lying in bed watching TV, but he didn't let his fingers linger.

"Umm." I swallow again, but it does nothing to rid the ball of lust forming in my throat. "There's leftover pizza in the fridge."

He's at the side of my bed now, forcing me to angle my head to look up at him.

"I'm not hungry for pizza." His voice is almost a growl, and the only way I can respond is by nodding and licking my lips.

He doesn't reach for me though. He doesn't yank the comforter that's hiding my bare legs away. He doesn't crush his mouth to mine and tell me all the dirty things he wants to do to me.

Instead, he turns away, crosses the room again, and pulls on his jacket minus his leather cut.

"Let's go grab something to eat."

I ignore him, keeping my eyes low as my fingers press into one of the yellowing bruises on my arm.

"I'm not hungry," I mumble when the silence grows too big around us, and I feel forced to speak.

"Come on," he urges, his hand appearing in front of my face. "The fresh air will do you some good."

"I don't want to go."

"I can't stay trapped in here with you tonight."

I ignore the desperation in his voice. I have to. Otherwise I'll mistake it for something else like I did just moments ago. He doesn't want me. He just has a fucked-up sense of obligation to me for some reason.

"Then go back to your clubhouse. I'm sure the things going on there are more entertaining and better suited for your needs."

"There's nothing at the clubhouse I want." His fingers curl, insistence in the long digits as he flexes them for me to take.

"No." I slap his hand away and avoid looking back up at him. "I don't need a fucking babysitter, and I'm tired of the damn sympathy."

"Kaci." My name from his perfect lips is a warning.

With my spine so straight it makes my hips ache, I look up at him and point to my face, indicating the bruises that are beginning to heal, but are far from gone. "I'm not going to leave and do something stupid. The party guys don't really go for the visibly damaged. They are more into a blank canvas they can fuck up themselves."

His jaw ticks as he clamps his teeth together. It only makes looking at him that much more difficult. He's fucking gorgeous, and if I lean in, I bet I could smell his cologne and the late spring air clinging to his clothes from the ride over. Just the scent of him is addiction inducing.

"We're going to get something to eat." His lips barely move with his words, and I'm wondering if I've finally pissed him off enough, finally managed to break through his ungodly level of patience.

The blanket is snatched back, revealing my bare legs, and by the further hardening of his jaw, I can tell he sees the tiny slit of fabric between my legs, exposed from sitting Indian style.

"Get dressed," he hisses before turning away and walking to my fridge.

Like a petulant child being forced to go to early Sunday morning church with her parents, I stand from my bed and rip my tank over my head. My nipples furl the second the cool air hits them, but I don't bother to cover my chest, and I definitely don't miss his eyes widening as I slowly walk to my single dresser to grab clothes.

"Fuck you," he spits angrily as he glares at me and reaches for his leather vest. "I'll wait for you outside."

I jolt, standing in place when my door slams closed. It feels like an eternity passes, but my need to see him, to apologize for whatever the hell he thinks I've done motivates me to grab some clothes. Like a fool, I carry them into the bathroom, and realize once I see myself in the mirror why he was in such a rush to get away from me.

Blemishes, contusions, and discolored skin greets me. I press a soft finger to the boot mark on my side. My eyes scrunch and my lips form a flat line, but it doesn't stop me. I press three fingers into the injury as a reminder. Every man that walks the face of the earth is a piece of shit, and TJ isn't excluded from that. If anything, he's even more fucked up than the rest, nurturing me, trying to get me to trust him, all part of his game until he tears me apart.

Knowing this, I dress in a rush, ignoring the scream from my ribs as I tug a long-sleeved shirt over my head. I don't bother with makeup to cover the fading bruises on my face. I want people around me when they see us together to be disgusted, to think that he beats me and I'm the idiot who has stuck by his side. I do run a brush through my hair and braid it down my back so it doesn't get tangled on our ride on his motorcycle, though.

I take one final look in the mirror, assessing my overall appearance. The smile that spreads across my face isn't a surprise. Agony and being hurt is what I live for. It's what gets me out of bed each day, and I just know that TJ is going to be the one to give me everything I need.

Right before he puts an end to all my pain.

Except, when I pull my apartment door open to join him, he's already gone.

Chapter 18

TJ

Leaving her apartment last week was the only recourse I could come up with. My plan at the time didn't include staying away for a week solid, but that's what it took for me to get my head on straight.

But as I stand in front of her apartment and look up to her single window, I realize a week wasn't even close to long enough. My thighs burn to run inside and punish her for what she's doing to me, for what she's been doing to herself. With determination in my stride, I climb the stairs and unlock her door with the key I made weeks ago.

Soft music hits my ears the second her body comes into view.

She's dancing.

In the middle of her apartment, she's swaying her hips to the music, letting her hands roam down her body in soft sensual caresses as Chris Isaak crones about wicked games from her cell phone. I hated this song when my dad played it growing up, but suddenly it's become my favorite.

Her blonde hair sways unrestrained down her back. With her eyes closed, teeth biting into her plush lower lip, I watch, entranced and mesmerized by her bare legs and the soft swell of her ass as she turns away from me. I want nothing more than to sink my teeth into the delicate flesh.

It isn't until she faces me again, her sultry, but dilated, green eyes focusing on me, that I fully understand what's going on. She urges me to step closer, holding both hands out, but my eyes search the room instead.

The rolled-up bill and powder residue on her kitchen counter are all I need to see to comprehend why she's so playful, and why she's reaching for me now when she never has before.

A week ago she wanted me gone, wanted nothing to do with me, only saw me as caregiver, and nothing more. She wasn't thankful or appreciative of the amount of time I spent with her, of the times I saved her from herself, but I can't pin all my anger on her.

I gave her too much space, too much time to think, and all that shit stops now.

I go to her, watching her mouth fall open on a breathless sigh as I press my body against hers. Her fingers find my hair when I grip her naked hips with punishing hands.

"Hi," she whispers against my lips.

Alcohol taints her breath, the relaxing agents of whiskey fighting with the coke she has snorted.

"I missed you."

Her words cut me to my soul. I grip her harder because I know those words would never leave her lips if she weren't high as a fucking kite. The tiny whimper escaping her throat lands in my balls, drawing them up tight to my body as my cock thickens and pounds against the zipper of my jeans.

"Kaci," I pant against her lips, needing her and unable to do what really needs to be done.

Never drunk and never high. It's what I told myself every time I wanted to take her. She has to be aware, has to make that cognizant choice herself. I won't be like the assholes she seeks out for punishment at the parties. I won't take advantage. I won't even touch her delicate skin without her sober and begging for it.

All of it lies.

My mind wars with my body as her hips continue to sway to the music. The brush of her body against mine slowly melts my resolve.

This wasn't my intent. Wanting to hold her like this, needing to push my dick against her belly were the reasons I stayed away. I'd needed to find control, something I lost the second I stepped inside this room.

She arches against my chest when my tongue snakes out and brushes her lip.

She whimpers, relaxing into my hold for only a second before her body stiffens and her palms, no longer tugging at the hair at my nape, run down and push against my chest.

"No." A single word without fire behind it at all.

Standing in her own apartment, she's pulling the same shit she did at the bar, the exact same act I don't doubt she's pulled each and every damn time she's been at one of those parties searching for someone to hurt her.

When I pull her harder against my chest, I wonder how long the other guys took to lose their cool. I want to be better, to last longer, but she's testing my limits, and the glint in her eyes means she knows it.

"Stop," she pants, but it turns to a moan when I dig my fingers into the flesh of her ass again.

I'm at an advantage, fully clothed while she's in nothing but a thin tank top and a scrap of lace pretending to be panties.

"Kaci," I say against her lips once more, but she doesn't give in. She doesn't open her mouth to grant the entrance I'm begging for. Instead her fingernails dig into my chest. My shirt barely serves as protection from her attack, but I'm not hindered.

"I'm not playing this game with you, gorgeous." I fist her hair, tugging until the long column of her neck is exposed and she's whimpering.

"Please don't," she rasps when my tongue, obviously not good enough for her mouth, traces the fluttering pulse point at the base of her throat.

Her back bows, the movement causing her body to tease and taunt me further as her lush tits press against me. She must realize the contact because she swivels her hips against me as much as the curvature of her body will allow.

The room has fallen silent as the songs ends. The only seductive sounds around us now are the harsh pants from our mouths and her keening cry when I sink my teeth into her shoulder. It's not enough to hurt her or draw blood, but that doesn't stop the goosebumps from radiating down her arms.

Her mouth says stop one more time, but her hips never stop moving against mine.

"Enough," I spit, pulling her back up to standing and releasing her.

"TJ?"

I hate the waver in her voice and the doe eyes she's blinking up at me.

"Is this a game to you?" My words are harsh and accusatory.

"I wanted you to stop."

Her eyes never leave my lips, and fuck if they don't tingle at the attention.

"Stop?" I huff, my hands raking over the top of my head. "Okay."

I turn to leave, but her hand on my arm stops me. With my jacket still on, I can't feel the warmth of her embrace, and I fucking hate it.

"Dance with me."

I turn, finding her arms open, and I'm every part the damn fool my father told me I was because I walk right back into her fucking arms.

I kill.

I maim.

I torture.

Yet, this pixie of a girl is controlling me. I only allow it for now because cold has replaced the warmth on my chest from where she was, and I hate the chill it forces over my skin even though I'm fully clothed.

"There isn't any music."

"We don't need music," she whispers. "Move with me."

I should feel like an idiot, standing in this girl's apartment, my hips swaying and moving to a song only she can hear in her head, but I don't let it slow me down. My fingers find her ass again, and I pull her against me with a grunt when her warm lips tease my neck. I bite my lips to stop the moan that needs to escape. I refuse to give her the satisfaction.

I slide a leg between her thighs, rolling her body so she feels the friction against her clit. With nimble fingers, I pull the strap of her tank away and nip at her shoulder.

"Kaci," I pant against her warm skin.

Just like last time, she tenses a single second before she pushes against my chest. I don't relent this time. If games are what she wants, I'm willing to play this time.

I dig my teeth into her shoulder hard enough to bruise, deep enough to leave my mark on her body long after I'm gone.

"Don't," she whimpers while her fingers dig harder into my clothes.

"That's enough, gorgeous." I pull my body from hers, but only far enough to reach between us and use my free hand to rip open my belt.

"Wh-what are you d-doing?"

She's realizing the tables have turned. She's not the one in charge, and sorry for her if she even believed she was for a second.

"Down," I command adding pressure to her shoulders while my hand still grips her hair. My cock is out a second later. "We're playing *your* game."

Her knees hit her hardwood floor with enough force that a wince creases the corners of her eyes, but this is what she does isn't it? I can't feel sorry for her, can't back away now. This is, after all, exactly what she expects of me. What she expects of every man she comes in contact with.

Her eyes widen further when I pull my knife from my belt.

"Is this what you need?"

She doesn't answer, but her gaze never leaves my blade until it's out of her line of vision and running down her neck. Her breaths increase in speed, the hot air teases the head of my cock like a caress.

"Suck," I command, shifting my hips a couple inches closer until my dick is resting on her perfect fucking bottom lip.

Her mouth clamps shut, and her hands push against my thighs, but I'm not backing away now. I reason that doing this after a couple of lines of blow and some alcohol isn't the same thing as lacing her drink and stripping her naked while she's unconscious. She may not be in her right mind, but neither am I.

"Suck," I repeat, drawing in my own harsh breath when her lips turn up in a sinister smile. The devious look on her face is enough to make me pause, but only briefly. "Bite me and I'll slit your fucking throat."

I twist the tip of my knife into the flesh near her collarbone, not enough to draw blood, but enough for her to heed my warning.

"I'm waiting." I move my hips, my cock pulsing hard when my pre-cum coats her lips.

I've got her by the hair, threatening her with my knife, and yet as she looks up at me, wide green eyes shining, and opens her mouth as if this entire situation was of her own making and I'm giving her exactly what she wants. We both know she's the one in complete power. She dominates me from her fucking knees with one simple suck.

I jolt, hips pulling me from her mouth with the power of her initial contact. Her cheeks blaze, tongue sneaking out to lick my taste from her lips.

"You're not going to top me from down there, beautiful."

My knife clatters to the floor, forgotten in an instant as both of my hands reach for her. I twist my fingers into her hair at her temples and pull her forward. Her gasp of surprise is silenced with my cock as I shove it in hard and deep. The muscles in her throat squeeze my head, and it takes all of my power not unleash on her. I have no rhythm, no steady pace. It's one more thing she's stolen from me. Years of experience and hundreds of mouths previously wrapped around my cock no longer matter. I'm brand new, once again that thirteen-year-old boy fucking a club whore for the first time, only that chick no longer exists either.

It's as if, until this very moment, my dick has never had human contact before. I'm starved for her, for the intensity of her actions and the way she makes my heart race with the simplest of touches.

The sound of her gagging doesn't slow me down. It only serves as the new song we're dancing to, my breaths rushing out to form the chorus of our erotic song.

Something changes. I can feel the electrical current in the room shift at the same time her fingers stop digging into the front of my thighs and she shifts them to clasp my legs from the back. She's no longer pushing me away. Now, she's clinging to me, pulling me in deeper.

Avoiding the sight of her swallowing me whole is the only thing keeping me from exploding down her throat, so I keep my eyes tilted to the ceiling until the burn in my nuts is so bad with the need for release that it can no longer be ignored.

"Jesus fuck," I grunt when I give in and lower my head to observe her servicing me.

Head tilted back, throat taking everything I have to offer, she's the most immaculate thing I've ever seen. Unpainted lips wide and encircling my cock, I watch as tears flow freely from the corners of her eyes as I stab into her over and over. Her chin is drenched with spit, and all of that is amazing, but it's the hollows of her cheeks as she legitimately participates in my brutality that sends me over the edge. For a half of a second, I'm indecisive, unable to choose between pulling out and marking her face with my cum, or blowing down her throat.

The warmth of her mouth and the hand sneaking up my thigh to grip my sack make the decision for me. I punch deep and unload, my cock jerking erratically against her tongue. I blow so fucking deep in her throat she doesn't even have to swallow when my oversensitive cock falls from her lips.

Chapter 19

Kaci

TJ is smiling down at me, and the softness on his face and in his bright blue eyes is almost enough to make me forget about the pain in my knees and the urge to grin back at him, but then his hand reaches down and softly cups my cheek.

"Don't," he warns when I jerk my head away so fast I end up sprawled on my ass.

Shame washes over me. I wasn't supposed to enjoy his pleasure. I wasn't supposed to soak my panties the second he shoved me to my knees and commanded me to open my mouth. I had no right to be on the verge of coming when he threatened me with that fucking knife. Remembering the weapon, my eyes dart to my left, spotting the shining blade lying by my hip.

"Nope," he hisses and pulls me up before I can wrap my fingers around the hilt. "What were you planning to do with that, pretty girl?"

Pretty girl

Gorgeous.

Beautiful.

All the fucking pet names are enough to make me go mad.

"Baby," he whispers, his fingers cupping my jaw exactly the same way they did when I was still on my knees and reeling from his assault.

Last fucking straw.

"Don't." With all the force I can muster, I push against his chest. "Leave me alone."

"Not a chance in hell."

He pulls me against his chest, holding me tighter when I try to fight him. His punishing grip around my back is stronger than he's ever held me before, and only then do I know that all the other times, I could've gotten away from him. Had I actually wanted to leave his arms, he would've let me go. The story is a little different now as he holds me tight enough it's becoming difficult to get an adequate lungful of air.

"Let me go," I beg, but he only holds me tighter.

I know exactly what this is. Aftercare. He took advantage of me, and some hidden soft spot inside of him is urging him to make sure I'm okay. Deo did the exact same thing. He'd brutalize me, then try to hold me. It only served to ease *his* guilt. The comforting touches, his fingers rhythmically sifting through my hair were to calm his demons, not make me feel at ease. I fell for it the first time, but then the next night he returned and hurt me even more.

I squeeze my eyes closed, forcing myself to try to calm down, but the embrace is too much. It's too reminiscent of the past. Not once, not one of the assholes from the party got me as close to that time in my life as I am right now. I'm trembling, part in fear and part in need for him. It's the latter that renews my strength.

"Get off me!" I roar, so close to his ear, he has no other choice but to loosen his hold.

I'm barreling toward my bathroom, assuring myself that if I can only make it inside and lock him out, I can wait to freak out until he leaves.

"Don't think so." He's grabbing me again, pulling my back against his chest, and I hate the feel of his hot breath on my skin. "I'm not done with you yet."

I whimper at his threat but stop struggling.

"Please," I plead.

I repeat the word over and over. At first, I'm begging for him to release me, to let me deal with what happened between us in my own way, but the meaning of the word changes when his rough hand tugs up my shirt and he grips my breast punishingly.

"I don't want to hurt you."

"Yes you do," I argue.

The slap to my breast weakens my knees, but he holds me steady. Fire blooms on my skin, radiating from the sting of his hit. The red flesh tingles before I feel my pulse settle at the injury.

"You liked that."

"I-I didn't," I stammer.

A biting slap hits my other breast, and I moan like a whore. His lips turn up against my neck in a wicked smile.

Arousal isn't allowed. It's punished and treated like a sin. Slaves aren't granted pleasure and showing it only results in harsher treatment.

"Get out of your fucking head, Kaci." Two successive hits, one to each breast, bring me back to the present. "Where are you?"

Two more hits.

I want to answer him, but the burn from his slaps are just too decadent.

One hand holds my hip with brutal force while his other reaches up and pinches the stinging nipple on my right breast.

"Where. Are. You?" He pinches and releases with each word.

"H-here," I manage. "I'm here."

His hand leaves my tits too soon, but his probing fingers begin to trace lower. I bite the inside of my cheek to keep from mewling as he sweeps under my panties.

"God, you're fucking perfect," he praises as he dips a finger between my folds, no doubt finding me drenched.

Once again, I try to pull away because I'm unable to keep my arousal a secret.

"Don't fucking move," he growls.

My panties are ripped from my body. The abrasion left behind on my hip will serve as a memento from tonight. I grow wetter with the mere thought of looking at it tomorrow in the mirror.

"Ah," he moans before sinking his teeth hard into my earlobe. "Fucking your mouth turned you on."

It isn't a question, so I don't bother to lie. He's pushing two thick fingers into my core, so there isn't even a point in lying to him right now. My body tells him everything he needs to know.

"I've waited so fucking long to touch you like this."

I can't handle the reverence in his voice, or the fact that his hands have transitioned from harsh grabs and slaps to reverent caresses.

"Let me go," I spit.

"Too sweet for you?" The taunting lilt of his voice contradicts the continued softness in his touch between my thighs. "Just thought I'd be nice and return the favor. Give a thank you for the epic suck off, but I don't think *nice* is what you need. Is it?"

I yelp in surprise when suddenly I'm tossed onto my bed. I bounce twice, and when I land, TJ is already between my thighs. His jeans are still around his thighs and the heat of his once again thick cock arrows to my pussy like it's one step ahead of the game.

Of their own accord, my hips swivel, and a shameful cry rushes past my lips at my inability to control my own body.

"No." Cruel fingers grip my jaw until TJ forces me to look him in the eye. "Don't close your eyes. Don't fucking think. And don't you fucking dare picture anyone but me. Watch."

Obeying his command, my eyes follow him as he slides down my body. Every ripple of his abs bumps over my clit as he makes his way down my body.

"Don't be nice to me," I beg.

He nods, one soft dip of his chin, and suddenly we're on the same page.

"I wouldn't dream of it."

I thought we were in tune with each other, but then the single light in the middle of my ceiling glints off the blade of his knife. I don't even know when he picked the thing up from the ground, or maybe he keeps more than one on him at all times.

"Do you trust me?"

My head shakes.

"Smart girl." The blade trails over the inside of my thigh, and I jerk suddenly at the misplaced tickle. "Be still, or I might hurt you."

"You wouldn't." I'm not daring him, but what would be the purpose of this man saving me only to nurse me back to health, then to turn around and hurt me again. "What the fuck!"

I feel a burn on my inner thigh, and when I look from his face to the wound. It's already welling with a dot of blood.

"Don't," I whisper when his tongue starts at my knee, trailing a hot wet path toward the injury.

First, he cut me, now he's going to lick my blood? This fucking changes everything.

"TJ."

He doesn't listen, and it only takes a split second before his tongue slowly, in one fluid motion, licks the droplets away. My pulse pounds ferociously in my clit at the sight of my blood coating his tongue before he closes his mouth and swallows. His eyes flutter closed on a groan, and it's a long moment before he opens them again. When he does, his pupils are dilated and the devious look in his eyes sets me on fire.

"You liked that?" His tongue sweeps over the wound again, but the cut is so small a single dot of blood is all he gets. I begin to tremble with the notion that he may hurt me again so he can get more.

"I didn't."

"And yet," his tongue licks higher, and the rush of his breath over my center is all I can focus on, "you're glistening."

"I-I'm sorry." The apology is expected, but he frowns anyway.

"How far can I take you?"

I don't answer him, but I'm certain I'm going to shake right off the bed with the shiver that has settled into my spine.

"This far?" The tip of his blade traces my outer lips.

"TJ," I gasp, legitimately scared he's going to slip and do some real damage. That thought amps up the shaking even more because more damage may be exactly what he's after.

"This far?" he continues, ignoring my plea. The tip of his blade maps out a path over my clit. "I did promise to make you come this way."

I'm so fucking close. The threat, the pain, his mouth so close to my core, all of it is too damn much, yet also not nearly enough.

"I remember you said you wouldn't come."

I whimper in duress when he pulls the knife from my skin.

"But I love a fucking challenge."

With deft fingers, he turns the knife in his hand, pressing the hilt at my entrance.

"More than that though," his head lowers, dangerously close to being right *there*, "I want to feel you, taste you on my tongue when you explode."

His puckered lips suck at my clit the exact second he shoves the hilt of his knife into my pussy, and I see fucking stars. My body convulses, pussy sucking on his knife at the same tempo his lips work on my clit.

"Jesus keep going," he hisses, and my body obeys for what seems like years until I'm wrung out, muscles aching as if I'd just run a marathon.

The knife and his mouth disappear, and I don't bother opening my eyes when he shifts his weight. The clank of his belt hits my hardwood, and I expect him to pounce on me and slam his thick cock inside of me, but it doesn't happen. When I open my eyes, all I see is his back disappearing into my bathroom.

Then the lock flips into place.

Chapter 20

TJ

I taste her when I close myself in the bathroom.

I taste her when I climb into her shower.

I taste her when I grip my cock.

And I can still taste her on my lips when it only takes five punishing pumps for me to coat the wall of her shower with my cum.

I could've fucked her. How easy it would've been to just ram inside of her as the last convulsions of her cunt distracted her.

Yet, I didn't, and fuck if I don't feel like I deserve a gold medal for my restraint.

The rough towel I drag over my body after stepping out of her shower is a harsh contrast to the silkiness of her pussy against my mouth and the delicate flesh of her thighs under my fingers.

"In due time," I promise myself in the mirror before I unlock the door and step out into her room.

The covers are tucked under her chin, probably giving her a false sense of security, and as I suspected she would, she avoids looking directly at me.

"I didn't use all the hot water." She hurries off the bed when I bend down to grab my jeans, and then the bathroom door slams.

I go to settle on her bed, and the wet spot left from her orgasm taunts me. She came so fucking hard it left *me* with spots in my vision.

Nothing will ever be the same. How can it? What she showed me tonight is only but a glimpse of what we could have together. Sure I've cut women before, and they've enjoyed it. I'm like a fucking surgeon with a knife, knowing how deep I can go and where to cut to minimize pain but maximize blood loss. Never, not fucking once have I leaned over and licked any away. I'm not thirsty for it. I get off on it coating the skin, not ingesting it. That changed tonight, epically.

Kaci stays in the bathroom for over an hour, and by the time she opens the door, I can tell by the look in her eyes that she expected me to be gone.

"Hey," I whisper.

She gives me a weak smile before grabbing some clothes out of her dresser and disappearing into the bathroom again. My stomach grumbles, reminding me that I came over to try the going out thing with her again. Unless she's left without her cell phone, she hasn't stepped out of this apartment since she was attacked three weeks ago. As much as I like the idea of her not going anywhere without me, I also know it's not good for her head to be stuck in here day after day.

Knowing she isn't going to want to leave now, I pull out my phone and order delivery. Just as I'm submitting my credit card information, the door opens again. Her damp hair hangs in clumps over her shoulders, wetting her t-shirt and making the furl of her nipples more prominent.

I swallow down my need and give her a quick grin. She settles on the other side of the bed, and it rubs me the wrong way. I purposely situated myself on her side of the bed so she would come to me, but stubborn as always, she keeps her distance.

"I ordered subs. Should be here in thirty minutes."

She nods in response before pointing her remote at the TV. The laughter of the audience on a sitcom serves as a distraction until the food arrives. Without a word, we eat and pretend there aren't a million words we should be saying to each other right now.

I hold out my hand for her trash when she balls the paper up. She places it in my hand, making sure her skin doesn't touch mine. I can tell she needs the space, so I'll give it to her for now.

We go back to watching TV, but the silence is eating away at me. I'm feeling like Dr. Phil before the words even come out of my mouth, but I want to help her get over what happened to her. The destructive path she's hell bent on walking is dangerous and a risk I'll no longer allow her to take.

"I know what happened in Honduras and Venezuela." The confession is low, and she doesn't respond immediately, which leaves me wondering if she even heard me over the raucous laughter coming from the TV.

"You don't know shit," she says long moments later.

She continues to watch the TV, and I continue to watch her. To anyone else, others who hadn't spent days watching as her face transforms with each of her emotions, she'd appear calm and unaffected by my words. I know differently. It's in the slight crinkle in the corner of her eye, and the almost invisible tremble in her chin. She's hurting, probably being tortured with what happened every day since she returned home. I can relate, and as much as I don't want to talk about my fucked-up past, I know I can use it to try to reach her. Maybe if I show her my gaping wounds, she'll do the same.

"I killed my mother."

She doesn't move, doesn't turn her head in my direction, or ask me to clarify, but she's listening. I just know she is, so I continue.

"My dad was a real bastard. He started the Ravens Ruin MC in Miami, but after he fucked the cartel over and got Lynch's mother killed, he hauled ass to Sutton, and laid down roots. My first memory of him is walking in to see him plowing into some chick while my mom sat in the corner and watched. She wasn't happy. I remember that much, but she wasn't doing anything to stop him either. He was cussing her, using words

I didn't even know the definition of at the time, but the gist was easy to understand. He'd take what he wanted from whoever he wanted because he was the king, and no one went against the king in his castle.

"I was two, maybe three at the time, but I knew from that moment that men were allowed anything. As a little shit, I used it to my advantage. I got extra ice cream, more time at the park, even permission to stay up later than normally allowed, all with simple little manipulations I learned from my father.

"I think I loved her. I remember the serenity I felt when she'd hold me to her chest and rock me to sleep as a little boy. I also remember the fear in her eyes when I'd repeat things to the women around the clubhouse I'd heard my father say."

I don't look at Kaci as I speak, but I watch her hand as she lifts the remote and powers off the TV.

"I thought I was a bad motherfucker, and the guys in the club loved me. They'd laugh their asses off at my antics. Apparently *'come suck my cock, whore'* is hilarious to bikers when it's said by a four-year-old kid."

"That's not funny at all," Kaci whispers.

"I know it's not. I mean, I know that now, but back then I wanted to be just like him. He yielded so much power from the men around him. I was his pride and joy. I think it was hard for him to look at Lynch, and it wasn't until the day he died that I realized why."

Kaci settles her back against the headboard, but I hate the distance, so I pull her against me. She doesn't fight it. With her head on my chest where she belongs, I continue.

"My father never loved my mother. I'd always thought it was because he didn't have a heart or the cocaine he snorted like it was his job fucked him up, but honestly, he never got over Lynch's mom. He'd bought me a toy gun when I was six, and I knew in my soul I was a real Raven then. I was a badass with this little cap gun."

'That looks great in your hand there buddy, but you won't be a real man until you have hair on your nuts.'

"That's what he told me earlier that day."

Kaci snorts a laugh, but I can tell she's appalled by my father.

"Seriously, I couldn't fucking wait to get hair on my nuts. I wanted to be a man exactly like my father. I idolized him. Later that day, the DEA raided the clubhouse." Her hand flexes against my side, but I ignore it and push forward. "They rushed in. At the time, I thought there were a hundred guys swarming into our home, but police didn't scare me, because I remember my dad saying he wasn't afraid of them a million times before. I lifted that tiny cap gun with steady hands at those fuckers, yelled 'die pigs', and pulled the trigger."

Kaci tenses against my chest, and I allow my hand to trace down her spine for a few seconds before I begin again.

"My mom must've predicted what was going to happen because she jumped in front of me, taking three bullets to the chest."

Kaci gasps, and her hot tears soak through the front of my shirt, but she doesn't placate me with empty words.

"My dad was wailing, yelling at the police, losing his fucking mind, and seeing him lose it made me lose it too. I was bawling like a baby, trying to tug my mom into my lap, like holding her would stop the red stains from spreading across the front of her shirt. It wasn't until my dad looked in our direction and realized my mom was dead and not me that he stopped crying. He didn't bother to wipe the tears from his eyes, but the sobbing stopped like someone had flipped a switch, and he smiled at me. His lips turned up in a proud smile as I sat there with my mom's dead body on my tiny lap."

Kaci's shoulders shake with silent sobs, but the comforting hand on her back is all I can manage right now. I'll fucking lose it if she raises her head and gives me any kind of fucking sympathy. I don't deserve it. I live with my choices every fucking day.

"After the dust settled, Lynch, he's eight years older than me, came to my room to talk to me. He told me that one day this club would be his, and what happened to my mother wouldn't happen in the club then. I believed him. Even when he went to prison, and things got so much worse, I held out hope that things would be better, eventually. Now they are."

"No more violence?"

I chuckle at Kaci's soft-spoken question.

"We are the most violent fucking people you'll ever meet."

She doesn't stiffen in my arms or pull away like I expect, but not looking into her eyes right now is killing me, so I cup a hand under her chin and urge her to look up.

"I'm sorry about your mom," she whispers, and her sincerity is almost enough to make me break.

I clear my throat and press my mouth to hers instead. She opens on a sigh, her tongue sweeping over mine with sweetness. I groan, but don't deepen the kiss. When I pull away, she's looking at me like she's never seen me before in her life.

"Kaci?"

"I want you to leave and never come back."

She pulls out of my grasp and locks herself into her bathroom. I do the only thing I can manage at the moment. I shrug on my jacket and my cut and get the fuck out of there.

Chapter 21

Kaci

I'm torn in two directions.

On one hand, I feel free for the first time since TJ pulled me from that guy's arms at his clubhouse. He hasn't been here in two weeks, and the freedom has been much needed.

On the other hand, I miss him more than I would ever admit out loud. I miss the sound of his voice, the feel of his body against mine in bed, and if I let myself think about it long enough, I miss what happened the last time he was here.

It was his story, and the way he looked in my eyes like he was in pain and I was the only one who could ease that for him that has kept me from reaching out to him. I can't be that person, even when deep down, I know he's the only person who can ease my own pain. Two broken, fucked-up people together will only mean more agony and heartache for both of us. Damaged people don't heal others. Trying to put someone back together with your broken pieces only leaves you with less than what you started with. It only causes more problems.

Even though I'm different now. Even though the thought of leaving my apartment at night literally makes my skin crawl, I can't bring myself to go to him.

I've only left once in the three weeks since TJ carried my battered and bruised body home. I walked to Tito's yesterday in broad daylight, and I looked over my shoulder and shook the entire way to the restaurant.

He did this to me.

Before he came along, I was always the commander of my own destiny, and I hate him for taking that from me. Just like I hate the sureness in my finger as it hovers over his name in my phone.

I press call and cancel just as fast.

"I don't fucking need him," I grumble, but I never drop my phone. I never toss it to the side and get up from my bed. I don't rush into my bathroom and tug on slutty clothes and pile a pound of makeup on my face. I simply hold the device in my hand and wait until I have enough courage to let the call go through.

My bruises are gone now, and it physically makes me sick to look at myself in the mirror. Without the injuries, the only thing I can focus on are the circles under my eyes from night after night of restless sleep, and the girl staring back at me urging me to find happiness.

What I need is a distraction, and if I'm too chicken shit to leave my apartment, there's only one recourse.

I hit call on the phone, and rather than end it immediately, I hold it to my ear. It only rings twice before the call is connected, but TJ doesn't say a word, and for that I'm thankful.

I didn't know what I was going to say to him. I've been going back and forth between begging him to come over and ripping him a new one for what he's already done to me. When the situation arises though, I don't do either of those things.

"I was wearing a one-piece swimsuit and a cover-up the day he took me."

TJ doesn't speak, but I know he's still there from the static on his end of the line. His clothes rustle as if he's moving, and either the wind or his breath comes through the microphone.

"His name was Deo." I clear my throat, unsure if I can get all of this out, already knowing I will regret it. "He told me he could tell I was a virgin by the way I walked. I remember thinking, even through my fear, that there was no way to tell if someone was a virgin that way, but then again he found me and his speculation was true."

My tongue slips out, wetting my bottom lip.

"He said virgins were the cream of the crop. They brought the most money at the auction, so he was always excited to get one. Virgins were what he sought out, and I just happened to catch his eye on the beach that day.

"Ten thousand dollars. That's what the guy paid to rip into me. He left me broken, bleeding, and begging for death. Before he walked out, he pressed his lips to my forehead and assured me the experience was worth every penny."

He doesn't speak, but his breaths are now rushing out, echoing in my ear. I inwardly wonder what his reaction would be if he knew the full truth. He shouldn't be angry on my behalf. The effort is lost on me. I don't deserve it.

"I was eighteen, and even though I thought I knew it all, much like most kids that age do, I realized I didn't know anything. I was guarded, protected every day, reminded how good girls behaved because my dad had political aspirations and didn't want me to ruin his chances. When Deo came in later, he praised me for making his customer so happy. I was certain he'd gotten what he wanted, and he was going to let me go home. I knew it in my soul that the worst was over, and even as horrible as it was, I would heal. I would move past it.

"I don't know how long I'd been there, but Deo came to me every night. He used me, and even though he was rough, he had never raised a hand to me. He didn't strike me the first time until I asked when I was going to be returned to my family.

"According to him, I was ungrateful for the life he had given me. He was raging on and on about pets biting the hand that feeds them. The next night Deo didn't come, but other guys did."

I try to clear my throat again, but the lump doesn't dislodge. I haven't even been able to discuss these things with the therapist my mother insisted I see when I got home. I have no clue why I'm spilling my guts to the man who threatens me with a knife and forces himself on me as well. I shake my head, clearing it of those thoughts. TJ is nothing like Deo and his band of abusers.

"I don't know how much or if he even charged the guys that came to my room night after night."

I hear growling coming through the line, but TJ doesn't speak a word.

"Deo's punishments got worse. He didn't come to me often, but when he did, he beat me for having sex with the men he allowed into my room. The first time I told him I didn't have a choice. I learned after he broke my wrist that night it was just better to take what I was given than disagree with him. I'd never win in a fight against him.

"Every day I'm reminded that had I only worn a two piece that day, had I looked less innocent, things would've been different."

"Kaci."

I hate the sound of my name on his lips. It's nothing but a reminder of the way Deo used to say it when he was hurting me.

"Please," I beg. I'm unable to explain to him. As hard as it is to give him the larger details of my time in Venezuela, there's no way I can break it down for him.

"Don't say my name." It's all I can manage.

Silence once again fills the phone.

"Now I get to choose," I continue before all my courage dries up. "I get to choose the party, the guy. I control my life. No one understands. Not that I have anyone who even gives a fuck."

The growling gets louder, but I ignore him. This conversation isn't about saving his feelings or acknowledging his misplaced emotions.

"I don't have any friends. My parents might as well not even exist. I have nothing to prove to anyone but myself. Going to those parties, deciding whether or not I tilt a cup up to my lips, it's the only thing I have. I choose my path. Of course, the guys think they're smarter than me. No one in their right mind would go to a party and intentionally have themselves drugged to the point of incapacity, right? Who's crazy enough to do that? But I know who's in control. Even drugged and unable to defend myself, I'm the one in control."

Just hearing the words out of my own damn mouth makes me realize how psychotic that is.

"I'm on the shot. Wouldn't want to get knocked up, you know? Nothing ruins a party like people staring at the pregnant girl snorting coke." A humorless laugh rushes past my lips, but I know nothing about this is funny.

Tears begin to stream down my face, and I don't speak for a long time. I weep with the phone to my ear. I cry for the eighteen-year-old girl who thought she had the world at her fingertips, only to find out there's nothing in this world left but pain and misery and shame for all the things I'm not telling him.

"And I liked what you did here last time," I confess once the sobs ebb. "How fucked up does that make me?"

"It makes you perfect."

My heart stops at the sound of his voice, and I cling to the hope that he actually means what he's saying.

"They made me this way." The tears begin anew.

"If none of that bad shit had happened, and we'd met at a different place in our lives, I'd still do the exact same things to you, and you'd enjoy them. They didn't make you. This is just who you are."

I ignore his words. There's no point in focusing on what could've been or arguing with him that he's wrong. It's the pain of what I've lost that guts me. For the last six years I've lived in misery, slowly distancing myself from family and friends who didn't understand why I just couldn't *'get over it already.'*

"I told myself I didn't need you, that I didn't want you. I was sure when I asked you to go that I wouldn't miss you. I'm tired of lying to myself." I take a deep breath before continuing, "I do miss you, and I fucking hate myself for it."

I hang up the phone, my eyes burning from the tears I should never have cried in the first place.

My head jerks up at the first sound of knuckles on my door, but I don't bother to get off my bed.

Why should I?

He has a key.

Chapter 22

TJ

I grin to myself when I have to pull out the key to unlock her door. At least she's locking it now. I've been watching her apartment almost every single day, waiting, hoping, and praying she'd make this call. I've grown discouraged over time, but it hasn't stopped me from parking my bike down the road and begging the devil to make tonight the night she actually reaches out.

She doesn't say a word as I enter, relock the door, and strip out of my jacket and cut. They fall to the floor, and I don't give a shit for even a split second about the disrespect I'm showing my club when I leave them where they land and cross the room.

"I—"

I press my fingers to her lips. "Shh."

Her story gutted me, much like, I'm sure, my story did her. She pushed me away, not sure what to do with all the information I threw down in her lap, but I know what I needed in that moment and didn't get from her. I was only bitter about it for a few days before I realized that what I needed wasn't something she could give to me at the time.

"I'm sorry they hurt you."

Her eyes slam shut, but it doesn't hold the tears that continue to streak down her face. I pull her head against my chest and wrap my arms around her shoulders. She doesn't fight me, but she's not settling into my comfort either.

"I'm sorry they stole things from you."

Her shoulders heave with her sobs, and her hot tears soak through my shirt.

"I'm sorry they took your power and your ability to say no."

She pushes against my chest, and I allow it. Asserting dominance after what she's confessed tonight just isn't in me. She doesn't go far, only pulls her head back so she can look up at me. Fuck me for loving the red rimming her eyes and the now silent tears as they cascade down her flushed cheeks.

"When was the last time someone pleasured you without pain?" She has to know I'm including our time together. My fingers have itched to smack her tits again. My teeth have ached with the need to bite her perfect fucking skin, but none of that is what either of us need right now.

"Never," she whispers.

She attempts to hang her head, but I refuse to let her be ashamed of that. She's not responsible for what those pieces of shit made her do, but she has to know she doesn't have to be that person. Regaining control and power doesn't have to be about accepting the abuse she puts her body through. She can be powerful and safe at the same time. She also has the right to like every form of sexual pleasure regardless if others deem it deviant.

"Let me," I lick at her lips. "Let me make you feel good."

"Turn off the lights," she urges as I reach for the hem of her shirt.

"I want you to watch me. I need you to see *us*." I refuse to let her hide from me.

Her head nods as if she believes she's answered a question. I can only relinquish so much power here. I have my own demons after all. In my gut, I know what I'm offering has the ability to end with epically disastrous consequences, but I'm not strong enough to resist. Offering her pleasure on the heels of hearing her confess her ten-month brutalization has got to be the worst decision ever, but the train has left the station, and it's only gaining momentum.

My hands tremble, betraying my inexperience in situations like this when my fingers ghost down her arm. I don't do soft and sweet. I'll get a girl off, but it comes as a consequence to my own pleasure, not as a response to hers. Somehow, deep inside, I know Kaci Stewart is different. She's one of a kind. She's everything I didn't know I needed, and everything I've fought against for as long as women have been trying to hitch themselves to me. For the first time in my life, I'm terrified of a woman, of what she can do to me, of what she means to me, but I shut down the voices in my head telling me to get my ass out of there and never come back.

"Undress me, please," I urge as she sits as still as a statue on her bed. She has to be an active participant in this, or she'll end up right back in her head. It's the last thing either of us need. Being rejected by her one more time may be what sends me into my own fucking spiral.

Her hands shake as much as mine as she reaches for my belt buckle, but I wait as patiently as I can manage as she slides the leather away. Warm fingers sweep inside my jeans as she works open the button, but I'm teetering on the edge as the sound of my zipper lowering echoes around the otherwise silent room.

"Jesus this is killing me," I confess, but when her lips tilt up in a soft smile, I know I'd stand on the edge of her bed forever if it's what she needs.

"Do you want me to suck you?" she asks, never taking her eyes off my cock as she pushes down my jeans and boxer briefs.

"I—" I swallow when the word comes out on a moan. "I want you to do whatever you want."

Her shaking fingers wrap around my dick, and I nearly lose it when her tongue swipes over her lips.

"I don't know what I want," her confession is softer than a whisper.

"Do you trust me?" I've asked her once before and her response was accurate, but I'm hoping she understands that asking again is situational.

"Y-yes," she responds.

I move into action, tugging my shirt over my head before bending at the waist to untie my boots. After kicking them off, my jeans and boxers are the last to be discarded. Before I climb on the bed, I grab a rubber from my jeans. It feels like I haven't fucked in decades, but in my head, I know the condom hasn't expired, so I toss it on her pillow before lowering my mouth to hers.

"We don't have to do this," I assure her before licking at her lips.

"I want to." She's breathless and still shaking, but instead of leaning away from me, she reaches up to wrap those trembling fingers in the hair at the nape of my neck. She did the same thing when we were dancing weeks ago, and the reminder has me pulling my head back to look into her eyes.

"No drugs or alcohol today?"

She gives me a wry smile, but she shakes her head no. It's all the confirmation I need. With my right arm, I swoop behind her lower back and urge her to lie down. I'm on top of her and between the opening she's allowed between her thighs an instant later.

"I haven't done this before." The words leave my mouth before I can stop them.

She chuckles. "I seriously doubt that."

"I mean—" I lick at her throat—"I haven't made love to a woman before."

She tenses in my arms, and I'm certain I've lost her, but the second my tongue touches the shell of her ear, she moans and settles in my arms.

"I have fucked more women than I can even remember, but I've never given a single one the attention I'm going to give you. I've never—" I turn us so I'm on my back and she's straddling my thighs. The black lace covering her perfect cunt is more picturesque than snow falling on the mountains. "Given a woman all the power."

Unable to resist, my hands cup the weight of her breasts, fingers teasing her pink nipples.

"I've never given in, taken things slow. I'm going to do my best, but if I get too rough or do something you don't like, I need you to tell me. This is about you, K—" My jaw snaps shut before I can say her name. She's asked me not to, and after thinking long and hard about our interactions in the past, it's the one thing that makes her shut down.

"All about me?" I groan when her hips flex and she scrapes the fabric of her thong down my bare cock.

"I'll have no choice but to make it all about you if you keep rubbing your pussy over me like that, because I'll come before we even get started."

She stills, her eyes refusing to look down at me.

"Tell me what you need," I urge.

"I want you to take over."

I've never heard such sweet words before in my entire life. In the blink of an eye she's on her back, and I'm rolling latex down my aching shaft. Resisting the urge to rip her panties from her body, I slowly tug them down her hips and toss them to the side.

I'm transfixed, eyes focused on the slick, glistening slit between her legs.

"Do you want me to taste you?" It's hard to speak past the saliva pooling in my mouth.

"No."

Disappointment is like a brick in my gut.

"I want you inside of me."

A groan erupts from my lips as I angle my cock and the heat of her pussy swallows the first couple of inches.

"Mmm." The sound of her pleasure drives me a couple inches deeper, faster than we'd agreed on. Slowly sinking the rest of the way into her is an exercise in restraint I'm not certain I can continue for long.

"Raise your leg up on my hip." The action does the exact opposite of what I needed, only clamping her down on me harder rather than relieving some of the pressure.

My only recourse is distraction, and I'm questioning this bright fucking idea when I cover her body with mine, slowing my hips, and licking into her mouth. My cock isn't listening, and my balls haven't gotten the memo.

"Touch me," I beg, groaning in her ear when her fingernails scrape down my back. At first it stings, but then heat radiates outward. The warmth makes me cling to her harder. Who fucking knew going slow could be better than pounding into someone? "How does it feel?"

"Amazing."

Her other leg laces around my hip, opening her just enough so I can drive all the way inside. She's tight and decadent, better than anything I've felt before in my life. Her breaths grow erratic. Her nails dig into me deeper, and I fucking love it. We're going to come together, and I know without a doubt it will be the single most erotic thing in my life to date.

"Come for me," I command in her ear.

Her hips shift as soft moans come from her mouth.

"I'm coming," she pants, but the energy I felt moments before is no longer there, and when her hips jolt, I can tell it's forced. My orgasm, *our* orgasm, the one that was supposed to change my life, rushes out of me, but the emotion that was behind it seconds ago fizzles.

Uncertain and begging to be wrong, I look down at her. When she looks away, I know for a fact what I felt in my gut.

She fucking faked it.

Rather than expressing what she needed, or telling me she was no longer into it, she gave me what she thought I wanted. Her throat works on a swallow, and a single tear trails down her cheek when I pull away.

I should hold her to my chest, tell her everything is okay. Ask her what she needs, and what can I do to make everything better for her. At least, that's what a nice guy would do, a guy with patience, one who hasn't been kicked by her over and over.

I'm no longer that guy, and as I pull myself from her body and climb off the bed, I realize I never was that guy. I don't even bother pulling the condom from my dick or tying my boots. I put my clothes on, and I'm out the fucking door a minute later.

If I can't do anything to make her life better, to ease her pain even a little, I don't need to be here. If she can't be honest with me, even in such an intimate moment, I'm no longer going to waste my fucking time.

I'm done.

I can't save her if she isn't willing to save her damn self.

Chapter 23

Kaci

"Perfect."

I pop my red lips in the mirror and give my hair a final spritz of hairspray. My outfit is perfect, exactly what I need for a night like tonight.

For days I let TJ walking out of here without a word bother me. It wasn't until I realized that he knew I faked the orgasm that things made a little more sense to me. I hurt his ego. His pride was wounded, and I figured he'd come back, but I haven't seen him in a week.

There was no way I could tell him that the thought of making love made my skin crawl. It's not really the thing a guy would appreciate. I couldn't tap him on the shoulder and beg him to fuck me harder or twist my nipples until I screamed to get me off.

Getting upset is his problem, just like him assuming what I needed. I never asked to be treated with a gentle hand. Hell, on the phone he threatened me, told me that even had I not gone through the shit I did all those years ago that he'd still get me off the same way he did before. I knew it was true the second the words left his mouth. I longed for his rough mouth or the handle of his knife fucking my pussy raw again, but then he barged in, saw my tears, and presumed. Big fucking mistake.

I can't rest it one hundred percent on his shoulders because I didn't give him the entire story. It was hard enough confessing what happened, admitting that I came twice the night my virginity was stolen from me isn't something I could ever voice. What kind of deviant orgasms after being abducted and hurt?

Hurting me when I came was Deo's favorite pastime. At first the punishment was more like foreplay for me. I relished the biting slaps and clamps all over my body, but after realizing those things actually brought me pleasure, he ramped up the pain until it was unbearable. Even my abductor knew I was fucked up and punished me for it.

"That is not what tonight is about," I mumble as I turn a bottle of tequila up and gulp the burning liquid. The courage I need doesn't come fast enough, so I turn it up again. And again.

Grabbing my phone off the counter, I turn to leave my apartment. I normally wouldn't take it with me for fear of losing it, but I'm not sure I'll be able to go through with my normal plans tonight, and I may need it to get an Uber back to my apartment.

I almost stumble back when I open my door and see fucking Detective Martin standing on my stoop with her arm raised to knock. She's not in a uniform, but the bulge of her gun on her hip doesn't go unnoticed.

"Didn't I tell you not to show up here?" I shove past her and take the steps two at a time to get to my car. I think better of it when I remember I just took several huge slugs of liquor, and I'm paranoid she smelled it on my breath when I passed her. Getting thrown in jail will derail my plans, so I pull out my phone and click on the Uber app. The party I'm attending tonight is only about a mile away, but there's no way I'm making that trek in these heels.

Her hand covers my phone before I can go any further.

"McGee asked me to bring you in."

Just the mention of the asshole detective makes my stomach twist in knots and my pulse rate double.

"What the hell does he want?"

If Detective Martin hears the waver in my voice she doesn't let on.

"Just has a couple more questions for you. Jump in, I'll give you a ride."

"I have my own car."

"Save your gas." She turns to her car, not bothering to make sure I follow her. In this instant I hate my upbringing, and the forced respect that was drilled in to me.

Don't be rude to police, reporters, or people who have money. My mother's words were drilled into my head as a child, no doubt an echo of what my father had expected of her.

The expensive watch on Deo's arm was the only reason I didn't walk away from him immediately on the beach that day. My politician father would've tanned my hide if I embarrassed him by insulting a possible constituent. It didn't matter that we were thousands of miles away from home and Deo's accent didn't sound anything like the other men who voted for my father, his training took over. He spoke to me, so I spoke to him. Somehow, he'd managed to get me to walk toward the parking lot without even knowing it. Seconds later I was being tossed in the back of a van and whisked away to almost a year of torture.

Martin clears her throat and snaps me out of my fucked-up trip down memory lane.

Just to be an asshole, I walk past the passenger side door she's holding open and climb into the back. She chuckles but closes the passenger door before rounding the front of the cop car and climbing in behind the wheel.

The first couple of minutes are spent in blessed silence, but true to form, she can't manage to ride all the way to the police station with her damn mouth shut.

Feeling her eyes on me, I make the mistake of looking up and catching her gaze in the rearview mirror.

"You look much better than you did last time I saw you."

I break eye contact and look out the window without responding, much the same way I did when she showed up and questioned all the bruises on my body.

"Where are you heading tonight?"

I don't say a single damn word, but for some reason, Martin is grinning like a crazy person when she opens the back door to let me out once we arrive at the station.

"Do you know how long this is going to take?"

"Now you want to talk?" She shakes her head as we walk up the short sidewalk into the front of the police station. "I'd suggest keeping that mouth shut a little longer."

I look over at her, certain I didn't hear her right, but she's already walking away.

"Ms. Stewart."

Goosebumps form on my arms at Detective McGee's voice. When I turn my head to look at him my hands begin to tremble. There's just something about this fucking creep that sets off all sorts of warning bells, and I'm fairly certain none of them have to do with the fact that he's a cop.

My jaw snaps shut as he ushers me down the same hallway I walked weeks ago. I regret my choice of clothes, because even the blanket I had wrapped around me then covered more than my halter top and short skirt do tonight.

He doesn't speak at first. He just waves his hand, indicating a hard-plastic chair on the other side of an economical table. It's almost like he's looking through me, cataloging and analyzing everything that has happened since I left the station over a month ago. I immediately hate the sins TJ confessed to me.

"Tell me about the biker," he demands as if he's reading my mind. I don't respond, but he isn't deterred. "The one that's been coming and going from your place like he lives there? The Ravens Ruin MC is full of some scary guys. With your background, I'd think you'd avoid guys like that. Are they hurting you? Threatening you?"

I shake my head immediately.

"Then care to explain?"

I shrug, suddenly exhausted that everyone thinks they know my fucking story.

"Did you break up? I have reports that he hasn't been seen there in the last week or so." My nails suddenly become the most interesting thing in the world. "Several people at that party recall seeing a couple of scary guys go upstairs that night. Did your boyfriend get upset you were planning a little orgy without him and kill those guys?"

I pick at my new nail polish and bite the inside of my cheek but ignoring this piece of shit cop isn't possible.

I finally look up at him. "You seem to be forgetting that one of those guys drugged me that night. I doubt I was in that room with them because they wanted to make sure I was safe from harm."

"So you don't care they were murdered, their bodies ripped to pieces only a couple of feet from your unconscious body?"

His ears are beginning to turn red, and it's clear he's barely holding onto his anger.

"Not even a little bit," I lie, because I do care some. I put them in that situation, but at the same time I also know that if it wasn't me, it would've been someone else. "Are you charging me with something? If not, I'm leaving."

"Sit down," he growls when I move to get up. "I'm going to tell you a little story."

Chapter 24

TJ

"You should've been here," Legs coos in my ear. I hate that she's right on top of me, but I also haven't bothered to push her away. "We learned tons of new self-defense techniques."

"False," Ronan says with a wide grin. "You stopped fighting the second Mac stuck that first finger in your ass."

"True," Mac adds from across the room. "I've never seen someone go from *don't do that* to *don't stop* so fast in my life."

Everyone in hearing distance laughs at their antics, but I ignore the memories of how much Legs likes her ass fucked and take another sip of my beer. I'm nursing it, and I could lie to myself and say I'm just not in the mood to get drunk tonight, but I know where I'm heading. The same damn place I've headed every night for the last week, and the week before.

"We can go back to your room if you're not feeling it out here." Legs's hand skates up my jean-clad thigh, and I don't push her away at first but the closer she gets to my cock, the dirtier I feel. How fucked up is it that I have all of this willing pussy surrounding me, and they do nothing for me?

"Don't fucking touch me," I hiss when her too-long fingernails ghost over the zipper of my jeans.

Her head snaps back, and I fully understand her reaction. From the time she showed up here, she has been on my dick. Well, minus the hour or so she spent with my brother. I'm not the only guy she's been with since arriving, but she's been the one I've entertained most often the last couple of months. What Legs fails to realize is that almost every girl before her got the same amount of attention. I like pushing the girls I'm fucking, seeing how far I can take them and where their limits are. It's impossible to do that without getting to know them first. I'm not like my dad. He'd go at it full-force with a brand-new girl, not giving a shit if he took things too far. In his mind, there was no such thing as *too far*. I'm nothing like that.

"You know," Legs seethes beside me, "the next time you want to fuck—"

I glare at her over the top of my beer. "You'll stick your ass in the air exactly how I like."

Her lip twitches, and I can't tell if she's trying not to smile or if she's getting ready to snarl at me. It could go either way, honestly.

"Sweetheart," Ronan, ever the hero, cups his hand under her jaw and turns her face toward him. "I've been thinking about this talented mouth of yours since I saw you licking Xena's cunt earlier. Could I convince you to give me a little attention?"

The second Legs drops to her knees in front of Ronan, I'm off the couch and out the damn door.

"Where's the fire?" As much as I want to plow past my brother and his woman, I respect the bastard. It has more to do with his help when I was younger and less to do with the fact that he's now the club president.

"Just gonna go for a ride." I keep walking further into the parking lot.

"On four wheels instead of two?" He angles his head at my hand on the door of the SUV.

Yanking my hand away like I touched fire, I look up at both of them. Lynch's classic, who-gives-a-shit smile is in place, but there's something about the eyebrow raise and small smirk playing at the corner of Zoe's mouth that tells me I'm not as slick as I think I am. Bikers don't choose to ride in a cage. We prefer the freedom of motorcycles for a reason, and it's out of character for me to select the SUV rather than my bike.

"Be safe," Lynch grunts.

Zoe winks at me before she lets her man turn her back in the direction of the clubhouse.

I hesitate for a long moment before unlocking the vehicle and climbing inside. For another couple of minutes, I sit inside before pressing the ignition switch. When I crank it and pull toward the gate, I let myself sit idle and talk to Pete and Sonic about absolutely nothing for ten minutes. It's almost as if I'm trying to find something to keep me away from Andover tonight. My obsession with Kaci has gone too far. I've enjoyed her pussy melting on my tongue and sliding into her incredible body, but I should be immune to her by now.

Yet, every night I climb inside of this SUV and drive over to her apartment. Some nights I spend parked right in front of her place, daring her in my mind to open the fucking curtain and see me waiting down there. Most nights I park a few blocks away and hide in the shadows to stare up at her windows. I only started to do that because there have been more patrols near her house since they found the dead body in the dumpster a couple weeks ago.

I'm twenty miles outside of town when I get the first notification on my phone. My foot grows heavier on the gas pedal as I pick it up. Within minutes she's stationary and another notification is sent, placing her right in the middle of the fucking police station. For a split second I wonder if she's gone to them, finally spilling her guts and sharing all the things I confessed to her, but when I get to Andover and drive past her house, her car is still in the drive.

She's on the move again by the time I get to the police station, so I sit across the street and wait for her to settle. She doesn't go home like I hope. Her tracker stops at a house across town.

I should go home. She's hell bent on putting herself in these situations. I've tried over the last damn month to get her to seek something different, something less violent, less likely to get her killed, but she seems determined to end up in a dumpster herself. Even as hard as I try, I may not be able to stop that from happening. I have duties back at the clubhouse. I can't sit and watch her every second of every day.

My foot is tapping wildly on the floorboard for fifteen minutes before I give in and put the vehicle in drive. This is the last fucking time I exert any amount of energy on Kaci Fucking Stewart. I vow to myself that tonight is the very last night I will ever drive to Andover and wonder what kind of trouble she has gotten herself into. Knowing it's my last trip, I park under a broken streetlight a few houses down from where her tracker indicates.

I strip out of my cut and aim for the trees beside the house. Only a couple drunk people can be seen on the porch, and as I approach, I realize this party is a lot tamer than the others she's been to. Without missing a beat, I swing my body up into the tree at the far end of the house. Fewer people means I'll be easily identified if I barrel through the front door, so I climb the tree until I'm close enough to jump on the small balcony.

The entry door lever is cheap, making it child's play to break and gain access to the house. Thankfully the doors open up to an unoccupied upstairs den. The hallway leading to the staircase is lined with four doors. One is open revealing an empty room. Another is a bathroom. My pulse is pounding in my ears when I open one door, surprised to find it empty. The last door produces exactly what I think it will. Kaci is spread out on a bed, as some piece of shit lowers his head and swipes his tongue up her slit. It would be hot as fuck watching her get pleasured by another guy if it were something that she actually wanted. I don't imagine she's given him permission, seeing as she's passed the fuck out.

The guy, probably stoned himself, doesn't even notice the door open or me standing there glaring at him. I don't have time to think or worry about my knife. I'm on him, snapping his neck in the blink of an eye. I feel cheated as I step over him and lean down to get closer to Kaci.

The scent of her pussy invades my nose, and if she were awake, I'd mount her right here and now.

"This shit ends today," I grunt as I pull her skirt down to cover her cunt and scoop her in my arms.

Getting her out of that fucking house is harder than I expect. The climb down is ten times more difficult than the climb up empty-handed. The first scream happens as I am rounding the house and carrying Kaci to my SUV through the shadows. By the time I get her buckled and climbed inside myself, I can hear the sirens. The first flashes of red and blue appear just as I am turning off the road.

I drive out of Andover, not even bothering to stop by Kaci's house. There isn't a damn thing left of that life that she needs anyway.

Chapter 25

Kaci

My body jolts when I hear the slam of a door. Even before I open my eyes, I already know I'm not at home. A small smile plays at my lips as I take a mental inventory of my body.

The familiar headache is pounding in my skull, but other than lying in an uncomfortable position, I feel fine. The realization depresses and thrills me at the same time. A small beam of light pushes against my eyelids, forcing me to open them slightly to figure out where it's coming from. A shadow descends a flight of stairs to my right, but it isn't the unknown man walking toward me that makes my pulse skyrocket. I'm looking up at him from behind a metal grid. I'm caged, surrounded on all six sides by thick metal iron.

"Where am I?" I ask the man and get no response.

From the sun filtering in from up above him, I'm pretty certain I'm in a storm shelter, but they aren't common in Massachusetts, so it terrifies me that I've been transported someplace different. Pine and bleach fill my nose as the guy draws closer. Bleach was only used in my previous abduction to clean up blood. My mouth dries in fear.

"Are you fucking kidding me?"

He doesn't have an accent, but that doesn't mean anything. Several Americans worked for Deo, and it wasn't until I was rescued that I even knew I hadn't left Honduras.

"Help me," I beg, but my pleas evolve when he steps closer to the cage. "Don't hurt me."

A second man slowly makes his way down the stairs. With him blocking the light, it's easier to see the first guy.

"I'm going to fucking kill him!" he roars before the familiarity of his leather vest sinks into my terrified brain.

"Wow," the other guy mutters as he closes the distance between the bottom of the stairs and my imprisonment.

One of them reaches up and pulls on the light, and even though I try, I can't keep my eyes from squinting. The two men stare down at me. One is lost in anger, but the other one smiles down at me like I'm a treat being offered to him. My eyes dart to his vest first, letting me know he's Hornet, the road captain. The scowling guy is—

My eyes dart from his leather to his face. Green eyes stare back at me, and if TJ hadn't mentioned Lynch was his brother, I never would've guessed they were related just by appearances. His complexion and hair are darker, nothing similar to TJ's blonde hair and ice-blue eyes. Don't get me wrong, he's just as gorgeous—

I shake my head violently. I've been abducted. This guy's looks are the last thing I need to concern myself with. Good looking doesn't mean morally sound. Deo was incredibly handsome, but I've never met a more brutal man in my life.

"Please let me out."

"Did you know anything about this?" Lynch ignores me, but points as he speaks with the other man.

Hornet chuckles and shakes his head. "Nope. I mean. I'm not surprised, but I didn't have a clue."

Not surprised? Does TJ do this often? Why does that thought make me jealous?

"I don't want to be in here." I look all over the cage for a door, and my disappointment grows when I see a huge lock through the latch.

"Do you know who she is?" This question comes from Hornet in a way that makes me think he does know who I am.

I'd fully expect Lynch to be the one informed on what TJ's been doing. Not only is he the president, but he's also his brother.

"Should I?" Lynch asks, his brow creasing.

"I think she's the girl that got beat up in the garage last month."

I don't confirm or deny, because I don't know which way would benefit me better.

Lynch could probably bite through steel with the tension forming in his jaw. In the next second, he tugs on the string to the light, and I'm once again encased in darkness.

"Please don't go," I beg, but they both turn and ascend the stairs without another word. The door slams shut, and silence surrounds me.

What have I gotten myself into?

Uncontrollable tremors rack my entire body. I can't even hold onto the cage without my knuckles banging against the metal grid above. I don't know how much time has passed, but I'm still in the same clothes I was wearing when I left the police station. It could be hours or days if TJ saw fit to keep drugging me. I have no way of knowing.

"He won't hurt me," I assure myself. If I was in danger, the guys who just left would've hurt me. They could've, if they wanted to.

We are the most violent fucking people you'll ever meet.

TJ's words from weeks ago force me to realize that I may not be as safe as I want to believe.

With this realization, I do exactly what I did the first time I was taken. I look around the cage for a way to escape, but once it's obvious I'm stuck, I settle. Lying on my side so I can face the door, I take deep breaths and calm my heart rate. I made mistakes the first time, and I refuse to do the same again. I have to conserve my energy and stay sharp. An opportunity to escape won't happen until they pull me from my confines, so there isn't any point in getting agitated before then.

My eyes flutter closed as I try to imagine myself someplace else. Instinctively, I want to think of a warm beach and sand between my toes, but Deo ruined that for me years ago. My teeth grit when TJ comes to mind, his body over mine, his kiss-swollen lips turned up in a smile. Refocusing, I picture myself alone in a cabin surrounded by foot after foot of soft snow.

***

"A body like this will bring thousands." The rough timbre of his accented voice makes my skin crawl.

Just when I think things can't get worse, his finger trails down my cheek and over my arm. I've been here for days, but I've been mostly left alone. He hasn't touched me since he shoved me in the back of that van.

"You're almost beautiful enough to keep for myself."

I shiver, unable to imagine what the worst outcome will be.

"Please let me go."

His fingers stop, gripping my naked hip, and a pained cry escapes from my lips. "I just stopped by to say thank you."

"Th-thank you?" The question in my voice is clear.

A sinister smile spans his face. "For not letting anyone fuck you. Virgins bring in a lot of money."

My knees nearly buckle, but he steps closer. His erection pushes against my stomach, and bile rises in my throat.

"Please don't!" I yell before screaming out in pain as my fingers tangle in the panels of the cage.

I'm not back in Deo's dungeon, but realizing that now doesn't keep the tremors from shaking my body violently.

"Let me out!" I scream, face angled in what I'm hoping is the direction of the door. I'm in complete darkness, and it fucks with my head more than being able to see what may come for me. I yell over and over until my throat is sore and the only sounds I can make come out as rough coughs.

Instinct takes over, and I revert right back to the things that didn't save me in Honduras and Venezuela. I grip the metal and try to break it open. I don't stop until my fingers are bleeding. I lean back and kick at the door, hoping to somehow break the lock. By the time I give up on that, my feet hurt so much I doubt I'd be able to run away if I get the chance.

My shoulder is next, ramming into the cage like a battering ram over and over with as much leverage as I can manage in the tight space. By the time I give up, I'm bruised, exhausted, and wondering why I even care what happens to me. The sobs come without warning, and I pray to a god I no longer believe in to make my death quick and painless, even though it's more than what I deserve.

Memories of Seth's cute little face carry me into unconsciousness.

Chapter 26

TJ

I'm barely out of the damn shower when a fist hits my bedroom door. I knew this was coming. I just figured I'd have a little more time. The guys never go into the basement unless they have business to attend to, and those issues that would bring them below the clubhouse are usually discussed in church or at least brought to me since I'm the enforcer of the damn club.

"What's your problem?" I snap when I pull my door open to find my brother standing there. If this were a cartoon, smoke would be billowing from his ears while a whistle blew in the background.

"Explain yourself." His voice is a little too loud and bordering on too disrespectful for me to ignore. President or not, I'll take his ass to the ground just like I used to when we were kids. I don't imagine anger and a show of force are going to help me in this situation, but I've never been one to back down.

"It isn't a big fucking deal," I assure him, barely containing my rage.

My fingers tingle with the absence of my knife, but with how angry Lynch is right now, I don't imagine pulling it just for my comfort is going to come across the right way. Stopping myself from using it would be another issue.

Briar's door snaps open, but my brother doesn't even divert his attention. He's safe in this clubhouse, and he damn well knows it. He doesn't give a shit if he has an audience for whatever it is he needs to say. The more people who hear about it now just means less people he'll have to tell later.

"Not a big deal?" he snaps as his eyes narrow on my naked chest. "Are you fucking kidding me? Since when is having a girl locked in a cage in the basement not a big fucking deal?"

Realizing there won't be a problem, Briar backs out of the hallway and closes his door. I hate that Lynch didn't see him. In nothing but sweats, I know for a fact he was just banging our little sister. If Lynch had seen him, maybe he'd be able to focus his anger elsewhere. Giving his blessing or not, being approached by a half-naked Briar while our sister is in his room might have tipped the scales in my favor.

Ignoring my big brother, I go back into my room and get dressed. He stands, fuming, in the doorway as I drop my towel and shove my damp body into clothes.

"Who is she?"

"Is it the girl that got beat up here a month ago?" I look up from lacing my boots to see Hornet standing a foot or so behind Lynch.

The question doesn't faze Lynch, so either they've already had this conversation, or he deduced the same thing.

"Who is she to *you*?" Lynch clarifies when I glare at Hornet like he's betrayed me. "You'll fucking talk to me."

He shoves his arm across the hallway when I try to walk past him.

"Lynch," I warn, but he doesn't budge. "She's the girl that was in the room when Briar and I went to take care of Molly's business in Andover."

"What?" Hornet and Lynch snap their eyes at me. We all know the implication of this information.

"She witnessed you kill three men?" Concern laces my brother's voice. "Do we have heat coming?"

"No," I shake my head and push past his arm.

They follow me down the hallway, but don't say another word as I lean against the bar and hold a finger up. Mac slides a beer across to me and then grabs one for the other two.

"She didn't recognize me." I tilt my beer back for a long pull before I lower it and tell them the truth. "I've been spending time with her. She was at the bar when we got back from the cartel run. She was here the night Hornet found that guy beating the hell out of her."

"The bar was invite only," Lynch says. He wasn't in town that night, but he knows how we run things around here. He wouldn't let his girl go out in an uncontrolled environment when he was so far away.

"I invited her."

Lynch's beer slams down on the bar top. "Have you lost your fucking mind?"

I shrug, unable to fully deny it. "I think I may have."

"Oh shit." Lynch frowns first before a slow smile spreads across his face.

"What?"

"You've fallen for her."

"Have fucking not," I hiss without missing a beat. "She's just determined to get herself killed."

Lynch angles his head, and Hornet takes the hint. Mac disappears just as fast.

"I haven't," I repeat. "She's fucking broken."

Lynch just watches me. He tried this shit when I was younger, staring me down hoping the atmosphere around us got so uncomfortable that I would spill my guts just to relieve the tension. It didn't work on me then and it sure as hell isn't going to work now.

"Just because you and Briar fell down in some love hole doesn't mean all of us are going to."

He grins around the lip of his beer bottle.

"Will you need help getting rid of her body then?" Every muscle in my body stiffens. "I don't really approve of killing females, but if she found out who you are, I guess there's no other way around it. I can get Ronan to help you. Nothing seems to bother that fucker."

"That won't be necessary," I grunt.

"So you can dispose of her on your own?" Lynch shakes his head, the devious glint in his eyes not matching his brutal words. "You'll need help."

"No one touches her but me." My words come out on a growl, and the fucker beside me has the damn audacity to chuckle at my response before he stands up.

Leaning in close to my ear, his humor is suddenly gone.

"Better than anyone else, you should know that I won't tolerate a snitch or someone bringing heat down on my club."

He isn't lying or exaggerating. He killed our father to protect the Ravens Ruin MC and was willing to kill Zoe when he thought she'd betrayed him. Kaci's death wouldn't even make him bat an eye, and I'm pretty sure if I became a complication, he'd take my life too.

"Just keep it in mind," Lynch says after downing the last of his beer. The echo of him slapping it back down on the bar follows him out of the room.

Regret swims in my gut. I never should've brought her here, but one way to keep her from betraying us is to never let her leave. My smile stays on my face until the sun sets and I make my way to the basement door.

"Let me out," she hisses the second I turn on the overhead light.

"No."

"This isn't right." I don't say anything. "You can't just keep me down here."

She sounds more scared than I expected her to. I'd anticipated anger and irritation, but the fear in her voice is a shock. It only proves how broken she is. I've spent hour after hour with her, and she still doesn't trust me.

"TJ!" she yells when I merely stand a few feet away and stare down at her.

"Promise me you'll stop going to those fucking parties."

"No."

I don't know where she's drawing her courage from now, but she should know this isn't something I will negotiate on.

"You're not getting out of that fucking cage until you agree to stop trying to get yourself killed."

"I'm not going to lie to you."

My lip twitches with her honesty even though that truth is the last damn thing I want to hear.

"You are so fucking stubborn," I growl. "Why can't you just stop getting yourself hurt?"

"Why can't you just walk away and leave me to my own damn life? I didn't ask to be saved." She frowns and looks away.

I don't know if she's referring to years ago when Cerberus pulled her out of Hell in Venezuela, or when Briar and I caught her in that frat house with four men looming over her.

"You're not just hurting yourself." I feel like I'm arguing with a toddler over the negative health benefits of sticking a fucking fork in the electrical socket. Just like a three-year-old, she can't see the dangers in what she's doing because the thrill is all she's focusing on.

She huffs, her head turning until her empty green eyes look back up at me. "No one gives a shit about me."

"That's not true." My mouth is suddenly dry, but I do my best to keep my posture stiff and unassuming. I can't confess my feelings to her when I don't understand them myself.

She somehow understands the battle I'm fighting inside as evident by the sudden glint of deviousness in her eyes.

"I don't give a shit about a single person on this earth, myself included." Her tongue snakes out and licks at her lower lip as her eyes narrow in challenge. She's purposely exploiting the emotion she can read but I'm unable to express, and her words cut me deep.

Does she want me to hurt her? Is she trying to prove that no one will tolerate the nastiness coming from her beautiful mouth?

"Let me go." She sounds almost feral, but isn't a cage where wild animals belong?

"I can't do that." Her eyes dart to my hand when I pull my knife out. The snap of the blade locking into place when I flip it open echoes around the room.

"Wh-what are you doing?"

"Why are you afraid? Wouldn't this be easier than slowly dying or being brutalized over and over at those damn parties?"

Heat *and* arousal wash over her as her eyes stay trained on the shiny blade. God she's fucking perfect, but her being turned on right now isn't what either one of us need. It only feeds exactly what she's after.

"I hate you," she seethes, no doubt a means to propel me into action. She wants me to hurt her. She wants me to get her off. She needs both, but that isn't on the calendar of events right now.

"Do you have any idea what it does to me each and every time you show up at one of those parties?" I take a step closer. "Any clue how it makes *me* feel?"

I take one more step. Standing right in front of her, I shrug out of my t-shirt. I didn't bother to put my cut on since Lynch was up my ass.

"It feels like this."

Without hesitation, I slash my knife across my stomach.

The pain is fucking orgasmic, but it's her wide eyes and mouth hanging open that makes me almost come in my jeans.

Chapter 27

Kaci

"No!" I reach for him as blood blooms on his skin, but the grid of the cage isn't large enough for me to get my entire hand through. "What are you doing?"

"I'm a psychopath. Why do you care?" His knife draws across his skin again, and both wounds seep blood down his abdomen.

"Stop!" Tears are burning my eyes. "You yawned too!"

Confusion marks his brow just as he's lifting his knife to cut himself again. "What?"

"A few weeks back at my apartment. I yawned and you yawned too. Psychopaths don't yawn empathetically."

I'm sobbing when he cuts himself again.

"You really need to stop getting your info from binge-watching Netflix."

"Please stop," I manage through my tears.

"Why?" TJ dips the tip of his knife into the blood on his stomach and draws on his skin with it. "This is what it feels like on the inside when you put yourself in danger. You hate me. I just thought you should know what you do to me."

"Don't!" I yell again when he runs the knife twice more over his stomach. The blood is too thick, making the number of wounds hard to distinguish.

"I don't like bleeding on the inside, Kaci. So I'll bleed on the outside *for you*."

He's right. He has to be a fucking psycho, but that doesn't stop the tears from falling or my gut from clinching with the way he's looking at me right now. He's begging me with his eyes, telling me I'm the only one who can stop the pain.

"TJ!" His knife stills midway through another cut. "Hurt me. Hurt me instead."

His head shakes as a tear forms in the corner of his right eye. "I need this. It's the only thing that keeps me whole on the inside."

It isn't until I really look at him and let his words sink in that I see the hundreds of razor thin marks all down his arms and across his pecs. They seem to glow under the single light hanging from the ceiling. I have no idea how I missed them before.

"And I need what I do," I confess. I reach for him again, fingers pushing through the grid as far as the cage will allow. "Please. No more."

"You stop, I'll stop," he barters once again.

"You're asking too much of me."

"Promise me." He holds his hand up to silence me before I can refuse him once again. "Promise that I'll be the only one to hurt you."

A dark thrill runs through my blood, excited by the idea, but I don't answer him immediately.

"And what about you?"

"Just the idea of your hand on my knife drawing my blood makes my dick hard."

Instinctively, my eyes drop to the bulge at the front of his jeans.

"So we—" I swallow, attempting to dislodge the lump in my throat. "So we only hurt each other?"

Is that what I need? Or is that just handing my power over to him? Would I even be able to give him what he needs? I've never been big on sadism. My desires tilt to the other side of the spectrum.

"I won't drug you and fuck you."

"I won't stop telling you no," I counter and love the way his eyes narrow. "Sometimes I may need more than just what you have to offer."

I told him I wouldn't lie, and this is my whole truth. One man may not be enough to give me what I need.

"I won't fucking share you." His ice-blue eyes are mere slits as he looks down at me. "But I'll find a way to give you what you need."

As if we've somehow sealed the deal with no paperwork, his knife clatters to the floor as he reaches for the combination lock keeping me trapped. In the next minute, I'm pulled from the cage and TJ is ripping at my clothes. My tits spring free from my tank top, but he doesn't let his hands pause until I'm standing in front of him completely naked. I don't bother trying to cover myself, but it does take a lot of strength to keep from reaching out to him.

"I can smell your pussy from here," he hisses in my ear as he crashes his body against mine.

I don't shrink away this time. I don't let shame swim in my gut for being turned on at the sight of his blood transferring to my stomach and breasts.

"Look," he urges just as his fingers tangle in my hair and he forces my head down. His other hand, covered in blood from his wounds, trails down my stomach. "Absolute perfection."

Harsh breaths loudly escape his lips as we both watch his fingers slide down my slit and disappear.

"Oh fuck," I moan as he pulls back his hand and my arousal, along with traces of his blood, coat his fingers.

"I'm not going to be gentle," he warns as I reach for his belt buckle.

"Please don't be."

Anticipation swims through my veins as he takes a step back. My hands, trembling with need, fall to my sides as I watch him strip. His eyes focus on my body and the blood left behind on my skin as he methodically strips every scrap of clothing away. Not only are we physically bare to each other, I feel as if we've crossed some invisible line that will at least feed our devious hunger for pain and humiliation.

"You need to tell me if it's too much," he says as he drops his jeans to the floor. His bright blue eyes are nearly black, the irises having been taken over by feral, dilated pupils.

I shake my head no. "I need you to be rough with me."

A hiss slips through my lips when he tangles his fingers in my already matted hair. My head jerks forward until our noses are touching and our breaths are mingling. "You'll tell me if it's too much."

My head nods, and it's not really a lie because what he does to me will never be too much. I only worry that, like last time in my apartment, he won't be enough.

"Do you want me to start by fucking your mouth or tongue fucking your pussy?"

"Fuck my mouth."

Without warning, he slaps my right breast. "Wrong answer."

"Eat my pussy," I whimper.

He hits my right breast again in the very same spot. I'd be amazed by his accuracy when he hasn't pulled his eyes from mine, but my flesh stings too much.

"Also a wrong answer."

"Jesus," I nearly scream when he lands two hits to my other breast.

"Repeat. After. Me." My breasts burn, and my pussy slickens when he punctuates each word with stinging slaps. "Whatever. *You*. Want. TJ."

"Please," I beg, and not for him to give me what I want, but because he's inching toward my limit and he damn well knows it.

Being drugged and unable to hand myself over to someone is different from actually speaking the words.

"Say it," he urges as his talented fingers twist my already burning nipple.

"Whatever you want," I tell him so quickly it sounds like a single moan.

"You missed a word."

I'm going to die. The pleasurable pain, something I thought I'd never actually have is going to kill me. I can't fucking wait.

"Whatever you want, TJ," I hiss.

"Mmm." His gratification rumbles from his lips. "I love the sound of my name coming out of this pretty mouth."

My blood boils, breath hitching at the realization that I now have a means to manipulate him.

"I don't want either," he hisses.

He spins me around, shoving my face against the wall as rough hands pull my hips, forcing my ass out. He slams inside of me without warning, and I kind of hate how wet I am for him. He's thick, filling me impossibly full, but the slide is too easy. It's decadent enough that my toes curl against the concrete floor.

"Fuck," he grunts. The feel of my body engulfing his cock seems to be too much for him. His hips stiffen as he releases my hair and grips my throat instead. It's not enough to obstruct my breathing, but tight enough to let me know who's in charge. My back arches as he urges me to straighten until my head is on his shoulder. Only then do his hips move again. "Fuck, fuck, fuck."

I'm liquid in his arms. I don't think my own muscles are even holding a pound of my weight up. He's doing all the work, using his strength to impale me with his cock in a relentless tempo.

"Goddamn it," he bellows, and suddenly I'm released and pushed to the floor.

I don't have a second to protest before he shoves his cock in my mouth. The pulse in my clit pounds at being denied in the same rhythm he stabs into my mouth with.

"I'm going to spank your ass for this," he grits out, frustration evident in his tone as he rips his cock from my mouth. "Ride me."

"Mmm," I whimper when he's on his back and I can sink down on him once more.

"If you make me come too soon, you're in for a world of hurt," he cautions.

I move my feet, shuffling them forward an inch or so to get better leverage when my toes hit metal. An evil smile tugs at the corner of my mouth when I look down and see his forgotten knife. Leaning in, I swipe my tongue over his bottom lip and pick up the knife. His eyes are half-lidded, and my tempo never falters.

He doesn't even see the knife until I'm holding it to his chest, and even then, he doesn't look afraid.

"You coming too soon, isn't my problem." I swivel my hips with him buried all the way inside of me. My pleasure is betrayed when my own groan slips out.

"This tight pussy is one hundred percent your fault." As if I didn't have a knife against his skin, he grips my hips holding me above him and slams into me a half dozen times.

Lost in my own pleasure, the knife slips. I don't realize I've cut him until he hisses.

"Fuck, baby. That doesn't help. It'll only make me come faster."

TJ suddenly sits up, and I'm terrified I pushed him too far as the knife clatters back to the floor. He's grinning as he grips me on one hip and at the nape of my neck and uses his own strength to piston me up and down on his dick.

"Oh, God," I groan as an orgasm slams into me. My legs tremble. My feet tingle. Hell, even my hair seems to stand on end, completely turned on by this man.

"That's much better," I hear him grumble in my ear. He allows my release. He lets me ride every wave my body has to give before he concerns himself with his own. "I'm going to come."

I wish I had it in me to double my efforts, to give him more pleasure, but my legs are too languid to work right. His teeth dig into my shoulder at the same time I feel his cock kick deep inside of me. It's several more pulses and an endless time before he releases his grip on the back of my neck.

He doesn't shove me off him as I anticipate. His grip on my hip loosens a fraction, and his other hand swipes damp hair from my eyes. "Did I hurt you?"

"Yes." A smile spreads across his gorgeous face with my answer. "Thank you."

Chapter 28

TJ

She is fucking perfect.

Her submission, then her fight. Man, this woman is everything I've ever needed.

"I came inside of you," I confess, brushing my lips along her cheek. "Didn't even consider a condom because I was so worked up."

Only now does she stiffen.

"I'm clean, baby," I vow. "I get tested very often because of the way I like to do things."

"I don't know if I'm—"

I pull my face away from hers. "You're clean, too. They tested you when you went to the hospital over a month ago."

Her brow draws in, and a frown plays on her lips. "And just how do you know that?"

I shrug, too far past expert stalker level to care. "I hacked your medical files."

"Of course you did." She huffs, but she's either exhausted or doesn't really care because she's still plastered against me. Either way is fine for me because I love the warmth of her skin against mine.

"You need to get some rest."

"Mhmm," she agrees and snuggles deeper in my arms.

"Fuck, I wish I could take you upstairs," I tell her as I stand and walk back toward the cage.

"What are you doing?" She's questioning me, but she doesn't fight me when I open the door and urge her to get back inside.

I don't answer until the lock is back in place.

"You faked your orgasm," I remind her as I bend to scoop up my clothes and begin to dress.

"I fucking did not!"

"Not today. No, today you came like a fucking goddess on my dick." Her cheeks pink and fuck me if I don't want to pull her out and take her again. "Last time at your apartment. You faked it."

Her jaw snaps closed.

"You need to learn to ask for what you need." Her arms cross over her chest. The crate is barely tall enough for her to sit Indian style. "Or at least not fake it when I'm inside of you."

She doesn't argue with me, merely huffs several more times as I take a seat in the single chair in the basement and pull my phone out.

"I need a shower. I don't think staying in this cage with cum dripping out of me is a good idea."

"I think my cum inside of you is the best idea ever," I counter. "Just the thought of it being there makes my dick hard all over again."

"We should fuck again then."

I don't pull my eyes away from my phone. "Doesn't seem like much of a punishment for faking it."

"You can slap my tits some more."

"Also not much of a punishment."

"I want you inside of me," she purrs.

The shifting of her weight in the cage draws my attention, but I do my best to look disinterested when my eyes find hers. "I'm already inside of you."

Her eyes narrow at the reminder.

"Take me upstairs and let me clean your wounds."

The offer is tempting. The thought of her small hands running soap over the superficial slices on my abdomen also makes my cock kick in my jeans.

I'm seconds away from giving in when my cell phone chimes a text.

Virus: We need to talk

TJ: Later

Virus: I have more info on that chick

TJ: Be right there

"I'm hungry." Her attempt at vulnerability doesn't affect me.

"I'll get you something to eat."

"I need coke."

"No, you don't."

"I need liquor."

"You don't need that either."

"Where are you going?" Kaci cries when I stand and walk toward the stairs.

"I'll be back. Think of how much of a bad girl you've been, and we'll discuss it when I get back."

"I'm going to cut your fucking heart out if you leave me down here again."

I turn back, basking in the joy of her smile when she thinks I'm going to release her.

"I can't fucking wait," I tell her right before pulling the string on the light and walking away.

"TJ! How long am I going to be down here?" she asks when I'm halfway up the stairs.

I don't turn back in her direction. "I'll send someone down with something to eat."

She's still calling me every curse word in the book when I close the basement door.

"I hear you've got a pet." Xena nudges my shoulder with hers as I step into the hallway. "When do we get to play with her?"

Before, the thought of anyone touching Kaci made me see red, but I don't immediately toss out the idea of Xena and maybe some of the other girls playing with her. Quick images conjured of Xena getting a taste of just how sweet Kaci's pussy is makes me want to grab her and get right to it, but I have other things to take care of first.

"Grab her something to eat," I tell Xena as I walk past.

"Of course," she responds, and the eagerness in her voice stops me in my tracks.

I turn back before she wipes the wicked smile from her pink lips. "Touch her pussy without my permission, and you'll never get to play with her again."

"Sure thing," she agrees. "I'm a patient girl."

We part ways, Xena heading into the kitchen as I make my way to Hornet and Virus's office. My concern increases when I walk in, and Virus makes eye contact immediately. Normally I'd have to wait for him to beat the level he's playing on whatever game is interesting him at the time.

"Your dad was a piece of shit, right?"

I raise an eyebrow at Virus as I take the seat behind Hornet's desk. Virus was absorbed into the MC after Lynch killed our dad, so he never had the displeasure to meet him.

"Probably the worst guy you could've ever met. Be glad you didn't."

"Was he *sell his daughter to sex traffickers* bad, though?"

"What?" I snap up from my relaxed position and glare at him.

"You told me you wanted more, that I needed to dig deeper. So I did." He must register my anger because he licks his lips nervously like I'm going to kill the messenger, and I just might. "People do what they've always done. If something happens and they benefit from it, even if it had horrific outcomes, they tend to repeat things to try to replicate the results. Royce Stewart won his mayoral race after his three-year-old son choked on a toy. Seven years ago, he announced his intention to run for Congress but wasn't met with much fanfare. He wasn't very good at his job as mayor."

"Can you get to the fucking point," I snap.

"On a whim, I looked into his finances. Three weeks before your girl was abducted in Honduras, her father paid five grand to have her taken."

My head snaps back. "Five fucking grand? That's nothing."

Virus shrugs. "They would've taken her for free. Mr. Stewart is a chump that got played if you ask me."

He has the decency to look ashamed when I growl at him.

"Are you sure? What did the payment show up as? Steal a Girl Inc. or something?"

"No." He points at his computer screen, but I hold my hand up to let him know I'm not interested in watching how he came to his conclusion. "I can go step by step, but the gist of it, after ten layers of bullshit, is that he paid someone that has ties to the guy they busted running the sex den in Venezuela."

"All because he wanted to win a fucking political race?" I understand killing someone because they pissed you off. I have murdered people for looking at me wrong or stealing Ravens Ruin dope, but to win a race? It's unfathomable to me, and I have loose morals.

"The fucked-up part is that he lost. His opponent ran on the premise that if Stewart couldn't take care of his own damn family what business did he have taking care of a state."

"She doesn't know," I mutter more to myself than to him.

She wouldn't go to her parents' house if she knew. I don't know everything about her, but I do know that.

"You going to tell her?"

My knee bounces and sweat blooms on my forehead just thinking about relaying that news. "I should just fucking kill him."

"It's not your kill."

I don't realize Virus said it rather than it being in my own head until I look and see him watching me.

"It's hers."

"Jesus!" I hiss standing from the chair and running my hands over the top of my head. I pace the short length of the office in a bid to calm down, but it only seems to agitate me more. "What is it with everyone around this motherfucker having daddy issues?"

"It's what makes us who we are," Virus answers.

"Would you tell your girl?"

Why am I even asking him this shit?

I feel helpless. She's already broken. This news may be what finally sends her over the edge.

"I don't feel like there's a one hundred percent right answer here, man."

And that solves that. He doesn't have a damn clue either.

Chapter 29

Kaci

My head jerks up, more from being startled awake than fear of the unknown. I shouldn't trust TJ, but there's just something about the light in his eyes that makes me believe he'll never truly hurt me. He's nothing like Deo and the men that hurt me before. Instinct tells me he's different, even though just like before, I've been abducted and locked in a basement.

Slender legs are showcased at the top of the stairs. Most people would be relieved to know that even though it's not TJ coming back, a woman is here. I personally know that women can be ten times worse than the men in situations like this.

The door doesn't close behind her as she makes her way toward me, but I recognize her just from her stature.

"Xena?"

I shield my eyes as if it will help with the light haloing behind her.

"Just a minute doll." The light clicks on, but she doesn't give me but a brief glance before turning back to the stairs. She rushes up them, closes the door to the outside, and rushes back down. "You seem to have gotten yourself caught."

Her bright blue eyes sparkle as she looks down at me and the predicament TJ has placed me in.

"Seems so." She reaches for the lock on the front of the cage. "What are you doing?"

"Don't you want out of this thing?"

"Did TJ tell you to let me out?" Now, I know I sound like a crazy person.

"He told me to bring you something to eat."

"But he didn't say let me out?" She shakes her head. "I'm not getting out until he says I can."

"Even if I can help you escape?"

"He'd still find me," I mutter. "Running now will only make things worse later."

"Do you want to escape him?" She flips her long black hair over her shoulder as she waits for me to respond.

She'll be waiting a long-ass time because I don't really have an answer for her. As a matter of fact, I have done my best not to think about the what-ifs for years, and TJ is one of those things I've shoved in that box. Wanting him and needing him temporarily is very different from thinking I'll have something with him long-term.

"Does he do this often?" I ask instead of answering her question.

Xena bites her plump lip. Amusement shines in her eyes, letting me know that she's well aware that I avoided the question.

"I've been here for years, and I can't think of a single time he's caged a woman down here." She looks around the empty room as a shudder runs through her. "But, a lot of things happen down here that us women don't hear about."

"Where am I?"

"In the basement." Pinching my lips together, I glare at her. "In the basement at the clubhouse."

The tremble in my hands from earlier renews, but I shove them under my thighs, so she doesn't see my fear.

"What's wrong?" She crouches down in front of the cage so she can look me in the eyes. I must not have been quick enough.

"The last time I was here—"

She holds her hand up, interrupting me. "That guy wasn't a member, and he'll never bother anyone again. The guys here would never hurt someone like that."

"What?" I ask when she scrunches her nose up.

"Things were bad up until a couple of months ago, but Lynch is the Prez now, and the women are safer." She clears her throat as if she's said too much and stands. "I didn't know what you would like, and I'm not much of a cook, so I hope you like PB&J."

"I can't eat," I tell her.

"You have to be hungry." She lifts the tray from the chair and sits down before repositioning it in her lap. "I also brought a couple of bottles of water. I think you've only been down here like a day or so, but I imagine you're thirsty."

"I can't drink either." My throat seizes in rebellion.

"Sure you can. TJ *told* me to get this for you."

She pushes the end of the bottled water through the grid of metal, and my mouth runs dry seeing the perspiration drip from the cold plastic.

"I can't." Using the tip of a single finger, I push the bottom of the bottle so she can't tempt me any further.

"Are you like going on a hunger strike?"

"No." I lean in closer like the room is bugged and I'm afraid someone is listening in. "There isn't a bathroom down here. Not even a bucket."

Her nose scrunches as she jerks her head back a few inches, the thought of using a bucket disgusting to her. If she thinks that's bad, she would die with some of the stories I could tell. "A bucket? He's not going to make you use a bucket."

"If I drink that water, I'll need one quicker than I already do."

She pushes the bottle back through the hole. "I don't think you'll be down here that long. Drink some water at least."

I fidget with anticipation. "Did he say he was going to let me go?"

I take the bottle of water when she offers it again, but her quick snort makes me take pause before I can twist the lid off.

"I don't think he has any plans to let you go, sweetheart."

"H-he's going to kill me?" Why is that the first place my head goes even after he hurt himself and begged me to stop putting myself in harm's way?

"TJ isn't one to see out women to kill. If you're down here and not up there," she points to a rope hanging from a rafter I hadn't noticed before, "there's a good chance he's planning on keeping you, not hurting you."

My throat works on a rough swallow at the sight of the menacing rope and the shadow it casts on the far wall.

"Do you fuck girls?"

"What?" My eyes snap from the noose to Xena.

"Do you fuck girls?"

"I-that's-wh—"

"When I asked the question, I figured it was a simple answer, but from the way you're acting, I'm beginning to think it's a little more complicated than a yes or no." Xena stands, placing the tray back in the chair and inches closer to the cage. "I can ask different questions."

My palms slicken with sweat, and I don't know if it's in fear of the memories or arousal from exactly the same.

"Has a girl ever gone down on you?"

"Why are you asking me this stuff?" The words come out as if I have gravel stuck in my throat.

She shrugs. "Just curious. Don't want to answer?"

"Yes."

"Yes, you don't want to an—"

"Yes, a girl has gone down on me."

"Did you return the favor?"

"No." I don't elaborate. I don't know why I'm trying to hide my past, but I don't feel like going into in-depth explanations about how I was tied and gagged when it happened.

"So you've never eaten pussy?"

"I didn't say that." Her lips thin as if she thinks I'm playing a game and she's growing agitated. "I have gone down on a girl before."

"Did you enjoy it?"

So much so, just the thought right now is making me wet. "I didn't hate it."

"I can work with that." Her tongue brushes over her bottom lip. "TJ said I can't touch your pussy without permission."

"I don't think that's a good idea right now."

She laughs hard before a smile stays on her pretty lips. "Honey, he was talking about *his* permission, not yours."

Maybe she expected me to be offended, but honestly, I like the idea of TJ controlling everything that happens to my body. His commands are what thrill me. I love it when he takes my choices away.

"I better get back upstairs. Are you sure you don't want this food?"

I shake my head. "Don't think it's a great idea."

"See you soon, Envy."

"Kaci," I correct before she goes far.

"That's your real name." She gives me another slow smile. "We all have club names. Well except for Molly and Zoe."

"Envy?"

"Yeah," she agrees. "There are going to be a lot of girls jealous of you."

"Of me? I'm the last thing they should be jealous of."

"Says the only girl that has TJ's undivided attention." With that, she grabs the tray, turns off the light, and makes her way to the stairs.

Envy.

I can't say that I hate the name.

Chapter 30

TJ

The whiskey I've been tossing back all night has done nothing to ease the guilt I have for not running down to Kaci and telling her what her father has done.

What good will it do?

That was Virus's parting question before I left him in the office an hour ago. I'll be honest. I don't know if it will do any good at all. The opposite, I'm certain will happen. I'm sure knowing that her father is solely responsible for the ten months she was abused, hurt, and brutally raped will be what finally sends her over the edge. She's already teetering there as it is, but I also know I don't want to lie to her, by omission or otherwise.

"You look like you could use another one."

I'd ignore Lynch when he sits down beside me, but my glass is empty, so he has a point.

I push the tumbler forward and let Mac fill it before drawing it back in.

"Want to talk about it?"

I grunt a no in his direction, but without even looking I can sense the smile on his face.

"I can tell you, from experience that it's easier if you just let it happen. Fighting it won't stop it. It only slows down the inevitable."

"What the fuck are you talking about?" I look over at my older brother who doesn't even bother to hide his wide smile. If I hadn't been present all the times he's made brutal examples of people since he met Zoe, I'd swear just by looking at him that he's turned into a pussy.

"Falling in love." He grins wider as he lifts his beer bottle to his mouth.

"I'm only fucking twenty. I'm not trying to fall in love."

"Twenty-one next week," the asshole reminds me, "and love doesn't give a shit how old you are."

"She's broken," I grumble, not adding that she'll be completely obliterated once she knows about her dad.

"You've said that before, but we all have shit we have to deal with."

A rough sigh escapes my lips. As much as I don't want to have this conversation with anyone, much less him, I need guidance.

"She was babysitting her brother when he choked on a toy and died," I confess, knowing this has affected her more than her abduction.

I honestly believe she sees her abduction as some kind of fucked up karma for not paying more attention to the kid that day.

"And you pointed the toy gun at the Feds, and they shot Donna."

Fuck. Hearing that out loud still stings all these years later.

"I mean," Lynch offers when I don't respond, "I think they came to the clubhouse with intentions of killing someone that day. It just happened to be your mom."

"She was abducted when she was eighteen. Right after she graduated, hadn't even had the chance to go to college or find out who she really is. She was held for ten months by sex traffickers."

"Fuck," he grunts, his eyes still on his beer bottle.

"She was a virgin," I continue.

"Fuck," he hisses again, and even though he's not looking at me, I don't need to see his eyes to tell his mood. His ears are turning red, and his knuckles are white from his grip on the beer bottle.

"I just found out that her dad sold her to those fuckers."

His eyes snap to mine. "Are you for real?"

I merely nod. "He sold her to enhance his run for Congress. He lost, and I think he regrets that she was ever found."

"So he had her abducted and then sent people to find her?"

"Cerberus found her when they were looking for another abducted girl." The memory of Virus telling me that Colby Davis killed herself after being rescued rattles around in my head, making me worry even more about telling Kaci the truth.

"Those fuckers," Lynch mutters.

We don't hate the New Mexico MC, but only because they haven't brought trouble to our doorsteps. They focus mainly on recovery, security, and reconnaissance. If we were dealing in skin, I imagine we would've tangled with them a time or two by now.

"No wonder she's fucked up. That's gotta suck knowing her dad was responsible for all of that shit."

My head is shaking before he even finishes talking. "I don't think she knows. She hasn't mentioned it. She went to their house a while back. She doesn't seem the type of girl that would have loyalty to parents that pulled this kind of shit."

"And I thought our dad was fucked up," Lynch mutters.

"Right?"

"What are you going to do?" I shrug. "Are you going to tell her?"

"If you found out this shit about Zoe—"

"Zoe blew her dad's head off when she found out she was a fucking pawn in that bastard's game," he interrupts. "Does she seem like the type who would want to do something like that? We could make those arrangements."

Lynch has the same damn mindset that Virus has. If Royce Stewart is going to meet the reaper for the things that he has done, it will be at

Kaci's hand. Lynch has all but laid down an order. If I had any thoughts of taking care of this for her, I might as well throw those out.

"I know what you're thinking, but if you don't tell her what he's responsible for and then kill him, she's going to feel even more misplaced guilt. Don't tell her if you don't want, but his death is her decision, and she can't make that call if she doesn't know."

"And if I tell her and she wants me to do it?"

"If she wants him dead and doesn't have the stomach to do it herself that's fine." A grin spreads across my face because I can convince her— "If you manipulate her and persuade her into believing that's what she wants when it really isn't, she'll hate you in the long run."

How in the hell does he fucking know what I'm thinking?

"I can't even imagine Zoe walking away from me. I don't think I'd be able to survive it if she did. I don't wish any of this on you man, but you have to make a call and fucking hope that it's the right one."

"What would you do?" I hold my hand up when he opens his mouth to argue about what Zoe went through. "If you were in this exact same situation, if *you* were me, what would you do?"

He shakes his head. "I don't have enough information to answer that truthfully. If I loved her, I'd tell her about what her dad did, but I'd also let her know how I felt about her because she's been through a lot and I imagine she'd want someone to lean on after that. If I didn't love her, I'd keep playing with her until I'd had enough, and I'd cut her loose. It would be too much drama for me to fuck with if I didn't care about her."

My gut clenches painfully at the idea of walking away from Kaci, but at the same time, I can't confess my love for her. I don't even know if that's what I'm feeling. I'm sure as fuck not going to ask Lynch what being in love feels like.

I drain my glass of whiskey and stand from the bar, still undecided what the final outcome of all of this shit is going to be.

"What are you going to do?" Lynch asks, swiveling his bar stool around so he can face me.

"I'm going to go shower and then get my girl out of the fucking basement."

"And after that?"

"I don't have a fucking clue, man."

Good-naturedly, he slaps me on the back. "Let all of this sink in for a little bit, and the decision will be the easiest one you've ever made."

I walk away from my brother thinking that he already knows what my answer will be, but just like with the situation with Kaci and her dad; it's one he's going to make me decide on my own.

Chapter 31

Kaci

I snuggle into the warmth engulfing my body for a long moment before I realize safety and comfort aren't something I'm ever afforded.

"Shh." The soft command only serves to make me tenser. I'm rigid by the time I get my bearings and realize I'm no longer in my cage. "I've got you."

"TJ?"

"I've got you, gorgeous. Just relax."

Even though it's the last thing I know I should do, I burrow deeper into his arms, burying my nose in the fabric of his shirt and breathing him into my lungs. He could be carrying me to my death, but I can't be bothered to worry about it right now from the comfort of his arms.

My eyes remain closed even as he pauses to open a door. Raucous laughter and the hard-hitting bass of music fill my ears and then begins to fade as he continues to walk. I don't bother to look up, and I'm even less concerned that I'm naked and people can possibly see me. The noise almost completely disappears when he opens another door and closes it with us on the other side.

"Where are we?" I ask when he stops moving.

"My room," he answers, making no move to put me down.

Given a couple of seconds longer, I could've guessed where we are. His scent, stronger than just his clothing, surrounds me like a blanket.

"Black sheets?" I mutter after I finally open my eyes and look around. "I would've guessed red."

He snorts in response as he continues to hold me and makes his way to a partially opened door on the other side of the room.

His bedroom is simple and shockingly vanilla, nothing like the dungeon I'd imagined due to his predilections. His bed, king sized of course, has a simple headboard and footboard, not the canopied, four-poster bed that would fit him better. The walls are bare, not covered in medieval weapons and chains.

"Your bed looks comfortable," I say on a sigh as we pass it.

"I know you're tired, baby. Let's get you cleaned up first."

My eyes squeeze closed when he flips on the bathroom light, and I bury my head into his chest again.

"Sorry," I say, pulling my head away when I remember the knife wounds on his chest. "Are you in pain?"

His bright blue eyes meet mine, and although they shimmer as he looks down at me, I can see the exhaustion as well. His eyes are rimmed in red as if he hasn't slept in days.

"My cock is *painfully* hard." He gives me a quick, wry grin before he tilts me so I can stand on my own two feet. "But, it seems to be that way all the time around you. Add in the fact that I had your naked body pressed against me, and it's kind of a given."

My eyes follow his hand as he adjusts himself in his jeans without an ounce of shyness before pointing over my shoulder.

"Use the bathroom. I'm going to run you a bath."

"What?" I look over my shoulder but make no move toward the toilet. "Can I have a little privacy?"

He rolls his eyes as if I'm acting like a bratty child but turns away from me to reach for the tub faucet. Knowing he isn't going to leave, I race to the toilet and make quick work of my business. It's not like it's the first time I've had to do this. I wasn't awarded a single second of privacy when Deo took me all those years ago.

"Lavender or vanilla?" he asks as I'm washing my hands in the sink. Peering up, I find him standing behind me holding up two bottles of bubble bath. His eyes are focused on my ass rather than meeting mine in the mirror.

"You don't seem like the bubble bath type," I tease, still standing bent over at the sink until his eyes leave my ass.

"Chicks seem to like it," he mutters absently with his eyes focused on the reflection of my bare tits. His lips part, breaths coming out harsher, and I know he's seeing the redness left behind from him smacking them earlier.

"Like Xena?" His eyes snap up to mine, confusion drawing his brow in.

"Jealous?" He turns, upending the lavender gel over the tub. More than double the amount needed pours into the rising water, and for some reason, he's hyper-focused on the foam as it begins to cover the top layer.

"She called me Envy," I tell him rather than addressing my feelings at the thought of him doing this exact same thing for others.

After placing both bottles back on the edge of the tub, he turns to face me. "Envy?"

His gaze, almost like a physical touch, runs down my body, causing an unsuspected warmth to run over my skin.

"She said a lot of girls around here are going to be jealous of *me*," I explain.

"Get in the tub," he commands, swallowing as if my body is too much for him to look at.

"Join me," I offer.

"I don't take bubble baths."

"Join me," I repeat, holding my hand out as I lift one leg over the edge of the tub.

He holds onto me until I'm lowering myself into the hot water. The bubbles pop against my skin as I settle, so I spread my legs in hopes of feeling the same fizz on my pussy. I expect him to turn and leave, but as I close my eyes, I hear him shedding his clothes, and then feel the water move as he steps inside with me.

"Lean back," he urges as he positions himself behind me, sandwiching my body between his long, muscular legs.

"I thought you didn't take bubble baths."

"You aren't them." His lips trace my pulse as it pounds in my neck.

"Them who?" I ask, regressing back to high school apparently. It's as if I need him to spell everything out for me. I don't want to make a mistake in assuming I know his feelings and intentions.

"The other women who have been in here," he answers. "The women who have been in my bed."

I don't know how to respond to that or what his expectations are. I have no right to wish he'd been untouched before now. He'd explained his childhood and the way he was raised in this clubhouse, but that doesn't stop me from being curious. He told me himself he's fucked hundreds of women, and I didn't have a problem with it when the words fell from his mouth, but after what happened in the basement earlier, I can't help but feel emotions I have no right to feel.

"Have you been with anyone since we met?"

"Yes," he admits without pause as his fingers begin to circle my nipple.

I cringe when tears burn the back of my eyes. Getting upset at his confession is a big red warning sign. I shouldn't be so involved that I give a shit about what he does in his spare time. His grip tightens when I move to stand up. I can get fucked by him. I can admit my desire for his brutal punishments, but the sweet routine including sliding against his wet skin in the tub is too fucking much. Being with him like this makes it impossible to separate myself from it all.

"I haven't touched anyone since before I pushed you to your knees at your place and rammed my cock down your throat. Not one fucking person since I tasted your decadent cunt. So, settle the fuck down."

"I d-don't care what you do," I stammer, but the tremble in my voice betrays my real emotions.

"Yes, you do." He punctuates his words with the twist of my nipple, and my lip bleeds from biting it to prevent the moan from escaping. "Would you like to watch what I can do with another woman? What she's willing to take from my blade to please me?"

My nostrils flare as I bare my teeth. "Only if you're cutting out her heart."

His silent chuckle shakes me, but his grip remains firm.

"I snapped the guy's neck before I pulled you off his bed at that last party. All he got before I showed up was a taste of your sweet cunt, but I couldn't help myself. Knowing he put his mouth where only mine belongs—" His muscles tense at my back as he draws in a long, harsh breath. "Every time I pull you from one of those fucking frat houses, my body count goes up."

I should feel bad that the guy at the frat party died. He was a pawn, a means to an end, but I put him in that situation. I know I'm evil when all I do is smile at TJ's dark confession.

"I won't tolerate another man touching you, tasting you, sinking inside of your wet pussy." For emphasis, he cups me between my legs, allowing his long middle finger to trace my slick lips.

"Wh-what about women?" I swivel my hips, goosebumps washing over my exposed skin when a long groan rattles in his chest. "Xena looked quite keen when she brought me something to eat earlier."

His finger plummets inside of me. "Did she touch you?"

"No," I pant. "She said she had to have your permission."

"Although I won't share you, it makes me so fucking hard imagining one of the girls sucking on that perfect clit of yours." His hips punch upward, letting me feel his hard cock at my back. "Giving them permission to bring you to the edge but not let you come."

"I don't need your permission to let anyone fuck me." I ride his hand, his finger buried deep, and wait for his retribution.

"Is that so?" I nod until his fingers leave my pussy and tangle in my hair.

A second later, I'm lifted and slammed down on his thick cock. A minute after that, I'm begging him for more and promising him the world as soapy water splashes all over the bathroom floor.

Chapter 32

TJ

"This is new," Kaci murmurs against my skin but doesn't bother to lift her head from my chest or open her eyes.

"What's that?" I ask as my fingers flex against her lower back.

"You're normally gone when I wake up."

I can't tell her I never fall asleep with a woman because it's happened more than once at her place and telling her I never stay overnight would be a lie too because she just woke up in my arms. I know it's my bed and everything, but I wouldn't have pulled myself from her naked skin if the fucking apocalypse came banging on the door.

As if I've conjured the Devil, a pounding fist hits my door three times.

"Church!" Briar yells from the other side.

Kaci startles from the unexpected banging, so I do what any man unwilling to admit his feelings would do, I hold her tighter and kiss the top of her head.

"So much for the blow job you were going to give me this morning."

I feel, rather than see, her smile against my skin. "You sound so sure."

Without warning, I flip her on her back, covering her naked body with my own. She moans when my teeth sink into her nipple. "I'd fuck your mouth right now to prove my point, but I've got to get to church."

I don't get up until my tongue and the press of my cock against her naked cunt makes her beg for me to slam inside of her. Her whimpers of distress are the sweetest fucking thing I've heard when I climb off her.

"You don't seem like the religious type," she muses, watching me as I tug on a pair of jeans. "Unless it's a devil worshipping thing."

Her eyes focus on my erect cock until it disappears behind the denim of my jeans.

"We aren't religious," I assure her, leaning down to press my lips to hers. "It's a biker thing."

Sitting on the edge of the bed, I tug on my boots as she draws shapes on my back with her fingernails.

"I need to come," she complains as I cross the room to the door.

My cock jolts in my jeans at the undiluted urgency in her voice, but I do my best to ignore it as I pull on a t-shirt and my cut.

"Be good while I'm gone." I know she can hear the warning in my tone, but her hand is moving under the sheet before I even leave the room.

"Took you fucking long enough," Lynch spits when I walk into the chapel.

"What's the big deal? I'm always the last one to arrive."

Lynch narrows his eyes at me but doesn't utter a word back. I don't know why I'm getting a reprieve without threats or verbal warnings, but I have a feeling he's trying to be sympathetic to my current situation with Kaci. I can't decide right now how I feel about it.

"We have a trip to Richmond in two days," Lynch begins. "Same amount as last time. I'm staying back this time. Briar, you'll team up with Mac."

The VP grumbles his distaste. That Irish fucker has struggled with keeping his eyes off my little sister, and Briar is fit to be fucking tied over the attention she draws from some of the men in the club.

"And I expect him to live through the drop-off," Lynch warns.

"I promise nothing," Briar mumbles.

Briar won't hurt the guy unless he does something to earn it, but Mac isn't an idiot. He'll probably shit in his leathers when he's informed he's going to be on the road, one-on-one, with Briar for several days. Mac hasn't patched in yet, so he will be kissing ass to the best of his ability until he has a little more say in the club.

"TJ you're back to New York, but you'll have Sonic with you this time."

"What the hell?" I look over at Ronan. We rode together last time.

"He's got shit here he has to take care of," Lynch says in a tone that challenges me to disagree. "Nothing changes for you other assholes."

A round of agreements echo off the walls.

Silence fills the room until I look back at my brother. "What are your plans for that girl while we're gone?"

"What do you mean?" I ask playing dumb.

"It's not the girls' job to tend to your caged pets."

"I bet Xena would love to tend to that pet," Hornet drawls.

"She's in my room," I inform the group. No one seems surprised. I'm certain they saw me carry her naked ass through the kitchen last night.

"Is she going home before you leave?"

"She isn't leaving," I tell my brother.

Lynch's eyebrow raises, and I fully understand his shock. There hasn't been a woman that's walked this earth that I couldn't turn my back on and walk away from, but Kaci isn't like any woman I've ever met.

"You plan to keep her a prisoner?"

"It's not anything different from what you did with Zoe."

"Zoe was in trouble," he counters.

"Same goes," I argue.

Lynch nods, understanding without having to go into details about why I can't let her return home right now. It's not that someone else would hurt her. She's a danger to herself.

"And if she tries to leave while you're on the road?" I don't answer him immediately. "I don't want to be put in the situation of using force to make her stay."

"I'll make sure she'll know the consequences if she steps foot off the compound."

Ronan chuckles from the other side of the table. "You sure she won't *prefer* your consequences?"

A grin tugs at the corner of my mouth. Ronan is well aware of how women respond to me. He's got a couple of girls in the club that beg him for his certain style of attention as well.

"I'll track her down if she leaves," I assure Lynch, and just the thrill of hunting her makes my pulse speed up.

"We need to talk about the other matter concerning Kaci," Virus adds, sitting up straight in his chair.

Like a real man, he looks me directly in the eye rather than deferring to Lynch to bring up this topic of conversation.

"Envy," I correct. "She hates people using her real name."

Several grunts of approval filter out from the men surrounding the table.

Not sparing any detail, Virus and I volley back and forth through my girl's past. All the way up to including the fact that her father paid a trafficking organization to abduct her from the beach during her post-graduation vacation.

"And what do you want to do?" Lynch asks me once all the shit is out on the table.

"I want to torture him, peel his skin from his body inch by inch until he begs me to end it all," I tell the group of men without blinking an eye. Most in the room nod their head in agreement, several speaking up to offer a hand if I need it.

"Prez—" Virus says on a sigh.

Lynch holds his hand up to silence him.

"But, I know this is her choice. She doesn't know, and I haven't told her yet. I don't plan on having that conversation with her right before we hit the road. I need all of you fuckers to keep your mouths closed, and trust that I will handle this situation with the level of respect that Envy deserves."

Everyone agrees, and when I look up at my brother, I see a glimmer of respect in his green eyes. Pride is something neither of us got from our father, and although the feeling is hitting me in the chest with that look on Lynch's face, I can't help but smile at him.

"Are you bringing her out of your room tonight?" Ronan asks with a sly grin.

"I haven't met her yet either," Virus adds.

"Kai has been chattering about her since he did shots with Xena last night," Professor interjects.

"What are you? A bunch of fucking women?" Lynch bellows from the head of the table. "He'll introduce her when he sees fit."

"And all you motherfuckers will keep your filthy fucking hands off her." I take my time to glare directly at each fucking man around the table. "Even if she tries something with you, you better back away."

Knowing laughter filters through the room.

"And if she asks you for any drugs, the answer is no. She's self-destructive." I don't have to say anything else before the guys at the table stop laughing. I have already explained why she was here, and how Briar and I met her. They know how serious I am.

I'm now the one filled with pride for the men in my club when they all nod their agreements. We're all brutal motherfuckers, but we band together and protect when we need to.

"But," I begin with a wicked smile, "I will bring her out of the room tonight for a little bit of fun. Ronan and Hornet, I'll need your help making her night one to remember."

Chapter 33

Kaci

When TJ doesn't come back after an hour or so, I just let my eyes flutter closed and sink deeper into his bed. They open again when the bedroom door is flung open.

"Who the fuck are you?" I hiss when I realize TJ isn't the one entering the room.

"Sassy," says a slender man as he walks in and sets a tray of food down on the dresser before turning back around to look at me. "I like it."

"Who are you?" I repeat.

"I'm Kai." His hand goes to his hip when I just continue to stare at him. "I'm Professor's pet."

"Pet?" What a ridiculous concept.

"Yes. Like you're TJ's pet. I belong to Professor."

"Bisexual bikers?" I huff a quick laugh. Just when I thought I'd seen it all. Even though I'm naked under the blankets, for some reason, Kai doesn't strike fear in me.

"Professor isn't bisexual. He's flat out as gay as they come, sweetheart." His tongue sweeps over his plump bottom lip. "I'm bisexual though."

He winks in a mischievous way, and unconsciously I'm tugging the blankets a little bit higher under my chin.

"Don't worry, doll. No one in this club will touch you without permission."

"TJ's permission," I qualify.

Another wink. "Exactly."

"And no one touches you without Professor's?"

His bright white teeth dig into his bottom lip. "I tend to get into trouble with that, but I think my man expects it."

I don't move a muscle to climb off the bed, figuring if I just sit still this guy will leave.

"I wouldn't advise you doing the same though," he says as he begins to sit on the edge of the bed like he owns the place. "Professor uses orgasm denial to punish me, and well, TJ has that damn knife, so his punishments may be a little more permanent than blue balls."

"What are you doing?" I try to slide further away, but he's sitting on top of the blankets, preventing me from moving.

"I made breakfast for you." He points to the tray. "Well *I* didn't make breakfast for you, but Vixen has PMS, and she likes to cook when that happens. The entire club benefits when it's her time of the month."

"And to think, I just sleep all day," I mumble when I look past him at the tray stacked high with pancakes, eggs, and sausage links. "Did TJ already eat?"

"TJ left," Kai says. "He probably won't be back until after the sun goes down."

My grip strengthens on the blanket. "He left me?"

"He left, doll. He didn't leave *you*. He'll be back." Kai springs off the bed. "Eat and get dressed. There's a party tonight, and you need to be ready."

I do what any girl would do in this weird-ass situation. I stare at him like he's grown two heads.

"Now!" he insists, pointing his finger at the closed bathroom door. "Get a shower. You have half an hour."

"I'm naked. I'm not getting out of this bed until you leave."

He snorts, humor sparkling in his eyes, but turns around and leaves. "Thirty minutes," he hollers from the other side of the closed door.

It's early afternoon. If there's a party going on tonight, it won't jump off until close to midnight. Kai may be a diva, but it won't take me hours and hours to get ready. Plus, I don't even know if TJ is going to want me here. Knowing all of this doesn't stop me from scarfing down the food Kai brought and rushing through a shower. I'm normally not one to get involved with anyone expecting friendship or anything of that sort, but there's something about being here in TJ's space and being invited to god knows what that has my blood thrumming with excitement.

I'm towel drying my hair with the bathroom door open to vent some of the steam from my shower when the bedroom door opens again.

"Now I see what all the fuss is about," Kai says, his eyes never straying from my tits. He seems enthralled, even with just the side-boob and perky nipple he's able to see.

I don't cower or cover myself and insist he leave. Doing that would show fear or shame, and I'm too fucking stubborn for that.

"Are you just going to stand there making my dick hard?"

"The inability to control your dick isn't my problem."

His lips twitch when I hang the towel on the rack and face him full on.

"You're bare." His eyes have left my tits and are now focused on the apex of my thighs. "Xena's going to be saddened by that."

"I don't have any clothes."

"I don't think anyone is going to mind."

It's my turn to snort at his ridiculousness.

"You don't think TJ would get upset if I prance around buck-ass naked?"

Kai shrugs. "He's never had a problem with any of the other girls showing and sharing his goodies."

My stomach roils.

"But I don't think anyone has been given free rein over his room either."

That last part barely softens the jealous rage I feel from his first statement.

"He's also warned all the guys away from you, and that's new as well." I don't know if he's saying this to make me feel better because I wasn't able to school the disappointment off my face fast enough or if it's actually true. "Let's not take any chances. Better get some clothes on."

"I don't have any clothes," I tell him slower this time just in case he doesn't compute information easily.

"Wear something of TJ's." Kai opens the door to the small closet and sweeps his arm inside, like I have permission to use anything I please. He must notice my face again. "The girls don't wear his clothes. Legs tried once, and I thought she was going to get the boot."

"So I don't think I should either."

"Yet, that sparkle in your eye, the one that's telling me you want to push his buttons, means that you will."

Since he's one hundred percent right, I slide past him and grab a well-worn t-shirt and a pair of sweats, not bothering to hide from Kai as I tug them on.

"How is it you look even sexier in those rags than you did completely naked?" He grabs my hand and tugs me toward the door. "Let's go, Envy. We have to get dolled up for our men."

I'm smiling at the nickname Xena gave me but stop dead in my tracks halfway down the hall when I see TJ round the corner with a small stack of clothes in his hands. His eyes widen as a slow, mischievous grin spreads across his handsome face.

"Looks like you don't need these." He prowls toward me, and with one single look in Kai's direction, my new intrusive friend makes himself scarce. "This just became my favorite shirt."

"I-I can ch-change."

His head is shaking back and forth before I finish my sentence.

"Don't you dare." His finger traces down the side of my neck until it reaches the furled bud of my nipple that's pressing against the thin fabric. "I don't know whether to spank you or fuck you."

"B-both?" I stammer.

His warm chuckle arrows straight to my clit.

"You make me fucking crazy," he pants against my ear. The breathy moan of his words is enough to force my legs to rub together. "How the fuck am I supposed to ride to town with a steel rod in my jeans?"

"You're leaving?" Panic is evident in my voice.

"I'll be back," he promises, never taking his lips away from the delicate skin of my neck. "Don't let anyone touch you while I'm gone."

"Please don't go," I beg, grabbing his hand from my hip and slowly pushing it past the rolled-up waist of the borrowed sweats. If he's fucking me, he won't leave. I consider it a win-win situation.

"You are an extraordinary temptation, Envy." I shiver, partly from the use of the nickname, but more so from the rough feel of his finger skating over my sensitive clit.

"Let's roll," someone bellows from another room right before TJ can slip his finger inside of me.

I groan my disappointment when he pulls his hand free, and it only serves to make him chuckle.

"I'm going to spank your ass for this when I get back," he warns before pressing a swift kiss to my lips.

"Can't wait," I tell him honestly as he backs away.

"Take care of my girl while I'm gone," TJ says to Kai who has reappeared in the hallway.

"I could suck that dick of yours and get you off in less than sixty seconds," Kai offers as TJ walks past him. "It would be a whole lot easier to ride that way."

I expect TJ to punch him in the face, but all he does is chuckle and shake his head as he walks away.

"Why can't he be just a little bit bi-curious?" Kai asks on a sigh as we walk to the end of the hall and watch several guys, including TJ, walk out the front door.

I growl my displeasure at his spoken fantasy, but deep down I'm curious what TJ would look like with Kai's lips wrapped around his cock.

"This is the spa," Kai says with a flourish as he leads me to another door and swings it open with a crash against the wall. This man clearly doesn't know how to open a door properly.

Grinning when I see Xena standing next to a table similar to the ones at the nail salon I go to when I get my eyebrows waxed, I give her a little wave.

"She's already bare," Kai says, and I laugh when I see Xena's face fall with disappointment.

"That's a shame," she mutters before turning around and flipping the power off on the wax pot.

"My boys need a little cleaning up," Kai says, crossing the room and flicking open the button on his cargo shorts.

"Nope." Xena walks past him closer to me. "Last time I tried that you cried for twenty minutes and ended up with one smooth ball and one hairy one. Professor wasn't pleased with me even though it was your damn fault."

"If you had balls, you'd understand," he mutters before settling in a chair on the other side of the room.

"Come on in, Envy. Let me introduce you to the girls," Xena says clasping my hand and tugging me in the direction of five smiling women and one that would be gorgeous if it weren't for the deadly sneer distorting her plump, painted lips.

She's going to be trouble.

Chapter 34

TJ

"That's perfect," I tell Ronan as we situate the cage in the middle of the living room.

"You actually think she's going to like this?"

"She'll learn to like it."

"I can't wait to see this shit play out." Ronan slaps me on the back as he heads outside.

Several girls are already gyrating on the laps of some of the men, but Kaci isn't out here yet, so I head in the direction of my room.

"You don't even bother to look and see who's at the door?" I ask when I walk in to find her with her back to me.

When she looks over her shoulder, her pouty, perfect fucking lips are a tangible tease to my dick even several feet away, I harden in an instant. "I figured it was either you or Kai."

"Excuse me?" I hiss as she turns around.

She's no longer in my clothes, but I can't even be mad that her lithe body isn't swimming in a pair of ratty sweats and the t-shirt I had every intention of ripping from her body. She's wearing a black bra that leaves nothing to the imagination. Just the sight of her nipples behind the floral-patterned lace makes my mouth water like a man who has been in the desert his entire life. As if that isn't enough, I'm struck stupid by the matching garter belt and lace-topped thigh-high stockings.

"Like what you see?" The purr of her words is almost enough to make me forget what she'd said.

"Why wouldn't it bother you if Kai came in here while you were standing there with your bare cunt in the breeze?" Jealousy isn't an emotion I'm familiar with, and it's clear in my tone of voice. Most women would cower, or rush to make excuses.

Not Kaci.

She merely stands there, seductively biting her bottom lip, eyes blinking innocently at me.

"I wasn't going to borrow Velvet's underwear. I don't have many limits, but I just can't wrap my head around wearing someone else's panties." She shudders as if tiny spiders are crawling across her skin with just the thought.

"Tell me about Kai," I demand through gritted teeth.

"He thinks I'm your pet."

I raise an eyebrow, and the fire she's been missing in her eyes since I walked in here returns with the power of a sun flare.

"I'm no one's pet," she hisses.

Her words don't faze me much. It's hard to concentrate on anything when the pink of her pussy is an amazing stark contrast to the black lace circling her thighs.

"Is that so?" I stalk toward her, and just like I presumed, she holds her ground, stubborn jaw tensing as I draw near. "You don't want to be owned?"

Her weight shifting marginally is the only thing that hints at her arousal.

"You don't want to be pampered? Taken care of better than any other woman in this club?" I grip her chin in my hand, tilting her head back until the delicate flesh of her neck is exposed.

"I'm not a possession," she breathes out on a harsh breath. "I can take care of myself."

I nip at her neck, and she yelps at the pain, but is smart enough not to jerk out of my grasp. Her nipples are puckered, her breaths are rushing out, and she whimpers each time I lean in to put my mouth on her skin. If I back away or trail my finger down her slit, I know I'll find her dripping down her thighs. I'm not scaring her; I'm seducing her.

"Did you not learn a thing in the basement? I expected a little resistance, but I didn't think you'd revert to your old ways so quickly." My mouth is a mere inch from her ear. "Do you need to be taught another lesson already?"

She moans exactly the way that makes my cock throb when I grip her chin tighter. Her eyes flutter close, and I wait for her to get mouthy again. Like the perfect specimen she is, she surprises me once again.

"Whatever you want, TJ," she pants on a rushed exhale.

"You are a superb fucking being, Envy. Are you ready for your punishment?"

"P-punishment?" She attempts to move her head. I imagine to look me in the eye, but I hold firm, not quite ready to stop licking the pulse point in her neck that is firing like an overused piston.

"You've already forgotten?" I taunt with another nip to her jawline. "Maybe because you didn't smell your sweet cunt on your finger, like I did every time I ran my hand over my face today."

"Oh… that." Her lips twitch with mirth, but she's smart enough not to take it any further.

"Yeah, *that.*"

She squeals when I suddenly release her face and spin her around, forcing her to bend over the side of the bed. The five, rapid-fire swats I land on her bare ass echoes off the walls.

"TJ!" she gasps as if she's offended. I'd believe it if she wasn't wiggling her ass for more.

"When will you stop fascinating me? When will I be able to go five minutes without this tight cunt of yours being my primary focus?"

She trembles, but the atmosphere changes around us. The edge of lust and greedy need slowly starts to dissipate.

Wrapping my hand in her long blonde hair, I jerk her up until her back is fully flush with my chest.

"My mom got me a dog once." My brows furrow in confusion. "It had an accident on the floor, and she got rid of it the same day."

"What are you talking about?"

"People don't always keep their pets," she says with the wrong emotion in her voice.

I need her hot, bothered, and ready to take my dick, not near sobbing and wondering if I'm going to toss her out like a puppy that can't hold its bladder.

"I'm not throwing you out." I grip her breast with the harshness I know she craves. "Besides, if you pee on my floor, I'll rub your nose in it while I fuck your ass."

She sputters a laugh at my ridiculousness. "I'm housebroken."

"Mmm." I run my nose down her neck. She smells fucking amazing. "Don't make me challenge your limits."

She tries to turn in my arms. "Hard fucking limit, TJ."

I'm not into watersports either, but she doesn't have to know that. I grip her hair harder, relishing in the near-silent moan that escapes her lips. Seems we're right back on track. "What happened to *whatever you want, TJ?*"

"Please not that," she begs.

"We'll see," I taunt before releasing her.

She bends over the bed without any urging from me, and I nearly lose my edge.

"I am so fucking gone for you, Envy. Your pussy. Your perfect tits. Even that filthy mouth of yours. I'll never be done with you."

"Please," she begs when my belt hits the floor, and the sharp rasp of my zipper being lowered fills the room.

"Don't rush me." I slap her ass another half dozen times, and by the sixth swing, she's pushing back so her ass can make contact with my hand sooner.

My knife is forgotten as it falls to the floor still in the front pocket of my jeans. I'm so far past the point of craving her, teasing her with it would end up being dangerous.

"TJ," she whines.

If I wasn't so close to blowing my load already, I'd force her to her knees and make her suck the pre-cum off the tip of my cock, but I have plans for that mouth later.

"Your cunt is so fucking greedy. So pink and fucking perfect, waiting for my cock like I'm the only thing it was made for." She whimpers with need when I swipe my thumb through the creaminess coating her lower lips, but it turns into a feral growl of hunger when I sweep it upward to her ass. "Like that?"

Her body, pushing against my digit answers for her as I circle it around the pucker.

"Hold that thought," I growl.

Like it knows exactly where it belongs, my cock lines up with her pussy without assistance. My knees nearly buckle when I sink inside her. The euphoric feeling of her cunt gripping me is just as strong as it was the first time. Only this time, I don't have to be gentle. I don't have to try to convince her with soft, steady thrusts that she's invaluable to me. I don't have to take my time because I'm unsure of when I'll get another chance.

I pull back and slam into her again. *This* is how we make love. This is what we both need. She cries out, still startled with how I fill her even when she knows what to expect.

"Hold still," I hiss when my cock tunnels deep and she tries to scurry away.

"TJ."

Her plea is all I need. I piston into her at the same time my thumb pushes through the tight ring of her ass. "So hot and so fucking tight. I can't wait to go balls deep here."

Her response is a garbled moan of need and terror at my words because her face is buried in the comforter.

"Touch your pussy," I command because I'm about to go off like a boy that's just sank into his first piece of pussy. "If I come before you—"

I don't have enough time to make my threat before her cunt pulses down my shaft, rippling in waves as her orgasm overtakes her body. She trembles, shakes, and convulses so hard I have to pull my thumb from her ass just to get a better grip on her hips.

Her head flies back as her orgasm renews. My smile is wide at the realization that it had the same effect as pulling a plug out mid-orgasm.

I don't have time to revel in the feel of her cunt clamping down on me because my own release is arrowing down my spine and drawing up my balls before exploding inside of her. I'm spastic, damn near having a seizure from overload for several long minutes after it's all over.

"Jesus fuck," I pant.

"That's a little too hard," Kaci whimpers, and I realize she's trying to get away from me.

"Shit." She's pulling off my cock and rubbing her hips where I held her in a death grip. "Is it going to bruise?"

"Probably," she whispers with a devilish grin.

Chapter 35

Kaci

"Where are we going?" I ask after TJ tucks his half-hard cock back in his jeans and clasps my hand. I don't bother to pull away, but I'm not very keen on leaving this room right now either. "I need to clean up."

"You're exactly how I need you to be."

He must sense I'm going to resist because he drops my hand and wraps his arm around my waist.

"TJ."

He ignores me as we make our way down the hall. Music blares loud and heavy from the front room, and my heart speeds up to match the pounding tempo. "Your cum is dripping down my thighs."

"Knowing that is why my cock hasn't bothered to deflate," he confesses against my temple.

I stiffen, every muscle in my body growing rigid when we round the corner of the hallway and the vast living area comes into view. It isn't the men and women all over the place or the fact that my pussy is bare for all to see that causes me to tense. The cum dripping from my thoroughly used pussy is now an afterthought. The familiar cage situated as if on display in the middle of the room is what makes my blood run cold.

"Play nice, Kitten," TJ soothes in a teasing voice as I scramble to get away from him.

"I'll scratch your fucking eyes out," I threaten as he all but carries me to the front of the cage.

"And I'll only make love to you from now on."

"You wouldn't dare."

"Once a week," he continues, "on Sunday afternoon, nice and slow."

His threat is more detrimental than whatever he has planned tonight.

Yells, whistles, and catcalls fill the room when people notice us walking in. Everyone seems to be entertained by our entrance. Well, all but Legs. Kai warned me away from her, telling me she was TJ's last plaything and not very happy to have been tossed aside.

I don't have the ability to worry about a catty female right now, however. Even over the raucous noise everyone is making, I can still hear the squeak of the hinges on the cage when TJ throws open the door.

I growl at his threat, but let him maneuver me inside, grateful for the pillow now in the bottom of the cage. Once inside, I take a moment to look around. Men, most wearing leather vests, crowd closer, praising TJ for possessing such a lovely pet.

Suddenly, I'm glad I'm in the cage rather than out in the open and easily accessible to all of these men. TJ has sworn that the men here would never hurt me or take me against my will. Xena professed the same thing, but their words give me no assurances right now.

"Go back to your whores," TJ says with humor in his voice.

Thankfully, the men listen, sitting in various locations around the room. Several women I met earlier and some I haven't been introduced to yet take up residence on their laps or at their feet. It doesn't take long before slurping and moaning filters through the room. Some of the guys are getting sucked off and are still holding conversations with the men beside them. It's like a free-for-all orgy around here, and by the looks of it, this happens all the time.

The one woman who makes my skin crawl pops up from the sofa and prowls toward TJ. He hasn't taken a step away from the cage, but there's no telling what he's going to force me to watch him do. My throat nearly seals shut, a lump forming so thick that I can't seem to swallow it away.

"I hope she likes the taste of my pussy," I mutter as I turn my head and refuse to look at them.

I know what Legs is feeling. I'm desperate for the attention he shows me, and I can't imagine the lengths I'd go to if I were in danger of being discarded.

"I'd love to taste your pussy."

Unable to watch what is about to unfold with Legs and TJ, I turn my head toward Xena as she crouches down to look at me. I smile at her, loving her inability to keep her thoughts to herself. She's flirted with me more than once but has never made a move to take what she desires.

Xena pushes a shot of golden liquor through the grid to me, and I smile wide before lifting it to my mouth.

"Go ahead," I taunt her. "But I have to warn you, it's filled with TJ's cum right now."

I don't bother to look up and get permission, because even though I'm in a fucking cage in the center of the Ravens Ruin clubhouse, I'm not his pet.

The burn of the alcohol is a lackluster replacement for the feel of his skin, but my desires don't seem to be top priority now.

"TJ wears condoms," Xena counters. "Always."

"Tell that to my pussy." I push the shot glass back through the cage and take the second one she offers me.

Xena's smile is wide and knowing as she tilts her head, indicating for me to look back at TJ.

"Touch me again without my permission, and you'll never see the inside of this clubhouse again." TJ releases the grip he has on Legs's wrist. As she walks away, he turns his attention to some guy beside him. She's an afterthought before she even makes it across the room. My eyes track Legs, but the sight of Kai with his mouth buried in some woman's crotch as some huge guy pounds into him from behind captures my attention.

Next, it's a breathy moan from the other side of the room that demands my eyes. Two women on their knees are taking turns sucking on a man's cock as he holds a conversation with Lynch, TJ's brother. Zoe, who I met earlier, sits on Lynch's other side and smiles down at the women as they pleasure the man.

"Does it turn you on?" Xena's voice is like the devious devil on my shoulder.

My tongue traces my lower lip as I nod, but my eyes never leave the action going on around the room. Everywhere I look, people are fucking and sucking and taking pleasure from each other. Some are being handled roughly, and before I met TJ I'd be concerned for their safety, but I'd bet my father's life savings that there isn't a dry pussy in this place. Each and every one of them is giving the others exactly what they want.

"Is this like some sort of orgy cult?" I whisper.

The scene playing out before me is something I've seen before, only these girls don't seem high to the point of not being able to protest, and the men are pleasuring them as much as they are taking their pleasure from them. Consensualness is the difference, and fuck if it doesn't change the atmosphere completely.

"We just like to have fun," Xena answers as she pushes another shot into the cage for me.

"I want to have some fun," I tell her before tossing the shot back.

As Xena stands and walks around the cage, my eyes once again drift to the action on the sofa. Kai is now buried in the woman he was eating earlier, and the man who I presume is Professor is still inside of him. It takes all the strength I can muster to keep my fingers out of my bare pussy as Kai shifts his hips back and forth, fucking into the woman on his forward thrust and taking Professor deeper when he pulls out of her.

My sense of propriety over TJ is the only thing that pulls my attention from the lustful things going on around me. Xena leans in close, her hand resting on his forearm as she whispers in TJ's ear. His lips turn down in a frown at first, but then lift in a menacing grin as she continues to talk, and they're sparkling with mischievous intent by the time she pulls away, and he looks down at me.

Without a word he walks around to the front of the cage and opens the door, offering me his hand to climb out. I falter at first, unsure if I want what he has in store, but another moan from across the room fills the air. It's the needy clench of my pussy that draws me out.

"Xena tells me you want to have a little fun," TJ whispers in my ear as he holds me to his chest. The erection fighting to escape from his jeans can't be ignored. "Is it okay to introduce you to a few people?"

I nod even though I don't think his introductions are going to include handshakes, full names, and casual small talk.

"Jump up," he urges as his hands go to my waist. I'm lifted from the floor, and my ass is settled on the top of the cage. He wedges himself between my legs, licking at my mouth before pulling his head back and looking me directly in the eyes. "You can stop this at any time. You know that, right?"

"What's going to happen?"

"Introductions." He gives me a quick wink before stepping to the side and turning to face the rest of the room. "Anyone want to introduce themselves to my girl?"

I watch in horror as half of the room starts to stand and make their way closer.

"Anyone with a pussy that wants to introduce themselves to my girl," he clarifies.

The men grumble and sit back down, but the women continue to advance, forming a line in front of the cage.

"So fucking perfect," TJ says as he grips one of my legs, holding me open. He bites his bottom lip as he sweeps his fingers over my soaked pussy. Gently, he pushes against my chest until I'm laid out on my back on top of the cage, ass so close to the edge, I fear I'd slide off if he wasn't holding on to me. "You may come."

I'm trembling, needing him in the worst way, but he steps to the side, his warm hands still on my leg as Xena closes the distance.

"I'm Xena," she says as if we haven't had numerous conversations in the past.

Instead of reaching her hand out to shake mine, she lowers her head over my snatch. My eyes dart to TJ, finding him staring down at my face as Xena's mouth covers my pussy. I jolt with the first touch of her tongue against my heated flesh, but within seconds I'm grinding down on her face. The woman has skills that rival TJ's absurdly talented mouth.

"You weren't lying," Xena says as she pulls her mouth back. My eyes drift from TJ down to the woman pleasuring me to find her grinning up at me. "I think the combination of your pussy and TJ's cum is the best thing I've ever tasted."

Anticipation rushes over my entire body when she lifts her hand, running it down my splayed thigh, getting closer to where my pussy needs her.

"Nope," TJ warns when her fingers sweep over my tender lips. "Mouth only."

I frown as her fingers disappear, but she more than makes up for it when she flattens her tongue and dives back in. She doesn't pull away until I come so hard, I see stars.

"Perfect," Xena praises as she nips at my inner thigh and stands to the side.

Mirroring TJ, she holds my other thigh as Zoe steps forward.

"I'm Zoe," the MC Queen says as she lowers her mouth to me.

Turning my head on the cage, I look over to find Lynch watching us. His eyes aren't on me, but on his woman's head as she devours me. There's no jealousy, malice, or warning in his gaze. I could be anyone else on the earth because it's his woman that turns him on. He only has eyes for her, and he allows this because it's what she wants.

Still wrung out from Xena's filthy mouth, Zoe pulls away before she makes me come.

"Nice to meet you," she says with a wink before bouncing away and right back to Lynch's lap.

"She's got a talented mouth, doesn't she?" Cold dread washes over my body as I look up at TJ. "Don't look at me like that, Envy. I've never experienced it. Never will. Just like Lynch will never lay a finger on you, but I've heard the stories of how amazing she is."

"She made me come once just from sucking on my nipples," Xena says, and the tension washes away as we both chuckle.

"I'm Vixen," another woman says just as her mouth engulfs my pussy.

I cum four times before the girls are done introducing themselves. When TJ tugs my hand until I'm sitting, I'm boneless, just a useless blob of skin.

"Not so fast," TJ says as I try to rest my head on his shoulder. "Do you really think it's fair that you get to soak the face of damn near every girl here while I'm left with a hard-on?"

"So tired," I whine as my eyes flutter closed.

"Every man in here is watching you, hoping that I'll share you with them as well."

I stiffen against his chest.

"I need to show them that you're mine."

I nod my consent, thinking he's going to lay me out and fuck me stupid. My pussy trembles with renewed delight at the thought, but instead of pushing me back down, he lifts me off the cage and pushes me to my knees. I look up at him confused as he pulls his impressive cock from the confines of his jeans and presses it against my lips.

"Show them that you're mine."

With my hands on my thighs, I open wide. TJ wastes no time shoving himself down my throat. My nose burns and my throat stings as he stabs into me, and I fucking love every second of it. The watery sight of his pleasure when I look up at him is almost enough to set off another wave of orgasms.

"You filthy bitch," he hisses as he pulls back, forcing his cock to fall from my lips. On my knees, I scramble after it, needing him back where he was. "Are you trying to embarrass me by making me come like a teenager?"

He lifts me from my knees, but he doesn't stop there. I'm floating through the air until he's laying me out on my back on top of the cage. His fingers are wrapped around my throat at the same time he slams inside of me. The rough intrusion after all the clit-only stimulation sets me off, and I come around his magnificent cock without further provocation.

Cheers ring out around the room as I squeal in delight. TJ smiles down at me, but the lust-filled grin is in stark contrast to the tightening grip on my neck.

"All I'll ever need," he grunts as he slams into me in a rhythm that's sure to leave indentions from the metal grid in my back for days.

"TJ," I moan, and like he can read every slight movement of my body, his fingers find me and strum my clit at a tempo that makes me explode again. Sound turns to an undecipherable hum, and my vision darkens around the edges until oxygen rushes back into my lungs when TJ pulls his fingers away from my throat.

His beautiful face twists in anguish as he comes, his cock jerking with the force of his own release.

"Jesus Christ," I hear someone mutter on the other side of the room.

"He came inside of her," another says.

"There's another one off the market," a girl whines.

"That's the hottest thing I've ever seen," an unfamiliar male voice praises.

"I never thought I'd see the day." This last one is in Lynch's familiar baritone.

TJ ignores them all. As if we're alone and didn't just perform in front of the entire club, I'm all he sees.

Chapter 36

TJ

"Hey."

I look down at my girl, terrified that I've taken things too far. She never told me to stop, but her neck is still red from the grip of my fingers. She came like a freight train, but that doesn't mean she's going to be okay in the aftermath. Holding my breath, I wait for the regret to show on her face.

Kaci grins back up at me. "Hey yourself."

Relief washes over me

"You're mine," I remind her. She squeezes her inner muscles, clamping down on my still half-hard cock. My eyes narrow as I push deeper inside of her.

"And you're mine," she coos.

And I am. She fucking owns every single bit of me, and I'm a better man for it.

"And now everyone knows it," I tell her as I pull back.

The second my dick is tucked back in my jeans, I reach for her again, helping her sit up on the edge of the cage. I wait for her next move, so I know what needs to be done. When her head tilts back, my lips find hers and my fingers move to her center on instinct.

Fuck, I love how damn creamy she is after I unload inside of her. She whimpers into my mouth when I slide two fingers into her.

"You're so fucking greedy." I pull my mouth away before sliding my cum-covered fingers into her mouth. Her eyes never leave mine as she sucks them clean.

The room erupts in cheers, and I smile when her cheeks flush a perfect shade of pink before she buries her face in my chest.

"Tell me you're fucking joking?"

With my arms holding Kaci against me, I look to my left and find Legs standing there with her hands on her hips, glaring at the two of us. Kaci isn't having it though, so I let my arms drop to her hips as she pulls her head back to see who is speaking to us.

I expect an argument, or should I say I hope Kaci stands up for herself, claiming me as her own and threatening Legs harm if she so much as looks my direction again, but all she does is frown at the most recent woman who used to take care of my cock when it got hard.

When she looks up at me, I realize none of that is needed. She doesn't have to prove a damn thing to me. I have an amazing woman in my arms, and there's nothing that can ruin tonight for me. She doesn't have shit to prove, and she knows it. Hell, every person in this room, with the exception of Legs, is well aware of where Kaci and I stand.

"Are you ready for bed, baby?" Kaci asks as she ignores the other woman.

She has never called me that before, and fuck if I don't love it on her lips.

"Are you sleepy?"

Her head shakes immediately. "I need more of your cum."

She's in my arms and being carried out of the room a second later. Xena understands the brief look I give her, and I know by morning Legs will no longer be an issue as far as my girl and I are concerned.

For all of her bravado in the living room, Kaci is dead weight in my arms by the time I close us into my bedroom.

"Wake up," I urge as I cross to the bathroom. "We have to get cleaned up."

It was hot as hell watching the girls suck and lick at her pink flesh, but I want her clean and smelling of no one but me. The shower hisses and sputters when I turn it on, and since I'm feeling generous, I wait for it to warm before stepping inside. It's not very easy undressing while she clings to me like a spider monkey, but I manage. I do have to rest her on top of the vanity to pull her garter belt and stockings off. Sighing in relief as I unclasp her bra, her head rolls on my shoulder.

Once we climb into the shower, she perks up enough to stand on her own, and we take turns lathering each other's body up and rinsing away the suds. I grow warmer with each and every touch she allows me, and by the time I turn off the water, my skin is overheated.

Her soft hand finds my cheek, and her tired eyes look up at me sleepily, and I'm fucking lost in her. She's my north, my guidance, my very reason for existing.

"You were made for me, Envy." A soft smile teases her lips as she looks up at me. "I lo—"

Her fingers immediately find my lips. "Don't say those things to me."

"I can't help how I feel."

"Don't tell me. Show me."

So I do.

I carry her to the bed, and I make love to her for hours the exact way we both need. We don't stop until my back is bleeding from her fingernails and my own hands have left bruises all over her perfect body.

***

"Baby," I whisper to Kaci as I push a strand of hair from her sleeping face.

She grumbles into her pillow as her face scrunches up from the hallway light.

"Envy," I coax, pulling the cover down her back and infiltrating the warmth she's created by cocooning into the blankets I was remiss to leave a half an hour earlier. I'm freshly showered and hating that I'm going to have to leave her for a few days.

"Why are you so hateful?" she complains and blindly reaches for the blankets.

"You're grumpy in the morning," I tease, letting my lips drift over her bare shoulder.

"Mmm," she hums, turning over so her breast is even with my mouth.

As much as I need to grab my shit and head outside, her naked body is too tempting to resist.

"I have to go," I whisper huskily before wrapping my lips around her nipple.

When her fingers dig into my scalp, I give her exactly what she's craving and bite down on the taut bud as it furls against my tongue.

"TJ," she moans, shifting her hips until the covers fall away from her legs.

The bite marks on her inner thighs lengthen my already half-hard cock.

"I have to go," I repeat, but my mouth doesn't leave her skin, and my eyes don't drift from the slit between her legs.

"Don't leave me," she pouts, and I love the sound of her begging. She did it several times last night.

"I don't want to." The confession is made as I make my way to her other attention-starved breast. "But I have to work."

"Where are you going?"

Her hips wiggle, and I lose my restraint as my fingers find the hidden heat of her luscious cunt.

"Jesus," I hiss when I find her drenched.

My free hand is working open the top button on my jeans when a throat clearing in the doorway pulls my attention.

Ronan is standing just outside of the room taking in the scene. "Briar is looking for you. All the guys are waiting outside."

"Fuck," I grunt as he walks away. "I have to go."

"When will you be back?" she asks as she reaches for the blankets and covers up her delicious body. I swear a wave of depression washes over me. Being gone from her is going to be absolute torture.

"A couple days."

"Days?" Fear fills her eyes as she reaches for me.

After sucking her wetness from my fingers, I lean over and take her mouth. Her lips, the way her tongue slides over mine, doesn't help my situation, but I'll be damned if I leave without it.

"Be a good girl while I'm gone and remember who owns you," I warn against her mouth.

She nips my bottom lip in retaliation, but there's a soft smile on her lips when she pulls away.

"Be safe and hurry back to me," she pleads.

I press one last soft kiss to her mouth. "Stay here where it's safe. I'll be back before you know it."

Chapter 37

Kaci

The next time I wake up, I don't know how long it's been since TJ left. I haven't slept as good as I have the last two nights in as long as I can remember. There's something about him, the safety he provides, and the calmness I feel in his presence that calms my soul.

It only takes about ten minutes of lying in bed alone for the boredom to sink in before I'm reaching for my phone to see if he has texted since he left.

The only message I have is from a number I don't recognize.

Unknown Number: Your mother killed herself yesterday. You will be expected at the services.

I don't know how I'm expected to feel in a moment like this, but a sense of calm surely isn't a normal way to react to news of a parent's death. I knew the time would come when she'd take too many pills, drink too much alcohol, all to try to forget the pain our family has been through.

I imagine most people would picture the good times they had with their parents. They'd remember happy birthdays and time spent smiling and having a good time. The only image my mind chooses to conjure is the tight, disappointed look on my mother's face when I walked across the tarmac after being flown back to the states by that New Mexico biker club. There were no tears of joy or warm arms of a loving mother waiting to encase me in their safety. A brusque "your father lost the election" was all I got when I was within hearing distance, then I was ushered into a car.

I climb out of bed and put on the sweats and t-shirt I was wearing yesterday before walking out of the room. Returning to my childhood home without my mother there as a buffer between my father and me is the very last thing I want to do, but ingrained family obligation dictates that I go. I'm reaching for the doorknob on the front door when I hear someone to my right.

"Bye, bitch. Don't come back." I look to see Legs standing off to the side with a horrific sneer on her face.

"Bye," I mutter like I would have if it were anyone else there.

By sheer muscle memory, I manage to order an Uber, go to my house, and grab my own car before heading to my parents' place. Somehow, all without even remembering the steps it took to do so.

Like an unwelcome guest, I knock on the door just like I have since I left home years ago. No one answers, so I knock again a little harder. This goes unanswered as well, but when I try the handle, the door opens easily. Feeling like an intruder, I step inside my childhood home.

On my way here, I'd anticipated people all over the place, dusting, straightening, and making the house presentable for a gathering after my mother's service. That's what happened after Seth died. People from all over came to grieve and offer their condolences on such a tragic loss.

When I walk into the foyer, the dark house feels empty, isolated, and cold. There's no longer any love here, nothing that draws me in and urges me to be the daughter my parents expected, not the disappointment I've become.

"Of all the people to die, it had to be your mother."

My father's words don't startle me. I knew he had to be around somewhere, and when I look over to the den, he's exactly where he always is, sitting in his chair with a bottle of liquor on the table beside him and a near-empty glass in his hand.

"But I guess she's been dead for a while. Her death is on your hands. She was never the same after you killed Seth." He tilts his glass up, emptying it down his throat, all the while staring across the room at the unlit fireplace. I'm not even worth his attention. My suffering, my loss doesn't even register with him. I'm not surprised, but I can't deny that it stings just a bit. Families are supposed to close ranks when tragedy strikes. We're supposed to hold onto what we have left, not point fingers and issue blame.

I've learned the hard way over the years that you can't reason with madness, so I clamp my mouth closed, biting the inside of my lip until I taste blood on my tongue. My silence and refusal to argue with him doesn't prevent him from continuing.

"They should've killed you." He scowls down at his empty glass, growing angrier at its lack of liquid relief as if someone else other than himself consumed the alcohol while he wasn't looking. He speaks again as he reaches for the bottle and refills his tumbler. "I should've paid the extra money that man asked for to ensure I'd never have to see your face again."

My eyes fixate on the man, who by all scientific processes is supposed to love me, if only by default. My head shakes back and forth, rejecting what he's just said, trying to convince myself I heard him wrong.

"Wh-what?" It's the only word I can manage past the burn of bile in the back of my throat.

He huffs with indignation before a slow, creepy smile crosses his aged mouth. He doesn't bother to look at me. His focus stays across the room as he lifts his glass once again to his mouth, drinking down half of the liquor he's just poured. At the rate he's been going for the last couple of years, I'm surprised he hasn't been hospitalized for liver failure.

"My political career soared after Seth was killed," he says as if he's talking to himself or recounting his memoirs to no one in particular. "It was the only consolation after losing my son. A part of me died that day with him, only to be replaced with a seething hatred for you."

Only now does he turn his head to look at me. His eyes sweep from head to toe, a look of disgust marking his once handsome face. His already flushed cheeks darken as his anger grows.

"I figured you'd die after being taken, and I'd never have to see your murderous face again. Imagine my surprise when I got the call that you'd survived and were coming back home? I paid five thousand dollars for those filthy bastards to scoop you up. The man I made arrangements with assured me you'd be hurt, fucked, and used until you didn't even know your own name. He swore you'd be lucky to last a month."

Tears burn my eyes at the realization of what he's saying, but somehow, I manage to keep them from falling. He doesn't deserve my pain. He's been the cause of my agony for many years. My self-destruction is due to his hatefulness, but I never imagined he was behind my abduction.

"Did Mom know?" Why this morsel of information is so important to me, I don't know.

He huffs again before taking another long sip of his whiskey. "Your mother hasn't known her ass from her elbow for many years."

"Dad?" He cringes at the word. "Why would you do this to me?"

His glass soars across the room, shattering to pieces inside the stone fireplace. I'd be shocked with the outburst, but they're commonplace where he's concerned. I'm more in awe that he has such great aim with so much alcohol coursing through his veins.

"You are the fucking spawn of Satan," he seethes as his blood-shot eyes find mine in the dim light of the house. "Your mother was nothing but a pregnant whore when I made the mistake of getting drunk enough one night to fuck her."

My skin is on fire, itching uncontrollably with every word he spits at me.

"She'd already manipulated herself into my damn head by the time I did the math and realized she'd been knocked up a month before I even slipped my dick into her." Without his glass, he now drinks directly from the bottle before struggling to stand from his chair. "The marriage was a farce from day one, a rush job to wed before she was showing, which would increase the chances of ruining my political career before it could really take off."

Swallowing does nothing to rid my throat of the lump formed there.

"Before you were even born, you were ruining my fucking life." His steps seem surer than they should as he closes the distance between us. "Do you know how damaging it is to my image for your coward of a mother to kill herself?"

My spine stiffens as I take him in from head to toe. He's no longer the man that strikes fear in my heart. He's a menace, a devious piece of shit who rules by scathing words and self-appointed power. He's the coward, treating me poorly to account for his own failures in life. He's a fucking bully for lack of a better word.

"You don't seem too far behind her," I spit as he gets in my face as a means of intimidation.

"You little bitch," he hisses as his hands reach up for my neck.

My eyes widen in shock as his grip increases to the point I can't get in deep breaths of air. Once again, I've underestimated him. He's never used his hands to wield his power, but it seems he's not above it today.

My fists pound on his chest, but the alcohol must keep him from feeling it because he doesn't budge. For one long moment, I let his fingers clench as his empty eyes stare back into mine. There's nothing in his dark blue glare that resembles a good person. He spoke of me being the spawn of Satan, but I think he's mistaken me for the man who looks back at him in the mirror every day.

With renewed strength, I shove at him. His hands loosen for a second before tightening again. When I shove at him the second time, I lift my knee and slam him in the crotch.

"I won't be your victim any longer!" I roar as he flies backward.

Drunk and unable to gain his footing, I watch as he falls. As if in slow motion, his eyes widen and his hands reach for me as if I'd keep him from falling on his ass after what he just did to me. He's wrong, but so am I. Falling on his ass isn't what happens, I realize, when he hits the coffee table with a sickening crack.

His eyes remain open as he slumps to the ground and his neck twists in an inhuman angle. Mouth gaping with a silent cry for help, the man who has done nothing but treat me horribly my entire life stares at the ceiling, dead.

Chapter 38

TJ

The ride to Richmond seems to be taking ten times longer than it ever has before. By the time we make a pit stop just outside of Philadelphia halfway into our trip, my back is already hurting, and my fingers itch with emptiness.

Pulling out my phone, I plan to shoot Kaci a super filthy text, priming her for some video chat action I have planned once we get to our hotel for the night.

She must need me as much as I do her because I missed a call from her twenty minutes ago. Instead of the planned text, I opt to call, the promise of her voice too tempting to pass up. The phone rings a dozen times before her voicemail kicks in. I call again and again, but she doesn't answer. Kaci doesn't always carry her phone around with her, so I call the next best thing.

"Hey, sugar," Xena purrs when she answers the phone.

"Can you tell Envy to get her phone?"

"Already missing her?" Xena laughs lightly, but from the sound of it, she's walking through the clubhouse. "I can keep her warm while you're gone."

Her offer makes me frown, but she knows better, so I chuckle. "You keep your hands off my girl."

"Afraid I'll steal her away from you?"

"Fat fucking chance."

"Hey, gorgeous." A knock on a door echoes through the phone. "TJ said yo—"

She pauses, and fear skates down my spine.

"What is it?"

"She's not here."

"She has to be there. I told her not to fucking leave."

"Does she always listen—"

I hang up the phone before Xena can even finish, and I'm calling her again. Over and over I call. Frantic and begging for her to pick up.

"What's wrong?" Sonic asks as he replaces the gas nozzle back on the machine.

I'm about to answer him when another desperate call to Kaci is answered.

"Baby?" I say when I'm met with silence.

"He's gone," she whispers so low I can barely hear her.

I break off from Sonic, uncaring that all the guys are gassed up and ready to hit the road again. They can fucking leave without me for all I care. The girl on the phone is the only fucking person that matters to me right now.

"Who's gone, baby?" I ask as I walk around behind the gas station, hoping it shields me from the noise of the traffic on the New Jersey Turnpike. It helps some, but not a lot. I cup my free hand over my ear to block everything out but her.

"My father had me abducted." She's stating a fact as if she has no emotion or is in shock.

"Fuck," I grunt, hating that she's discovered this and I'm not there to help her through it.

"My mom killed herself yesterday."

Once again she delivers the news the same way she would let someone know they have mail on the counter or they missed an unimportant phone call.

Confused, my brows draw in. "And your dad is gone?"

"He said all these things." Her voice cracks, the first sign of emotion before she continues, "He confessed to having those men take me, to hating me my whole life, to not being my real dad."

Shit. I didn't even know that part, but a lifetime of guilt swims in my gut for knowing the things I did know and not discussing those things with her while I had more control of the situation.

"He attacked me. I didn't mean to kill him, but I couldn't let him hurt me any longer."

Unease settles low in my gut, and I walk from behind the gas station and wave down Briar.

"Everything will be okay," I assure her as I motion for Briar to give me his phone. I type out a message letting him know what is going on, and that he needs to get my brother on the phone immediately.

"I have to call the police." Her voice is weak and too soft, nothing like the vibrant girl I've held in my arms the last couple of days. She's blossomed since I brought her to the clubhouse, and it kills me to hear the defeat in her voice.

"Baby, are you listening to me?" Silence fills the air again. "Do not call the police. We can take care of this without their help. Envy? Are you listening?"

"You're too far away," she finally says. "There's nothing you can do."

"Baby, I'm going to send someone to you until I can get there."

Briar's phone chimes, and he turns it around so I can read the message from Virus. It explains that he's traced her phone back to her parents' house.

"Kaci!" I snap. "Do not call the police. Do you hear me?"

"I'm so glad I met you, TJ."

Terror fills my bones with the defeat in her voice.

"You're the best thing that has ever happened to me," I confess. "I need you to be brave for me."

My eyes burn with frustration from being so far away as cold fear washes over me with how her voice sounds right now.

"I should've let you tell me you loved me last night. It would've been nice to hear."

"I love you," I scream, but I'm met with three beeps telling me that she has disconnected the call.

With shaking hands, I call her back immediately only to be sent straight to fucking voicemail.

"Lynch," Briar says and shoves his phone in my face before I can completely freak out.

"Go fucking get her," I hiss into the phone.

"We're leaving now," my brother assures me.

"Fuck, fuck, fuck!" I roar, pacing around in a circle. "She's in fucking trouble. I think she's going to hurt herself."

I have enough wherewithal not to yell that she's just killed her father since we are standing outside a very busy gas station.

"We're on our way," he assures me again.

"You're an hour and a half away. You may be too late. I'm coming home."

"You're going to calm down before you get back on your fucking bike." I hear an engine crank in the background. "Becoming roadkill isn't going to help her. I'm sending Ronan to meet the guys and pick up your product for New York."

"T-take Molly and Zoe with you," I stammer.

"I'm taking care of things here. I don't know exactly what I'm walking into over there, and I refuse to put our sister and my girl in any danger. Let the other guys know what's going on, and I'll see you back at the clubhouse."

"I can't live in a world where she doesn't exist," I murmur, my body already going cold with the fear of what she's capable of when left to her own tortured thoughts.

"No talking like that, brother. Let me handle this."

The phone goes dead, so I do the only thing I'm capable of, and I call her phone again. As anticipated it goes directly to voicemail, and that increases the terror settling in my stomach.

"I've got to head back," I tell Briar as I hand him back his phone. "Ronan will meet you guys at the hotel and head to New York with Sonic."

"I think you need to take a minute."

Somehow the hand on my shoulder is enough to stop me in my tracks before I can sling my leg over my bike.

My eyes find Briar's, and I'm so fucking grateful that he's here. He's like a brother to me, and the only man other than Lynch who can reason with me when I'm spiraling out of control.

"She killed her dad," I mutter. "She's going to hurt herself."

He's silent for a long moment. He doesn't tell me everything will be fine. We've faced too much shit in our lives to make assurances like that.

"You need to get home safely." His hand clamps on my shoulder again. "Tell me you're okay to ride safely."

I nod, knowing I can get close to halfway home before Lynch even makes it to her parents' house.

"I'll be safe."

"Fly like the wind, brother." He squeezes my shoulder one more time before releasing me so I can leave.

After three long calming breaths, I swing my leg over my bike and crank it. I don't look back as I get on the Turnpike and head for home, unsure if I'll live through the night.

Chapter 39

Kaci

Chills rack my body, but I've given up trying to fight the cold. Even the noises coming from downstairs aren't enough to pull me from the tub. The water went frigid long ago, and yet I remain, chilled to the bone and shivering, unable to move from this spot.

At first, I let my mind imagine that I didn't shove my father to his death, and any minute now he will storm up the stairs, spit more vitriol my way, and insist I leave his house and never come back. With my mother gone, there's nothing left for me here. I can't help but wonder if doing what she did would be best for me.

The noise below me could be the police, uniformed officers or that horrible detective from Andover ready to shackle my hands and feet as he proudly announces that I'll never see freedom again. Is that the best outcome? I need to pay for my sins, that much is clear. It's just deciding which steps to take that has me indecisive.

"Envy?"

With swollen eyes, I look up to see TJ's brother standing in the open doorway of the bathroom. Relief washes over his face, but that doesn't make any sense. He had to have seen what I did downstairs.

For some strange reason, I'm not afraid of him. He's not even trying to look at my naked flesh, but I still drag my knees to my chest and wrap my arms around my legs.

"TJ said you might need a little help here," Lynch continues. "Is everything okay?"

My head shakes back and forth before I drop it to my knees in shame. "I killed my father."

"I know, sweetheart. It'll be okay. We're here now."

"Zoe is lucky to have a man like you." My head, my thoughts, everything is all over the place, but he doesn't seem to mind. A small smile is on his lips when I look back up at him.

"And TJ is lucky to have you. How about we get you into some clothes and get you out of here?"

"I'm waiting for the police."

He stiffens, his lips forming a flat line on his face. "Did you call the police?"

I shake my head. "But they'll be here eventually."

A hand clamps on his shoulder, and Lynch shifts to the side as Kai appears.

"I got this," my new friend tells the MC president without pulling his eyes from mine.

Without another word, Lynch walks away. We listen to his heavy boots as they head back downstairs. Kai moves closer, tentative in his steps as if I'm going to freak out at any moment.

"I couldn't do it," I tell him when I follow his eyes to the razor blade on the side of the tub. "If I killed myself, I'd still just be Royce Stewart's daughter. Even when I was taken, it was more about him and less about me."

I sigh, hating the bitterness in my voice. I've never been one to play the victim, but my world is turned upside down right now.

"Poor Royce. It must be so hard to go on living with the death of his son, and then the abduction of his daughter," I mimic as if reading from an old newspaper article.

"You're shivering, babe. Let's get you out of the tub and into some warm clothes," Kai urges as he reaches for me.

I don't fight him as he touches me, sweeping his arms under mine and effortlessly lifting me from the cold water. My teeth are chattering as he wraps a fluffy towel around my back. I cling to the fabric, holding it to my heaving chest like a shield capable of protecting me from all the bad things that could happen.

"Did you guys call the police to come get me?"

Kai lifts my chin with the bend of his knuckle until my head is raised enough to look him directly in the eyes. "The Ravens Ruin doesn't call the police."

I nod in understanding, realizing I should've known that. They have a way of getting their own justice. TJ proved that more than once when he had to pull me from those frat houses. I can't even focus on what may happen now that I've committed the ultimate sin. Will they punish me for my misdeeds like they did the men who took advantage of me?

"Arms up," Kai urges as he unwraps the towel from around me and dries my body. Once he's satisfied, I let him dress me in the same t-shirt and sweats that I wore over here. Once again, I lift the fabric to my nose in an attempt to feel closer to TJ. Even in his absence, his scent lingers, and the familiarity assists in calming my nerves slightly.

"Where are we going?" I manage to ask when Kai guides me out into the hallway.

"Back to the clubhouse," Kai answers as we crest the top of the stairs.

"That's going to complicate things for them."

"It's where you belong," Kai assures me as he guides me down the stairs.

"Everyone in my family is dead," I mumble absently, watching my feet as we descend.

"We're your family," Kai whispers as he pulls me closer.

My masochistic personality shines bright when we make it to the foyer because I can't resist looking back into the living room, needing to see the reality of what I've done one last time. Only, my father isn't lying at an odd angle against the heavy, wood coffee table where I left him to scramble upstairs.

His lifeless body is strung up by a thick rope from the exposed beam running the length of the room. His eyes are still open and hauntingly empty. I can't seem to look away from the scene clearly recreated to tell a different story than the one I left behind a couple of hours ago. The tipped over chair under his dangling feet, and the spilled half-empty bottle of whiskey are nice touches, but deep down, I know it won't work. I've binged way too much on police procedural shows to let myself believe I've gotten a free pass. I don't even know if I deserve a free pass. Two wrongs don't make a right and all that.

Kai tucks me closer into his side and redirects me out the back door where a large, black SUV is waiting with the engine running.

"You're going to ride with these guys, and I'm going to drive your car back," Kai tells me as he pulls open the back door. I pull my keyring from the sweat's pocket and hand it over to him, giving him a final pleading look, trying to tell him I don't want him to walk away from me. The trembling renews the second he closes me inside and walks toward my car.

Lynch is behind the wheel, giving me a sympathetic look I don't deserve, when I turn toward the front of the vehicle.

A guy I recognize from the clubhouse, but never had a conversation with, turns to watch as I settle in the back seat and pull my seatbelt across my chest. The click of the belt echoes inside the vehicle, and I suddenly feel as if I'm on display with both sets of eyes watching me, waiting for me to lose it.

"Sorry about your dad," the passenger says.

"He wasn't my dad."

My eyes burn with unshed tears, the embarrassment of being emotional over a man who never cared about me forcing me to look away. The dreary rain that has moved in fits my mood perfectly. I don't bother to look back at the home I grew up in as we head down the long drive and out of the swanky neighborhood. I'd never felt whole here anyway, and I doubt I'll ever step foot back on the property.

There are no stops or detours. Lynch drives us right back to the clubhouse where Xena and Zoe are waiting for me just inside the front door.

"We got her," Xena tells Kai. Reluctantly, he releases me into their arms.

"Please no," I murmur, trying to cling to him, unsure why I feel so protected by him, but refusing to question it right now.

"Doll." His soft hands cup my jaw. "I'm already going to catch shit for being near you, naked in a tub. Let these girls get you cleaned up, and I'll come back."

I nod even though I doubt TJ will have a problem with Kai seeing me naked or watching me shower. TJ fucked me in front of the entire club after letting most the women put their mouths on me, after all.

Xena directs me back to TJ's room and straight into the shower. Xena strips as Zoe helps me out of my clothing. I wish I could be more help, but nothing seems to be working right. Every muscle in my body is heavy, sluggish, and not responding when I urge them to move. She cleans me with economical grace, never once crossing the line into inappropriate. I'm grateful for her help. I feel mothered. It isn't something I'm at all familiar with.

"Here," Zoe says as I step out of the shower.

In her palm is a white, oblong pill. I know what it is immediately. "No thanks."

"The Xanax will help you calm down," Xena offers with a small smile when I don't reach for it.

"I'm fine," I assure them even though I can't control the trembling in my limbs. I don't deserve to be numb right now.

Once I'm dressed in TJ's clean clothes, the girls leave, and I fall into Kai's strong arms once again.

Chapter 40

TJ

My feet barely touch the ground when I climb off my bike and sprint through the front door of the clubhouse.

"Wait," Lynch calls after me when I'm already halfway across the living room, arrowing toward the hallway.

I stop only because I'm frantic, and I don't want her to freak out any more than she already is.

"She's pretty shaken up. I don't know her well at all, but she's been trembling like a leaf since we arrived at her parents' house. Kai is in bed with her." My teeth grind together so hard my jaw aches. "Don't give me that alpha male bullshit. If anyone else got near her, she trembled like a scared Chihuahua. He's the only one that's been able to ease her nerves."

My hand skates over the top of my head in frustration, and it takes everything I have not to roar out my agitation, not because Kai is comforting her, but because I wasn't here to protect her from her piece of shit dad.

"Zoe tried to give her a Xanax, but she refused. She's only been sleeping for about an hour."

"What did you find at her parents' house?" I have to ask him because I need to know and don't plan on speaking with Kaci about it unless she wants to open up to me.

"There was a struggle from what I could tell. He fell and clocked his neck just in the right spot. It was a quick death. An honest to god freak accident from the looks of it."

"He didn't deserve that," I mutter, my hands growing increasingly antsy to get to her.

"We strung him up. If we get lucky, the police will only look at the big picture. He's been out of the political spotlight for a while according to Virus."

"Nothing exciting happens in Newbury. Two suicides in the same family in less than three days? That's gonna draw some attention." *Almost three*, my mind chooses to remind me of how Kaci left our last conversation. I was terrified of what I was going to find when I got here, blaming the tears running down my cheeks on the high speeds my bike hit on the way home to her.

"Virus is working on something to scramble the cell tower info related to her phone. So hopefully that'll be enough to keep them guessing."

"Hopefully." I turn away from him, but his arm reaches out before I can step away.

"You straight?"

"I'm good," I lie. I won't be able to say that with honesty until my girl is safe in my arms.

Although Lynch prepared me about what I was going to find, my blood still runs close to boiling when I open my bedroom door and find Kaci wrapped around Kai in repose. He doesn't jolt or fly out of bed with guilty movements. He simply raises his fingers to his lips, shushing me before slowly drawing himself out from under her. With more care and concern than I thought possible for the normally flamboyant man, he eases away from Kaci without disturbing her or waking her up.

The covers are pulled all the way up, so I don't have a damn clue what I'm going to see when they separate. Luckily for Kai, he climbs out of bed fully clothed. Even the soft fabric of his athletic shorts are flat, so he wasn't getting aroused by her when she was in distress. I should commend him for his restraint, because even with knowing what she's going through my cock kicks in my jeans at the mere anticipation of crawling into bed and replacing Kai in that spot.

My first instinct is still to punch him as he crosses the room, but I'd never want Kaci to suffer. If Kai in bed with her is what it took to calm her enough to go to sleep, then how can I be angry about that?

"Thanks, man," I tell him, clapping my hand in his as soon as he's close enough to touch.

He squeezes my shoulder, looking into my eyes, and I see her pain reflected in his. This girl has the ability to draw every single person in. It makes me even more protective of her.

"Anytime, handsome."

The door softly clicks behind Kai as he leaves, so the only light in the room is coming from around the edges of the window blind and the tunnel of illumination from the bathroom.

As fast as I needed to get back to her, I'm torn between getting a shower and washing the highway off me and stripping naked and crawling in bed with her. I frown when a clicking noise fills the silence in the room, but once I realize it's her teeth clacking together, my decision is made for me. She must've begun trembling again the moment Kai pulled away from her.

I strip out of my clothes, unconcerned that my cut lands on the floor disrespectfully. I growl in frustration when I try to push my jeans off without first removing my boots, so getting to her takes much longer than I want.

Stripped to my boxer briefs, I pull back the blanket and climb under it with her. My heart expands when she reaches for me in her sleep and presses her nose into my neck. The trembling doesn't subside immediately, and of its own volition, my hand soothes down her back until my fingers reach the hem of her shirt. With smooth movements, my fingers ease under the fabric so I can stroke her delicate skin from the nape of her neck to the top band of the sweats she's wearing.

She releases a ragged breath, and only then do I realize she's shaking because she's crying. As tears leave her eyes and skate down my neck and shoulder, I hold her tighter, whispering promises that she's safe, and I'm never letting her go.

I don't know how to make this better. Naturally, I want to grip her chin, insist she dry her eyes, remind her that her piece of shit dad doesn't deserve her tears, but she's also recently lost her mother, and she could be crying for her, for all I know. I contemplate rolling her over and eating her to so many orgasms that she has no choice but to let the endorphins take over and make her feel better, but she's in no position to fully consent right now.

I feel impotent, unable to give her what she needs. Emotional shit isn't my forte. At least it wasn't until today. I won't take it back. I won't tell her I freaked out and overreacted with my declaration while I had her on the phone. I meant every fucking word of it. I don't even know if she heard me say those three words I've never uttered to another human other than my mom and little sister before she hung up. I meant it then, and if she's up for it, I'll whisper them in her ear every night before bed. I'll yell them from the tallest tree on the compound if that's what she needs from me.

As I hold this amazing yet broken woman against my chest, I pray to a god I never believed in that this isn't what sends her spiraling so hard that I can't pull her back.

***

"I need to leave." Her words crush me, but the fact that she refuses to look at me while she breaks my heart makes it ten times worse.

I stop shuffling my clothes, and silence fills the room. My arms are shaking with unused energy and the urge to go to her and remind her why she's here to begin with. I don't imagine it would go over very well. She hasn't been very receptive to the attention I've tried to show her in the four days since the shit went down with her dad.

"Tell me what you need," I plead against her neck. My front is lined up with her back, but she no longer sinks into the comfort of my warmth.

After she woke up that first night when I made it back to her, she's been distant and antsy. It's as if she's waiting for the other shoe to drop.

She doesn't answer me, and if I'm honest with myself, I shouldn't expect her to. All I've gotten in the last thirty-six hours are one-word answers and silence.

Fear settles deep in my gut. The only hope I've been holding on to is the fact that she still reaches for me in her sleep, but her unconscious self isn't the one making decisions right now.

"I want you to stay," I tell her when she tenses against my body and stares across the room. "I need you to stay."

"You're not everything I need," she responds emotionlessly. "You can't give me that."

I don't know what that is, but clearly, she needs something, and I've failed her at anticipating her needs.

"Is it the cage?" I growl as my hand tangles in her hair and pulls her head back.

A long-suffered sigh escapes her lips, but that's her only response. My brain misfires before coming back online to think of ways to bring her back to me. I know what she needs. It's exactly what she sought out before we met.

I swallow thickly before releasing her hair.

"My birthday party is tonight. Leave tomorrow."

I know she can hear the desperation in my voice, and for once, I don't bother trying to mask it with sexual aggression like I've done numerous times with her before. I need her off balance for what I have planned.

Chapter 41

Kaci

I've checked the time on my cell phone a million times since TJ led me out here a couple of hours ago. He's frustrating the hell out of me, using half his time to police my alcohol intake and the other half ignoring me while he talks to everyone else.

I smile when I'm spoken to, but my skin is itchy and tingly with the need to get out of here. TJ has been underfoot like a clingy toddler for the last four days. He isn't the man he was before my last visit to my parents' house. I never wanted a man who doted on me and looked helpless when he didn't think I was paying attention to him.

The man who brought me here would know what I craved. He'd give me exactly what I'm looking for. Last week, TJ would've been able to pull me back from the edge. This week he seems more concerned about my mental health than anything else, except he can't see that his soft hands and sensitive nature are what's driving me crazy.

If he hadn't turned into whatever he is now, my issues would be gone by now. He should know I don't need him to act like some prince charming. I need him rough, insistent, demanding that I meet his desires. I need him to remind me of a safe word before he brutalizes my body with so much pleasure, I'm left drained for days. This is like that love making session back at my old studio apartment. I didn't want him that way then, and I sure as hell don't need that from him now.

The confession, him needing me, from earlier, I imagine would get most girls all gooey. What's not to swoon over? TJ is gorgeous on his worst day. He's a big tough guy all but citing fucking poetry right now. It does nothing for me.

Without a word, TJ stands, bending to push a chaste kiss to my lips before he walks away. The damn near platonic kiss is worse than it has been since I killed my father, and it makes me realize that he's already saying goodbye. For a man who has made all sorts of confessions, he sure is quick to lock the gate on all those emotions. He knows I'm leaving tomorrow. I figured the information would draw out at least one last rough fuck, a final session of dominance in front of his friends, but all it has done is make him withdraw from me.

I frown at his back when he walks across the room, smiling at some chick I don't know. I don't know what I expected out of him but pulling the girl against his side and disappearing with her down the hallway toward his room while she peers up at him like she's just won the fucking lottery, is not it.

"Tough break."

I look over to see that Legs has taken TJ's vacated spot beside me on the couch. I don't bother with a rebuttal. This chick hates me for the very same reason I hate the girl TJ just took off with.

"If you stick around long enough, you'll understand that none of these men are faithful."

"Speak for yourself," Briar, TJ's sister's boyfriend, says from the other sofa. Molly beams at his declaration and snuggles deeper into his side. They are fucking adorable, and a doting man is exactly what Molly needs. I have no interest in it, but a man that would just get up and walk away from me to fuck another girl isn't on my list of things that are okay either.

Anticipating that Legs is going to sit there and continue to taunt me, I grab two shots off the table in front of me and down them before standing and walking away.

"You need to leave her alone," I hear Molly chastise, but the energy is wasted on me. I won't be around long enough for it to even matter.

My phone is in my hand, typing on the Uber App before I make it to the front door. Waiting by the front gate for my ride away from this place seems like a much better idea than sitting beside TJ's last fuck buddy and listening to her regale me with stories of all the ways he's fucked her and hundreds of other women.

I'm attacked from behind before I can even understand what's happening. Two strong hands hold me while another set ties something around my eyes. I don't think to scream. For a long moment, I think someone is playing a joke on me. TJ said I was safe here. He assured me more than once nothing would happen to me at the Ravens Ruin clubhouse. I belong to him, and that the men here respected that.

As if reading my mind, the man behind me speaks. "TJ doesn't want you anymore. That means you're fair game."

My heart rate spikes as my mouth opens on a scream. I don't know if it's hearing that I've been cast aside by TJ, or the fact that these guys are going to hurt me, but agony washes over me.

A meaty hand covers my mouth, and my first instinct is to bite down. The man behind me howls in pain, losing his grip on me enough that I'm able to struggle away from them.

"She fucking bit me!" he roars.

"Get her to the garage," another man says from my left.

I've been in that garage before, and the memory makes my blood run cold. At the same time, isn't this exactly what I've been looking for? Wasn't I desperate to get away from TJ only moments ago, so I could put myself in this exact situation at one of the frat houses that never seem to let me down?

I spend too long analyzing and not enough time running because I'm scooped up, one person grabbing my upper body and the other wrapping strong arms around my legs. I'm swept up off the ground and carried. It seems like an eternity and mere seconds at the same time, until my feet are released. I fight them as two hands reach for my arms and pin them behind my back. A second later, they're tied so tight tingles run down my palms.

"I don't know why you're fighting." Whiskey scented breath fills my nostrils. "We saw how TJ fucked you in front of everyone. Seems like you were made for this."

"Admit it, Envy. You were made to take cock."

"I can't wait to see what all the fucking fuss is about."

Brash, cruel voices surround me, and I have no clue how I'm going to walk away from this unscathed. Things are different now. I'm not drugged. I didn't hand pick these people. I didn't have a hand in setting this up. It may be what I was longing for, but this is a far cry from the situations I've willingly put myself in before.

"First, she's going to suck my cock."

The only sound I hear over my harsh breaths is the release of a zipper before a rough hand grips my hair and forces me clumsily to my knees. I can't focus on the pain radiating up my legs from the impact with the knowledge of what is going to happen to me.

The whiskey breath is back, breathing down my neck. "You bite me, and I'll slit your fucking throat."

My heart stops. Those were the exact words TJ told me back in my apartment; only that voice doesn't belong to the man who brought me back from my darkness. Unbidden, my body responds much the same way it did then, and when his cock is pressed to my lips, I open up willingly.

A hoarse grunt echoes around the room when he shoves in as far as he can go, staying there until I begin to choke around him. He only backs away a few inches before he pushes me to my limit once again.

A pair of rough hands rip open my shirt before fondling my breasts with punishing grips as another person yanks my sweats down my hips. A surprisingly tentative finger sweeps at my seam, and my tears of shame soak into the fabric covering my eyes.

"You fucking slut," a man hisses in my ears. "You're fucking soaked."

My body was trained to respond to brutality. Getting wet for the men hurting me after I'd been abducted was self-preservation. Getting fucked dry just makes the assault worse. I'm reasoning with myself, trying to explain away the real reason I'm terrified and turned on right now. A psychologist would have a field day in my head right now. I don't even understand it myself.

The man attached to the dick in my mouth grunts again before pulling his cock free. Like a whore, I lean forward a couple of inches, tongue out looking for his dick.

A chuckle echoes around the room. Apparently, I'm entertaining him, or maybe he just knows me better than I know myself.

"Stand her up. I want her cunt."

As if he's the leader, I feel several sets of hands picking me up, doing his bidding. It's then that I realize I'm just feeding into my own victimization, so my will to fight is renewed.

"Get your fucking hands off me!" I roar, but I'm met with more strength than I can fight against. Fabric of some sort is stuffed in my mouth to staunch my wails as a handful of men carry me to a flat surface and spread me out on the top. I'm star-fished, my ass nearly hanging off the edge, and I freeze when I feel the heat of a man between my legs.

My muscles ache with the strain of trying to get free, but I freeze when a warm mouth covers my pussy.

My hiss is blocked by my gag, and I'm actually happy that my eyes are blocked so my captors can't tell how spectacular that mouth feels.

Who in the hell takes a woman against her will but tries to pleasure her first? I moan into the rag again as the hot tongue spears me open, but it's gone way too soon. My leg muscles flex in disappointment because I want him back.

"I bet she tastes fucking amazing," a man holding one of my arms says.

If my mouth weren't full, I'd offer myself to him.

Next thing I know, a thick cock is breeching me, taking something I didn't offer, no matter how ready my body is for the invasion.

How can I be terrified and blissed out at the same time?

Without warning, the blindfold is yanked away, and although with the blinding overhead light I can't immediately focus my eyes, I can feel my limbs being released one by one and see shapes of men as they walk away. When my vision renews, I find TJ standing between my trembling legs with his cock buried to the hilt inside of me.

"I'm everything you need," he growls before pulling back and slamming forward again.

Without warning, I come. My pussy spasms around him, rhythmically clenching and releasing his cock.

"That's my girl," he praises, never slowing the ravaging tempo of his snapping hips.

"TJ," I moan. "This-you-God-what?"

"Shh, baby. We'll talk later."

I don't think about my fucked-up needs, or how demented I must be to have gotten wet while being attacked. The only thing that exists in this world right now is the man who somehow knows and is able to give me exactly what I need when I can't even voice those things myself.

I come twice more before his shiny blade comes out to join the party, and as soon as the light glints off the metal, I know I'm in for one hell of a night.

Chapter 42

TJ

The early light of dawn is shining around the blinds on the window before we finally fall into bed.

"You seem relaxed now," I tell Kaci as I sweep the damp hair away from her face.

"You don't," she whispers as her eyes search mine.

"You said you were leaving today." I don't really want to have this fucking conversation but avoiding shit doesn't make things better.

A weak smile tugs at her lips. We're laying in my bed facing one another, but our bodies aren't touching. If I know her like I'm certain I do, she's still in that place where she needs to calm down before being touched again. We spent hours in the garage taking our frustrations out on each other before coming in and showering off the blood and cum before bandaging each other up. The last time I entered her pussy it was so swollen from coming for hours that I could barely push myself past the inflamed tissue. She came even harder that time than she did the entire night. This girl is fucking perfect for me, and I pray that she feels the same way about me.

"In the basement, you promised to give me exactly what I need." She blinks slowly, exhausted from the night's activities. "You proved it tonight. I should've believed you all along."

"It was a gamble," I admit. "I didn't know if it was going to be what you needed or what would make you finally leave me for good. You've been so sad lately. I didn't want to feed that because I don't think your dad is fucking worth it. I felt helpless."

"It's been a rough couple of days."

I reach for her again, my hand landing on the soft curve of her jaw. "We're meant for each other."

She doesn't cringe with my confession, so I continue.

"I wasn't complete until the day I found you in that room. We couldn't be us if my childhood wasn't fucked up and you didn't suffer like you did." I swallow a lump in my throat. This emotion is either perfect after what happened tonight, or completely misplaced, but my mouth just won't quit. "Everything that has happened has led us right to where we are. This is where we both belong."

"I wanted to kill that girl you walked off with."

I chuckle at the scowl on her face. Leave it to her to ruin my sentimental moment. "I knew what it would take to make you leave the clubhouse. I knew you wouldn't stay and fight for me." I press a finger to her lips before she can argue. "I also know you don't think you deserve to be happy. You've been second best, an afterthought your whole life."

Her eyes squeeze shut, but a tear still manages to slip out and run toward her temple.

"Look at me," I urge. When her bright green eyes open, wet with sorrow, I fall in love with her all over again. "You are so fucking beautiful. You are everything to me. I fucking love you, Kaci."

She doesn't cringe at the sound of her name this time. Her smile grows as she inches her face closer, and I meet her halfway. Our kiss doesn't turn fevered, but the biting, nipping, and tongue sucking are one hundred percent us. Soft, slow, and sensual just aren't what either of us needs right now. My exhausted dick kicks against my naked thigh, as I imagine it will do every time her mouth is on mine, but neither one of us make a move to do anything about it.

"You're not leaving the clubhouse."

A wicked smile spreads across her mouth. "What are you going to do if I try?"

"You already know."

Her pink tongue snakes out and sweeps her lower lip. "Your hands weren't the only ones on me last night."

The memory of my guys feeling her up, of Ronan dipping his fucking finger in her pussy is almost enough to force me out of bed to gut them. It was all planned of course, but seeing it happen made me frenzied for blood.

"I'll kill all of those guys later," I assure her.

"I don't want you messing around with other girls." She swallows, and it looks like the action causes her pain. "Don't use other women to make me jealous or get back at me when you're mad at me."

"You're more than enough woman for me," I assure her, "and a full-time job. I can't handle anyone else."

She snuggles deeper, so I take it as my cue and wrap my arms around her.

"I love you," I whisper against the top of her head.

She doesn't say it back, but she clings to me harder, and I know that it's her reassurance that one day she will say it. One day, she'll trust me completely, and know that I won't leave her, replace her, or walk away from her. It's my job between now and then to prove myself to her, and I'm one lucky son of a bitch to be given the opportunity.

Epilogue

Kaci

One Week Later

"You'll have to catch me first," I squeal as TJ chases after me. He's got that look in his eye, the confusing one where I don't know what his intentions are. I make it down the hallway and around the corner before he catches up to me.

"I warned you. Run from me, and I'll—"

We both stop in our tracks when we see the woman standing near the front door. TJ skids into my back, his arms somehow managing to wrap around my waist and pull me closer instead of bowling me over.

"Everything is fine, baby," he whispers against my temple as he unwraps his arms, his hand sliding down to meet mine.

"Can we speak privately?" Detective Abigail Martin asks with a pinched look on her face.

Several people are in the room, all silent, taking their cues from TJ since he's the highest-ranking MC member present right now.

"Why are you here?" I allow TJ to lead me to the sofa against the far wall. He sits, pulling me down beside him as if we're having drinks with an invited guest and not a fucking cop. I don't miss the fact that he's positioned himself between me and the cop.

"I'm afraid I'm here with bad news," she begins, but she's not looking at me. Her eyes are darting around the room as if she realizes she's outnumbered and regretting stepping foot in here without backup. She's got balls. I'll give her that.

"My dad messaged me last week about my mother passing. I was waiting for him to send me information about her services, but he must've forgotten. I've never been on the top of his priority list." TJ squeezes my hand in solidarity. We discussed what I needed to say if someone showed up here but doing mock interviews and facing the actual task are two different things. My hands are trembling, so I squeeze his back as a means to try to calm my nerves.

The detective frowns. "Your father was found deceased at his residence last week."

My face flinches with her news, but tears or a look of devastation aren't something I can manage. "What happened?"

"He took his own life." She offers the news with as little emotion as I asked the question.

"Same as my mom," I mumble, and the tears that well and fall down my cheeks now are for her.

I've realized over the last week, that my mother was weak. She trapped a man into marriage and probably regretted every second of it after his true colors came to light. I pity her, hating that she died, but knowing that she had found her own peace, that she was the strongest those last seconds before she died.

"We couldn't find another next of kin," the detective continues. "Your parents haven't been buried yet. That's why I'm here."

"There isn't anyone else," I inform her. "Their attorney or whoever is the executor of their estate should handle that. I'm certain my father left instructions. He was meticulous about business."

"We couldn't find a will. From what the Newbury police are telling us, everything belongs to you. You live in my jurisdiction. I'm only here out of courtesy."

My head is shaking back and forth. "I don't want it."

TJ wraps his arm around my back. "You don't have to decide anything today."

"Mr. Jenkins is correct."

TJ's eyes narrow as he turns his head to look at the detective, but I'm not surprised she knows exactly who he is. She's smarter than I'm sure most give her credit for That's why her being here for too long is dangerous to everyone around. She mentioned the MC once before at my apartment.

"And just who do we have here?" A genuine grin tugs at my lips when I watch Ronan walk up in all his handsome glory, strutting toward the pretty woman standing in the middle of the living room. His hands reach out before we can warn him. Both hands clamp down on Detective Martin's ass, and a look of bliss crosses his face.

Two of the women on the other couch chuckle while several of the guys grunt in warning, but none of them are faster than the female cop. With lightning fast reflexes, she swoops back and flips Ronan on his back. The air leaves his lungs in a whoosh, but he doesn't seem too concerned about the angle she's holding his wrist at or the knee she's got pinned against his chest.

Ronan looks up at her with a wicked grin. "Well, fuck me. I think I'm in love."

"Oh for fuck's sake," someone hisses behind me. "Here we go again."

THE END

Social Media Links

Marie James Facebook: Marie James
Author Group: Author Marie James' Stalkers
Twitter: @AuthrMarieJame
Instagram: author_marie_james
BookBub
Reader Email Share: HERE

OTHER BOOKS FROM MARIE JAMES

<u>Cerberus MC</u>

Box Set 1:

Featuring Kincaid, Kid, Shadow, and SINDICATE (exclusive ONLY to this box set) at a discounted price.

Box Set 2:

Featuring Dominic, Snatch, Lawson, and Hound at a discounted price.

Kincaid Book 1
Kid: Cerberus MC Book 2
Shadow: Cerberus MC Book 3
Dominic: Cerberus MC Book 4
Snatch: Cerberus MC Book 5
Lawson: Cerberus 2.0 Book 1
Hound: Cerberus 2.0 Book 2

MM Romance
Grinder
Taunting Tony

Standalones
Crowd Pleaser
Macon
We Said Forever
More Than a Memory

<u>LMLT SERIES</u>
Love Me Like That

Teach Me Like That

Hale Series
Coming to Hale
Begging for Hale
Hot as Hale
To Hale and Back
Hale Series Box Set

Ravens Ruin Series
Desperate Beginnings: Prequel (Book 1)
Book 2: Sins of the Father

Book 3: Luck of the Devil

Book 4: Dancing with the Devil

Made in United States
Orlando, FL
26 June 2025